"Joelle Charbonneau brings a professional's eye and experience to *Murder for Choir*, and readers will enjoy her heroine Paige Marshall's take on high school show choirs. Music and drama lovers who can't get enough of Rachel, Finn, Kurt, and the gang will have enormous fun with this delightfully witty take on 'Murder, She Sang.' Encore, encore!"

—Miranda James, *New York Times* bestselling author of the Cat in the Stacks Mysteries

No recital today . . .

Everything was quiet as I walked through the door that led to the back of the theater. The houselights were dark, but the work lights illuminated the grand piano on the stage. The lid was up on the piano, making it hard to tell if someone was seated behind it.

I walked down the steps toward the stage. Sure enough, I could see feet. Someone was sitting at the piano. I climbed up the escape stairs, walked around the piano, and felt the world tilt on its axis.

A backstage door slammed, and it echoed in the theater. On a normal day, the sound might have made me jump. Today, my feet were rooted to the floor. Slouched over the piano, head resting on the keys, was North Shore High's choir director, Greg Lucas. A microphone sat on the piano keys a few inches from Greg's mouth. I doubted he'd be speaking into the microphone anytime soon, seeing as how the microphone's cord was wrapped tightly around his throat . . .

Murder
for Choir

JOELLE CHARBONNEAU

BERKLEY PRIME CRIME, NEW YORK

THE BERKLEY PUBLISHING GROUP
Published by the Penguin Group
Penguin Group (USA) Inc.
375 Hudson Street, New York, New York 10014, USA

Penguin Group (Canada), 90 Eglinton Avenue East, Suite 700, Toronto, Ontario M4P 2Y3, Canada
(a division of Pearson Penguin Canada Inc.) • Penguin Books Ltd., 80 Strand, London WC2R 0RL,
England • Penguin Group Ireland, 25 St. Stephen's Green, Dublin 2, Ireland (a division of Penguin
Books Ltd.) • Penguin Group (Australia), 250 Camberwell Road, Camberwell, Victoria 3124, Australia
(a division of Pearson Australia Group Pty. Ltd.) • Penguin Books India Pvt. Ltd., 11 Community
Centre, Panchsheel Park, New Delhi—110 017, India • Penguin Group (NZ), 67 Apollo Drive,
Rosedale, Auckland 0632, New Zealand (a division of Pearson New Zealand Ltd.) • Penguin Books
(South Africa) (Pty.) Ltd., 24 Sturdee Avenue, Rosebank, Johannesburg 2196, South Africa

Penguin Books Ltd., Registered Offices: 80 Strand, London WC2R 0RL, England

This is a work of fiction. Names, characters, places, and incidents either are the product of the author's imagination or are used fictitiously, and any resemblance to actual persons, living or dead, business establishments, events, or locales is entirely coincidental. The publisher does not have any control over and does not assume any responsibility for author or third-party websites or their content.

MURDER FOR CHOIR

A Berkley Prime Crime Book / published by arrangement with the author

PUBLISHING HISTORY
Berkley Prime Crime mass-market edition / July 2012

Copyright © 2012 by Joelle Charbonneau.
Cover illustration by Paul Hess.
Cover design by Rita Frangie.
Interior text design by Laura K. Corless.

ISBN: 978-0-425-25137-9

BERKLEY® PRIME CRIME
Berkley Prime Crime Books are published by The Berkley Publishing Group,
a division of Penguin Group (USA) Inc.,
375 Hudson Street, New York, New York 10014.
BERKLEY® PRIME CRIME and the PRIME CRIME logo are trademarks of Penguin Group
(USA) Inc.

PRINTED IN THE UNITED STATES OF AMERICA

10 9 8 7 6 5 4 3 2 1

ALWAYS LEARNING　　　　　　　　　　　　　　　　　　　　**PEARSON**

For my students who inspire me each and every day.

Acknowledgments

Like any stage production, publishing requires a large cast to turn a manuscript into a book. I consider myself the luckiest girl ever that I am surrounding by amazing people who have helped bring this book to the shelves.

First and foremost I have to thank my family for all of their encouragement and support. I especially need to thank my mother for her smiles; Andy for his willingness to be my first reader (no matter how painful that sometimes might be); my son, Max, for his laughter; my father-in-law, Joe, for his unfailing belief in my talent; and my aunts, uncles, cousins, and extended family for their amazing cheerleading abilities.

Every day I thank my lucky stars to have the support and guidance of my amazing agent, Stacia Decker, and the entire team at Donald Maass Literary. Your unwavering faith in me is appreciated more than I can say.

I also owe a huge thank-you to my wonderful editor, Michelle Vega, for her love of this story and insightful help in making it stronger. Also, much gratitude to Natalee Rosenstein for her leadership, Paul Hess for his awesome art, Rita Frangie for the amazing art design (my cover rocks!), and to the entire Berkley Prime Crime team. You are all amazing.

Last, but by no means least, I want to extended my heartfelt thanks to the booksellers, librarians, and readers who pick up this book. You make everything possible.

Chapter 1

If Dante ever added a tenth circle of hell, this would be it. Prospect Glen High School's field house was packed for the third day of show choir camp. Choir students from four different high schools were tripping over their feet doing jazz squares, and I was stuck in the middle of it.

Two girls with bleach-blonde highlights and glitter makeup strutted by me, pointed, and giggled. Great. Even the high school kids were treating me like an outsider. I didn't think they were from my school's show choir program, but they might be. After two days on the job, I could only spot the fourteen kids in the top choir. They were the ones I was responsible for. The rest were assigned to Larry. As far as I was concerned, he could have them all. Too bad I needed the job.

"There you are, Paige."

I turned to see Prospect Glen's glamorous answer to Martha Stewart walking toward me. Felicia Fredrickson's brown eyes peered at me from under her frosted bangs. "Larry is looking for you. He could use a little help with the vocal clinic in the choir room. I think it's getting a touch out of hand."

Oh God.

Yesterday, a group of kids pushed the piano up against the storage room door with Larry in the room. Two hours passed before anyone realized he was missing. I could only imagine what was happening now.

According to Felicia, the camp was supposed to foster goodwill and bonding among the students. So far the Larry debacle was the only group bonding I'd seen.

I turned and hurried down the hall, Felicia trailing behind me. The music room was located in the Fine Arts wing of the high school, clear on the other side of the massive building.

"We really need to talk about this year's costumes." Felicia's heels clicked against the linoleum floor. "The last coach insisted the girls wear orange dresses with purple sequins. I don't care how good they sing, only a blind man or a football coach would award first place to a team wearing those colors. But there was no talking her out of it."

I tended to agree, but what did I know? Show choir was definitely not my area of expertise. Singing was. Real singing with good pitch and dynamic changes. From what I had heard so far, show choir singing was deemed impressive if it shattered eardrums.

"I don't mean to pester you, Paige, but we really do need to select costumes by the end of this week. While I was in Florida for the summer, I came up with the idea of using black and white with electric green and blue accents. North Shore High School wore black and pink last year, which means those colors are taboo this season." I must have given Felicia a blank stare because she reverently added, "They won most of the first-place trophies in the Midwest competitions."

"Why the rush?" I asked. "I thought the competitions were all scheduled for the spring." In fact, I was certain of it. Part of me was really hoping I'd get a call from a casting director so I could leave this job long before the competitive season began.

"We can't wait until the spring." Felicia's eyes widened with horror. "The choir always has their costumes made in time for the Fall Concert. That gives us time to make adjustments. The wrong fabric or a couple of incorrectly placed sequins can make or break a team's ability to execute their routines."

I'd have to take her word on it. In my performing experience, sequins rarely affected motor skills.

"So what do you think?" she asked.

I blinked. "About what?"

"Getting together to plan the costumes." She laughed. "The sooner the better."

"Can you meet tonight for dinner?" We could get the costume stuff out of the way, and I'd have a great excuse to skip my aunt's most recent culinary disaster.

"I have a date tonight." Felicia frowned.

Turkey surprise, here I came.

I mentally scrolled through my camp schedule. "I don't have to teach any sessions first thing tomorrow morning. Why don't we meet after breakfast and talk strategy?"

"That would be perfect." Felicia beamed, and I found myself smiling back. It was nice to have a friend, even if she drank the Show-Choir-Is-King Kool-Aid.

We reached the choir room, and I swung the door open to reveal chaos. The room was huge, with high ceilings and built-in risers that accommodated eighty-eight chairs.

Unfortunately for Larry, most of those chairs were currently unoccupied. A group of kids in the back corner were working on a tap routine. A few girls to my left were applying makeup, and the rest of the kids were doing what teenagers do best—flirting with members of the opposite sex.

Larry was sitting at the grand piano, working on the harmony of "Ain't No Mountain High Enough" with a group of boys. The song was to be part of the end of camp showcase on Friday, when parents and friends would come to see the campers strut their stuff. At the rate these kids were learning, they'd be ready to perform it around Christmas.

Stepping into the room, I watched several heads snap in my direction. Students I recognized from my choir nudged others near them, and the room quieted. The silence was gratifying.

Larry looked up from the piano with a slightly bemused expression. He spotted me near the door and smiled. "There you are, Miss Marshall. The sopranos are having trouble hitting the high notes. I thought you might be able to help them."

A bunch of teenage girls scowled at me. I was guessing they were the sopranos. Before I had a chance to answer, a voice behind me boomed, "Why don't I work with the girls?"

I turned and tried not to cringe as the director of rival school North Shore High's show choir, Greg Lucas, swaggered through the door. His arms were muscular, his skin perfectly tanned, and his teeth whiter than any toothpaste commercial. Too bad both his height and his personality were stunted.

The high school girls tittered and sighed. I rolled my eyes. Greg didn't appear to notice either reaction. As he shoved a silver pitch pipe into his pants pocket, his attention was focused on a beet red Larry. "This will give Paige a chance to see how a real show choir rehearsal is run. Right, Larry?"

Larry's eyes looked ready to pop. "Paige is a pro-pro-professional, Greg. She doesn-doesn't need help."

A few girls giggled at Larry's stutter. I gaped. I'd only worked with the man for a few days, but I'd never heard him trip over his words.

Greg walked over to Larry and clapped him on the shoulder. "I don't doubt Miss Marshall's professionalism. We're all looking forward to hearing her sing at tomorrow's master class. But I'm sure she'll be the first to admit that performing opera is totally different than working with a performance choir. Right, Paige?"

All eyes turned toward me. Crap. Plastering a smile on my face, I said, "Yes, opera is different, but my background is also in musical theater and dance. Larry wouldn't have hired me for this job if I wasn't qualified."

Truth be told, Larry hadn't been the one to hire me, but Greg didn't need to know that. Larry shot me a grateful look. His color was starting to return to normal—a very pasty white.

Greg shrugged. "Have it your way. Although let me know when you want to learn the ropes from a real teacher. I'd be happy to help." He leaned down and whispered something to Larry. Then, with a wink, he disappeared out the door.

With Larry looking like he was going to hyperventilate, I had no choice but to say, "Okay, everyone, let's get to work."

━━━━

Aunt Millie's bright pink convertible Cadillac was in the driveway when I pulled up to her house. The thing had white leather seats, gold rims, and the requisite fuzzy pink dice. All courtesy of the Mary Kay empire. Most women would look silly driving that vehicle. Aunt Mille and her car were a perfect fit.

I parked my blue Chevy Cobalt behind the Mary Kay Caddy and walked past the vibrant flower beds to the front door. In an effort to save money and travel time to my new job, I'd sublet my apartment in the city and moved in with my aunt. I was still getting used to the arrangement.

Don't get me wrong. Living at Aunt Millie's wasn't exactly a hardship. She had a miniature castle in Lake Forest. Her neighbors consisted of business moguls, several members of the Chicago Bears, and a former guitarist from the Monkees. Aunt Millie's house was small in comparison to her neighbors'—no indoor pools or basketball courts. Instead she managed to eke by with four bedrooms, five baths, and a gourmet kitchen that would make the chefs at Food Network salivate. Aunt Millie's house ranked high on the amazing scale. If it weren't for her beloved dog, the place would be perfect.

Quietly dumping my bag in the foyer, I cautiously crept through the house in search of my aunt. The cursing coming from the kitchen made her easy to find. Aunt Millie refused to hire a cook. She believed there was nothing she couldn't master when she put her mind to it. In the three weeks I'd been living with her, putting her mind to it had resulted in four burned pans, three visits from the fire department, and six phone calls to the local pizza joint. Judging by Millie's expression, today might be number seven.

Aunt Millie looked up from the cookbook she was squinting at over her pink-rimmed glasses. "How did it go?"

"Better than yesterday." I glanced around the kitchen for Aunt Millie's dog. "Where's Killer?"

Aunt Millie's pup was a prizewinning white standard poodle complete with pompon feet and tail. His name was Monsieur de Tueur de Dame. Or, in plain English, Mister Lady Killer. Millie called him Killer for short. Too bad the name fit the dog. Killer loved my aunt and hated everyone else. Aunt Millie thought it was endearing. I thought it was a reason to keep my rabies shots current.

Millie stood there assessing me. She was a sight to behold in her light pink cooking apron, polished nails, and perfect red coif. My aunt's style looked a lot like *Legally Blonde* on crack.

"He's in the backyard trying to attract the attention of Mrs. Wilson's collie." Aunt Millie sprinkled bread crumbs on top of her casserole concoction and gave a satisfied nod. She slid the dish into the oven with a smile. "So, how did it really go today?"

Sighing, I admitted, "Not great. The kids roll their eyes when I ask them to do breathing exercises, and the teachers aren't much better. I'm the outsider, and they have no qualms about letting me know it."

"This is only your second day. They'll come around." Millie took off her apron. Underneath was a tailored pink business suit that showed off the ample hips and the double-D cups I wished God had graced me with. I took after my mother's side of the family—A cup all the way. Millie smiled at me. "Once those kids hear you sing their attitude will change."

"I have to perform during the assembly tomorrow."

"That's perfect. What are you going to sing?"

Good question. I'd planned on doing something from *Carmen*. The Spanish-inspired music had lots of dramatic flare. But now I was rethinking the choice. From what I'd seen, these kids wouldn't be impressed by anything sung in

French. Maybe it was stupid, but I wanted to impress them. Which meant anything operatic was out.

"I don't know," I admitted. "What's your favorite show tune?"

"Honey, my taste runs more toward *Hello, Dolly!* and *Oklahoma!* Those kids aren't going to be looking for 'The Surrey with the Fringe on Top.' You need to sing something that will catch their attention and show them who's boss." She flipped the folded apron onto the counter and headed toward the door. "I have to get going. My bridge club asked me to bring the fall samples to the game tonight. I'm betting I come home with at least two thousand dollars in sales."

"What about dinner?" I pointed to the oven where Aunt Millie's mystery casserole was starting to smoke.

She smiled. "I'm sure it'll be delicious. Oh, and would you let Killer in when it gets dark? He gets a little anxious if he's alone outside after the sun goes down." And out the door she went.

While I was certain my aunt was wrong about the casserole, she was right about what I should sing. I needed something that showed vocal range, power, and a lot of style. Hitting the off button on the oven, I dialed for pizza and went upstairs to flip through my sheet music. By the time the pizza man rang the doorbell an hour later, I'd found what I hoped was the perfect song. Now if I could get Killer inside without losing a limb, things would most definitely be looking up.

———

"What happened to you?" Felicia's perfectly painted red mouth curled into a circle as she stared at my ACE-bandaged wrist. Around us the cafeteria was filled with screaming teenage voices and activity. Whoever decided to feed the kids doughnuts and coffee for breakfast should be shot. "Are you okay?"

"I tripped and fell. No big deal, I'm fine." That was my story, and I was sticking to it. Telling people my aunt's standard poodle pushed me down the stairs, then walked over my sprawled body to get back to his lady love was not an option. Thank goodness Millie's next-door neighbor was a doctor. While I wasn't thrilled that he'd witnessed Killer's victory over me, I was happy to learn my wrist was merely bruised.

Felicia smiled. "Good. Now, shall we get to work? I brought swatches."

Oh joy.

An hour later, I'd chosen a color scheme for my team's first costume—blue and white with green accents. The kids were going to need three costume changes, but this was a start. Felicia said I was a tactical genius. I wasn't sure genius applied, but the fashion police weren't going to pay us a visit.

"So, how was your date?" I asked Felicia as she packed up her fabrics and patterns.

"Not great." She frowned and gave the last of the fabric a hard shove into her shoulder bag. "The man was totally full of himself, and he wanted me to pay for my own dinner."

"I guess there won't be a second date?"

She shook her head and changed the subject. "Have you seen Larry today? I ran into him last night. He looked really unhappy."

Thus far, I'd only seen Larry in various states of concern so I wasn't sure why Felicia was worried. "I haven't seen him, but he said he was going to be filing music and working on lesson plans this morning. Did he say what was bothering him?"

She looked over both shoulders then lowered her voice. "Greg really got to Larry yesterday. I've never seen him so upset. I called him a bunch of times last night, but he never answered." She looked down at her watched and squeaked. "I've gotta run. See you at the assembly. I can't wait to hear you sing."

Heels tapping, Felicia barreled toward the lunchroom exit, leaving me wondering what I was supposed to do next. The assembly wasn't for another hour and fifteen minutes. The entire show-choir-camp student population was attending a dance class in the field house. Watching a bunch of high school kids practice jazz hands and jitterbug steps wasn't all that appealing, so I trekked over to the Fine Arts wing to see what Larry was up to. If he was as unhappy as Felicia thought, he might appreciate a shoulder to cry on.

Of course, for him to use my shoulder, I'd have to find him first. The lights were off in the choir room, and everything seemed to be exactly where we left it when we locked up last night. Larry's adjoining office was equally dark. I tried the handle. Locked.

I walked down to the hallway of practice rooms. They were strategically placed between the band and the choir rooms so that neither side could claim any more right to them than the other. A light was shining in one of the rooms at the end of the hall. I pushed open the door and watched two passionately kissing teenagers jump apart.

"Miss Marshall—" A diminutive, dark-haired girl sprang off the piano bench. "We were just practicing a duet. Mr. DeWeese said it would be okay if we skipped the master class."

This probably wasn't the duet Larry had green-lighted, but I had to give the girl credit. She lied like a champ. Her fair-haired duet partner, however, had turned three shades of red and looked ready to throw up. I recognized them both as kids from my choir, but I couldn't remember their names.

I gave the brunette a knowing look and then smiled. "I was trying to find Mr. DeWeese. Do you know where he went?"

The boy shook his head. The girl shrugged.

"You two should probably head over to the master class before your teammates wonder where you are."

The girl looked ready to fight me, but the boy said, "Chessie and I were just about to head over. Right, Chessie?"

Now I remembered. The boy was Eric Metz. He was good-looking in a gawky, boy-next-door kind of way and seemed friendly enough.

The girl was Chessie Bock. Senior. Star of the show choir and a girl Larry described as a huge pain in the ass. The confrontational glare she was giving me made me understand why. Big talent often equaled an even bigger ego.

Eric scrambled out of the practice room, giving me a big smile as he passed. Chessie's eyes narrowed, and her mouth curled into a smug smile before she strutted out the door. Lovely.

The rest of the practice rooms were empty, so I headed off to the one other place I figured Larry might be hiding. Prospect Glen's newly built auditorium had more bells and whistles than most of the professional theaters I'd worked in. The one-thousand-seat theater came equipped with four enormous dressing rooms, a state-of-the-art soundboard, and a fly system. It was a dream space. One I'd be performing in today.

Everything was quiet as I walked through the door that led to the back of the theater. The houselights were dark, but the work lights illuminated the grand piano on the stage. The lid was up on the piano, making it hard to tell if someone was seated behind it.

I walked down the steps toward the stage. Sure enough, I could see feet. Someone was sitting at the piano. I climbed up the escape stairs, walked around the piano, and felt the world tilt on its axis.

A backstage door slammed and echoed in the theater. On a normal day, the sound might have made me jump. Only, my feet were rooted to the floor. Slouched over the piano, head resting on the keys, was North Shore High's choir director, Greg Lucas. A microphone sat on the piano keys a few inches from Greg's mouth. I doubted he'd be speaking into the microphone any time soon, seeing as how the microphone's cord was wrapped tightly around his throat.

Chapter 2

I sucked in air and choked back a scream. Legs shaking, I crossed the ten feet between me and the piano. The ashen color of Greg's skin didn't give me much hope, but I had to check to see if he was still alive. Now that I was closer, I could see blood matting the back of his hair and a thick streak of blood on his shirt. He'd been whacked with something—probably the microphone. And he wasn't breathing.

Holy crap.

I reached for his wrist to take a pulse. My soul cringed as my warm fingers touched cold skin.

Nothing.

Oh God. Greg was dead.

Not sure what else to do, I dove into my bag and pulled out my cell. No bars. Slightly dizzy, I walked around the auditorium looking for a signal. I found one at the very back of the theater, underneath the sound booth, and dialed 911. I told the dispatcher what I was seeing and promised to stay put until help arrived. Then I called Larry. I would have called the school principal, but Larry's was the only number I had stored in my phone. Cheesy synthesized music played in the background when Larry answered. He must be in the field house for the group dance class. I told him about Greg and braced myself for hyperventilation.

Larry told me to stay where I was. He'd inform the principal and the other teachers, and then come help me deal with the police. No freaking-out. Well, that made one of us. I stood in the back of the auditorium trying to pretend a dead man wasn't giving a recital on stage. Every time I caught a glimpse of the piano, the coffee I drank for breakfast started to roll.

A few minutes later, Larry hustled into the back of the theater. He spotted me holding up a wall and trotted over. "The teachers are making sure the kids stay in the field house instead of coming down here for the assembly. Are you okay?"

"Yeah." No.

Larry patted me on the arm. "Do you mind if I go take a look before the police arrive?"

Before I could object, Larry trotted down the steps. He walked along the front of the stage and came to a stop a couple of feet from the piano. The way he studied Greg was creepy. Or maybe I was just impressed that he could remain so calm while I was ready to hurl. Still, I was relieved when Larry had his fill and started back up the stairs toward me.

Larry reached down to pick something up off the floor as the cops walked in the door. In the movies, the cops arrive within moments. In real life, they took twenty-three minutes. The two male officers were wearing blue uniforms and serious expressions. One was lanky; the other looked as though he personally kept the local bakery in business. I looked behind them to see if the rest of the cavalry was bringing up the rear.

Nothing.

Huh. I would have expected a man strangled with a microphone cord to warrant a bit more attention than just these two. *Law & Order* would have sent a team of people. Maybe murder was a bigger deal on TV than it was in real life?

"Are you Paige Marshall?" The skinny cop asked, walking toward me.

I nodded.

"You reported a dead body?"

Another nod. I pointed down to the stage. "He's seated behind the piano."

Prospect Glen PD's answer to the Pillsbury Doughboy blinked. "You mean there really is a dead body?"

Both men looked down at the stage with expressions of horror. I tried not to be offended that they thought I had placed a crank call. After all, this was a high school. The police department probably fielded calls about phantom murders and mayhem all the time.

"Please remain here," the lanky cop instructed, and the two of them trucked down to the stage. I heard one of them yelp "holy crap" while the other called a request for backup into his walkie-talkie phone. Five minutes later, I felt a small stab of satisfaction as two paramedics, four cops, and two men in suits came through the door.

The paramedics confirmed what I already knew. Greg was dead. I shivered remembering how cold he was to the touch. Larry patted me on the shoulder. After the two paramedics stepped to the side, one of the cops took out a camera and began clicking away. The men in suits circled the scene several times.

Finally, after the scene was recorded, a large, wide-shouldered cop in a light gray suit trotted up to the back of the auditorium. He raked a hand through his curly black hair, pulled out his badge, and nodded at Larry and me. "I'm Detective Michael Kaiser. The two of you found the body?"

"Larry was in the field house," I explained. "I was alone when I found Greg."

The detective pulled out a notebook and scribbled something. He glanced at Larry. "Could you please wait over there while I interview Miss . . ." Another glance at his book. "Marshall?" He pointed at the back row of seats at the far right of the room.

"I'm Paige's boss, Larry DeWeese. I feel it's my responsibility to stay and support her." Larry sounded more authoritative than I'd ever heard him. "She's been through a lot already."

The detective didn't look impressed.

"I'll be okay. They need to take our statements separately. Right, Officer?" I asked, pleased that my television-viewing preferences finally came in handy. Detective Kaiser explained that yes, I was right, and a dejected Larry trudged off to take a seat.

Once we were alone, the detective asked for my full name and contact info. I then walked him through my search for Larry, which led me to the auditorium and the events leading up to the arrival of the police.

"Did you know the victim well?" Detective Kaiser's dark eyes studied me with an intensity that made me jumpy.

"I met Greg three days ago. He's the director of North Shore High School's show choir program." I explained how Prospect Glen was this year's host of the camp in an effort to promote education, cooperation, and friendship among the programs. We both looked down at the body being moved from the stage. Cooperation and friendship were clearly not high on the list this year.

"Do you know of anyone who might have had a conflict with the victim?"

"Well . . ." My eyes roamed over to Larry, who was watching the floor show with a mixture of horror, sadness, and fascination on his face. He sniffled loudly. In three days, I'd learned that Larry was an uncoordinated dancer and a man who refused to kill wayward bugs that wandered into his classroom. The man was meek, nonconfrontational, and the only person I'd witnessed having a problem with Greg.

Yikes.

Fingering the boss as a murder suspect was a sure way to get fired, but I had to be honest. The detective was sure to hear about yesterday's run-in from someone. "From what I've heard, a lot of people had personality conflicts with Greg. Larry and I even had a confrontation with him yesterday afternoon." That sounded non-accusatorial, right?

The detective raised one bushy eyebrow. "What kind of confrontation?"

I explained the incident.

The detective wrote something down in his book. "Was that the last time you saw the victim?"

I started to nod my head yes, then stopped. "Greg was in the faculty parking lot when I got in my car to go home. He was leaning against a blue PT Cruiser."

"Did you see him get into the car?"

Nope. "He was still standing there when I pulled out of the lot." He even waved.

———

Larry's interview took a lot longer than mine. Probably because Larry had a lot to say. I couldn't hear what he said, but his mouth kept moving. And Detective Kaiser let him talk. By the time the detective waved me over, Greg's body had been photographed, processed, and removed by the paramedics.

"Miss Marshall, I was just telling your boss that I'll need you both to come down to the station and sign statements. I'm also going to need to talk to the rest of the faculty and some of the students who were here. Do you think you can arrange that?"

Larry puffed out his chest. "I'll have to inform Principal Logan." He pulled a bright green cell phone out of his pocket, pushed three buttons, then shook his head.

The detective gave him a puzzled look. "Can't remember the number?"

"Not my phone." Larry laughed. I could see why. The phone's case was decorated with pink and powder blue butterflies. Not something a male high school teacher would carry around. He shrugged. "I found it down there on one of the steps. One of the girls must have lost it during yesterday's assembly." He looked at Detective Kaiser's frown and stopped laughing. "Do you think the phone might be important?"

Detective Kaiser held out his hand, and Larry slowly dropped the phone into it. Red-faced, he dug into his other pocket, came up with a black cell phone, and stalked to the back of the theater looking for a signal.

"I thought you should know that your boss mentioned *your* confrontation with the victim." The detective's dark eyes held mine.

"*My* confrontation? As in just me?"

Detective Kaiser nodded.

"As in I had a reason to murder Greg?" I squeaked.

Another nod.

My fingers closed into a fist as I watched Larry talk on his phone. So much for trying to protect the boss. The man I thought was harmless was shoving me head first under the bus. Then again, cops were known to stretch the truth. Crossing my arms, I asked, "Why are you telling me this?"

He shrugged. "You both said there was a room full of witnesses. I'll be talking to them. If you're telling me the truth, you don't have to worry."

"And if I'm not?"

A Cheshire cat smile spread across his face. "Then you'll get to know me a whole lot better."

―――――

"Did you knock them dead today?"

I jumped as Aunt Millie whacked a head of lettuce in half with a butcher knife. She smiled at me and placed a tomato on the chopping block.

"I didn't, but someone did."

She stopped hacking with the knife. "What's that mean? Did you get bumped off the program?"

My aunt's word choice made me giggle. Not that Greg being bumped off was funny. It wasn't. In fact, I'd never experienced something so unfunny in my life. Clearly, I was coming unhinged.

"The assembly was canceled." I sat my purse on the floor and took a seat at the counter. "One of the directors, Greg Lucas, was murdered."

Aunt Millie's arm stopped mid-whack. "Murdered?"

I nodded.

"Do they know who killed him?"

"No, but they have a couple of suspects."

Aunt Millie's eyes gleamed behind her glasses. "Anyone I know?"

"Yeah." I blew a lock of hair out of my eyes. "Me."

"What?" Aunt Millie's eyes narrowed behind her pink-rimmed glasses. "If they think they can pin this murder on you, they've got another thing coming. You wouldn't hurt a fly." The knife glistened in the light as it swung wildly in her hand.

"I think they're just gathering information. The lead detective doesn't believe I did it." At least, I hoped not. I explained Larry's interpretation of the scene in the choir room, and Millie's cheeks turned the color of her hair. Whoops. I should have taken the knife away from her when I had the chance.

Aunt Millie brought the knife down onto the cutting board, sending bits of unsuspecting tomato flying. Right at me. Direct hit to the forehead.

Millie didn't notice. She marched around the counter, threw her arms around me, and squeezed. Suddenly, I couldn't breathe. "Everything will be okay," she said as I gasped for air. "Oh dear, you can hardly breathe you're so upset. Don't worry. My lawyer won't let them railroad you."

My aunt disappeared through the door, leaving a forgotten pile of mutilated vegetables behind her. I leaned my head on my still-bandaged arm, closed my eyes, and savored the quiet.

Then I heard it.

Nails clicking on the hardwood floor.

Deep, phone-sex panting coming closer and closer.

Finally, a low, menacing growl.

I opened my eyes. Baring his teeth from three feet away was Aunt Millie's baby and International Kennel Club Best in Show, Killer. On my best day, I couldn't outrun a purebred animal. Since today was far from my best, I decided to sit still and wait for Killer to get a grip.

The dog took two steps forward and parked his rump on the floor. His pompon tail thudded against the hardwood as his studied me. No doubt wondering whether he could eat me before Aunt Millie returned.

Somewhere beneath my seat, I heard Mozart begin to play. My phone was ringing. Killer nudged the purse with his nose and looked up at me. I eased myself off the stool and started to reach for the phone as Killer bared his teeth. Growling, he sprawled out on the floor with my purse underneath him.

Great. So far today I'd been pushed around by an unco-ordinated choir director and a poodle. That had to be a record.

My phone had stopped ringing, but I was determined not to be outmaneuvered by a dog. My ego couldn't take it. I stalked to the fridge and pulled out a piece of deli-sliced ham. Killer's nose twitched. Setting the ham on the floor near the patio door, I walked back to the stool and waited. The dog looked from the ham to me and back at the ham with a pathetic whine. Finally, unable to resist, he climbed to his feet and trotted toward his snack.

Score one for cured pork.

I grabbed my purse, found my phone, and flipped it open to see who had called. Larry. And he'd left a message. I punched a couple buttons and heard Larry's voice say, "Hi. I just wanted to let you know tomorrow's camp classes have been canceled." I'd figured as much, but it was good to know.

I was about to hit end, when Larry continued talking. "If you or another faculty member needs to reach me, call the Prospect Glen Police Department. One of our students has been arrested for Greg's murder."

Chapter 3

I walked into the Prospect Glen Police Department feeling more than a little out of place. The white-and-gray lobby was empty. The glass door to my left was locked, and the room beyond it was dark.

A bald man seated at a counter to my right looked up from his magazine with a frown. "We're about to close."

I blinked. Police departments closed? That seemed like a bad idea to me, but what did I know? Maybe they lured criminals into a false sense of security by shutting down the building.

Smiling, I said, "I'm a teacher at Prospect Glen High School. I got a call saying one of my students had been arrested."

"Nobody was arrested."

I jumped at the sound of the voice behind me and spun around. Detective Michael Kaiser stood in the doorway, an enormous cup of coffee in one hand and a McDonald's bag in the other. He raised a bushy eyebrow at me. "Did you come to confess?"

My heart thudded hard in my chest.

Detective Kaiser cracked a wide smile. "Sorry. Cop humor." He chuckled.

I frowned. "Larry said he was here at the station with one of our students."

The detective nodded. "We needed to ask Eric Metz a few questions. He's not under arrest."

"Larry said he was."

"Larry was wrong." Detective Kaiser's smile didn't reach his eyes. "Would you like to talk to Eric yourself? I was just bringing him dinner."

"You're bringing a murder suspect dinner?"

"I went out to eat and grabbed the kid a burger." Detective Kaiser looked uncomfortable being caught doing something nice for his suspect. He straightened his shoulders and headed for the door in the back of the room. "The food's getting cold. If you want to see the kid, follow me."

Huh. Not feeding a suspect seemed like a better way to get a confession. Maybe the kid wasn't really a suspect after all.

I hurried to catch up with Detective Kaiser as he walked down the hallway to a large open room filled with desks. I realized I was expecting the place to look like something out of a television police drama. Sadly, the back of the PGPD was a letdown. The walls were a bright white and decorated with photographs of Little League teams. Several desks had thriving potted plants sitting on them. A couple of glassed-in offices were to my left. No stale coffee smell. No dingy gray walls. Bummer.

Detective Kaiser directed me to follow him to a small

room to my left. Seated at a white table were Eric Metz and Larry.

Larry looked surprised to see me. Eric just looked stunned. The detective dropped the fast-food bag in front of the unblinking teenager.

"Paige, what are you doing here?" Larry stood up and rubbed his palms on the sides of his khaki pants.

I watched Eric slowly take the hamburger and fries out of the bag. His hands were shaking. "I got your message and was concerned." Larry had already tried to cast suspicion on me. I wasn't about to leave him in charge of *helping* one of our students.

Eric shoved some French fries into his mouth with a sigh.

"Do you need a drink, Eric?" I asked.

Eric looked up at me and nodded.

"Detective, could you get Eric a soda or some water?"

Detective Kaiser didn't look thrilled that I'd made him an errand boy, but he humored me and disappeared out the door. I sat down across from Eric. "Did you call your parents?"

"They're visiting my grandparents in Maine." Eric looked down at his food with zero interest. Never a good sign when dealing with a teenage boy. "I keep getting my dad's voice mail. The cell phone signals there are pretty bad."

"Maybe if you give Mr. DeWeese the number, he'll go call them for you. You really shouldn't be talking to the police without your parents around." And calling parents would keep Larry busy long enough for me to figure out why Eric had been brought in by the cops.

"Really? That would be great." Eric scribbled down the number and handed it to a less-than-enthusiastic Larry. Larry frowned as he walked by me to make his call.

Eric sucked down a bunch more fries and took a bite of

his sandwich. I waited for him to swallow before asking, "Why did the police bring you in for questioning?"

"The cops said they found my phone in the auditorium." Eric frowned. "Only they couldn't have. I didn't go in the auditorium this morning."

Knowing how cold the body was when I found it, I doubted the cops were worried about this morning. More like last night. Wait a minute. "What color is your phone?"

"Green with pink and blue butterflies," he said, trying hard not to look embarrassed. He failed. "Chessie gave me the cover. She said it's special to our relationship, so I have to use it."

That matched the description of the phone Larry turned over to Detective Kaiser. Still, what motive could Eric have for strangling the rival coach? This kid with ketchup smeared on his chin was hardly the homicidal-maniac type.

"Did you have a fight with Mr. Lucas?"

"No. But I wanted to." The pimple on Eric's forehead looked ready to pop. "The creep hit on Chessie."

I blinked. "He did what?"

"He waited for Chessie in the parking lot and offered to give her a ride. He said he had connections with the admission staff at all the right colleges and he could help a talented girl like her, but only if she helped him first." Eric pushed away the hamburger and fries, sending them skidding across the table and over the edge.

I couldn't blame him for not wanting to eat. Greg Lucas was at least forty years old. Chessie was seventeen. Yuck! If the guy wasn't already dead, I might have had to take a whack at him.

Instead of indulging in my righteous anger, I asked, "When did this happen?"

"Yesterday. After school."

Greg's parking lot loitering suddenly made sense.

Eric stood up and started to pace. "Chessie texted me after it happened."

Uh-oh. "And you texted her back?" He looked down at his shoes and nodded. "What did you say?"

"I might have said that I would make Greg Lucas sorry he hit on her."

Translation: In cool teenage texting slang he said he was going to beat Greg Lucas to death. And the cops had the phone to prove it.

The phone that Larry found in the auditorium.

Or did he?

Who was to say he didn't find it somewhere else and plant it in the theater to take suspicion off himself? He'd already pointed the finger at me. What would stop him from setting up one of his students to take the fall? Of course, that would mean Larry had something to hide.

"Okay, Eric. The cops have your phone, but that isn't enough for them to charge you with murder." At least, I hoped it wasn't. "Refuse to talk to anyone until your parents are here. They'll get you a lawyer and make sure you don't get charged for a murder you didn't commit." A murder rap wouldn't look good on college applications.

The kid sat down and nodded as Detective Kaiser walked in the door carrying a bottle of water and a can of Coke. He put both on the table and slowly studied the room. French fries were scattered across the floor like confetti. A line of ketchup streaked from the middle of the back wall to the floor where the hamburger had hit and slid to the ground. Housekeeping was going to be pissed.

They weren't the only ones. The minute Detective Kaiser wiped French fry grease off a chair and sat down, Eric said he wouldn't talk to the cops without his parents.

The detective told Eric he understood. Eric would have to wait here until his parents could be reached. Detective Kaiser then stood up and smiled at me. It was definitely not a happy smile. "Could I talk to you in the other room, Miss Marshall?"

Eek. "Of course, Detective. Do you need anything before I go, Eric?"

He looked up at me with tired eyes. "Could you call Chessie and let her know I'm okay?"

Promising to deliver his message, I gave Eric a sympathetic pat on the shoulder and followed Detective Kaiser into the hallway. The minute the door closed behind us, the detective leaned against a wall and crossed his arms over his chest.

Until this moment, I hadn't realized the detective was so big. His shoulders were massive, and I was guessing that under the white shirt and gray sports jacket, the guy was all muscle. And if the narrowing of his dark brown eyes was any clue, the man was ticked off.

"If I'd known you were going to screw with my witness, I wouldn't have let you see him." His voice was low pitched and dangerously calm. My dad used that same tone when I was a kid. Afterward, I wouldn't be able to sit comfortably for a week.

Instinctively, I edged up against the wall. "Eric is a minor." Unless he'd been held back a grade.

"Mr. DeWeese was willing to act as his guardian."

"Mr. DeWeese is the reason the poor kid is here in the first place."

"Which is one of the many reasons I called him when I brought in Eric Metz. I wanted to look into the coincidence."

Oops. "How was I supposed to know that?"

The detective sighed and raked a hand through his curly dark hair. "You weren't. In fact, you aren't supposed to be here at all."

"Well, Detective Kaiser, you're lucky I am. A defense attorney worth his retainer would get a judge to throw out any information you got from this interview. You don't strike me as the type who'd appreciate having a murder suspect walk on a technicality."

"Call me Mike."

I blinked. "Huh?"

My witty repartee made him smile. "My name is Mike. I figure if we're going to yell at each other, we should do it on a first-name basis."

That made sense. I held out my hand. "Nice to meet you, Mike. I'm Paige." Miss Manners had nothing on me.

For a moment the detective just stared at my hand. Finally, he relented and shook it. His hand was large and the skin a bit rough. The hand reflected the man.

Formalities over, I asked, "Where's Larry? I figured he'd be back by now."

"He was hungry. I told him I wouldn't start questioning the kid until he returned."

Good plan. "Did you get a chance to talk to anyone else who witnessed our run-in with Greg yesterday?"

The detective smiled. "The home economics teacher, Felicia Frederickson, backed up your story."

"That's good to hear."

"Makes me wonder why Mr. DeWeese's version of events was different."

"Did you ask him?"

He hooked his thumb into his belt loop. "I did."

I waited. The detective just looked at me. "And?"

"Your boss said you were new to the show choir community and he was so focused on your reactions that he must have missed the victim taking verbal shots at him. Your boss thinks you're the overly sensitive type."

"You don't?"

He laughed. "Anyone who can discover a dead body, be accused of murder by her boss, and show up at the police station ready to do battle for a student she barely knows is more likely a thorn than a wilting flower."

I was pretty sure I'd just been insulted, but I decided to let it pass. The guy had a gun. Enough said.

The two of us looked at each other, waiting for the other to say something. Huh. Guess the conversation had run out of possibilities.

"My work here is done. Call me if you get the urge to question Eric. I can be here in fifteen minutes." Ten if I let Aunt Millie drive.

Detective Kaiser grinned. "I don't think that will be necessary. But I do want you to call me if you hear anything you think I should know." He pulled a card out of his jacket pocket and held it out.

"Like what?"

"Mr. DeWeese was right about one thing. You're new. You don't have any preconceived ideas about the parties involved so you might hear something important that other people might shrug off." His smile remained, but his eyes were serious. Mike was in cop mode. "Humor me."

What the hell. I took the card and shoved it into my purse. With a jaunty wave, I trucked down the hallway toward to the front door. Happy to be free, I gave the door a shove and promptly set off the alarm. A minute later, Mike and ten of his friends came running. Do I know how to get a guy's attention or what?

———

"He might have a point."

"Who?" I'd just finished giving Aunt Millie the details

of my police department foray, leaving out the part where I set off the security alarm. It was my story. I was allowed to edit.

"The detective." My aunt shifted on the living room couch for a better view of her toes. Grabbing the bottle of nail polish off the oak end table, Millie set to work turning the ends of her toes shocking pink. "As an outsider you have a fresh perspective. Ask a few questions and see what happens. If you play your cards right, you could bust this case wide open."

Aunt Millie looked ecstatic.

I was horrified.

"I just want to keep my job." For now. I was still hoping a better gig would come along. One that didn't include a body count. "Larry was annoyed I showed up at the police station. How do you think he'd feel if I started asking people for show choir gossip?"

"That man needs karma to give him a swift kick in the ass." Aunt Millie put down the bottle of polish with a thud, causing Killer to look up from his perch on the floor. He glared at me as though his being awakened was my fault. Millie didn't notice. "Does Larry have a birthday coming up? I have a hair removal cream that was recalled last year. It's been known to cause rashes in some rather unmentionable areas."

Just mentioning Larry's unmentionables had me breaking out into a rash. Yuck.

My face must have said no, because Aunt Millie sighed. "Okay, no rashes. But let me ask you one thing. Do you think that Eric kid is a murderer?"

I'd only known the kid for three days, but I couldn't picture Eric doing anything more rebellious than toilet papering someone's house, and I told Millie so.

"That's what I thought. Which means a murderer is roaming around free." Aunt Millie patted Killer on the head, causing him to make throaty sounds of delight.

"Which is why I should stay out of it." Hunting down a murderer sounded like a good way to get killed.

Swinging her legs onto the floor, Aunt Millie gingerly stood up. "I'm not talking about playing Nancy Drew. I'm just saying it wouldn't hurt to keep your ears open and ask a few questions. No one would think twice. You're the new girl. You're supposed to ask questions. It's the only way you get to know people."

With that pronouncement, Aunt Millie hobbled on her heels out of the room, Killer trotting happily behind her. Leaving me to wonder if Aunt Millie wasn't on to something. I might not want this job, but I had it. My pride wanted to prove I could not only coach show choir but excel at it. To do that, I needed the kids to trust me.

I looked down at my watch. It was only eight o'clock, which gave me time to ask a few questions tonight. Getting Eric off the hook would go a long way toward convincing the rest of the students to give me a chance. And unbeknownst to Eric, he had given me the perfect place to start.

Chapter 4

"What do you want?" Chessie Bock's eyes narrowed to unattractive little slits as she glared at me from the open doorway.

"Eric wanted me to tell you that he's okay." I watched Chessie's face go from suspicious to concerned to pissed in a flash.

"Why didn't he call me instead of you?" Her lips pursed together, and her nostrils flared. Jealously wasn't an attractive look for Chessie.

"He didn't call me. I saw him at the police station. He's trying to get a hold of his parents."

She chewed on her bottom lip and nodded. "They're in Maine. Eric was supposed to go with them."

"But he wanted to come to camp. He told me."

"I wanted him to come to camp," Chessie corrected. "Eric wanted to go fishing with his dad. This is my senior year. I want to do better than place fifth. Eric's a great singer, but he has some trouble dancing. He needs all the help he can get."

Yikes. The guy was sitting in jail, and his girlfriend was dissing his moves. Not cool.

Chessie seemed to read my mind. "Someone like you wouldn't understand." She gave me a hard stare. "Our choir has to be way better than the others even to have a shot at winning. If it weren't for Mr. DeWeese, we would have won last year. He doesn't know how to play the game."

"What game?"

Chessie brushed a lock of dark hair out of her face and let out a frustrated sigh. "Look, Mr. DeWeese is a nice guy and a pretty good teacher, but he doesn't do the things he needs to do to get us to the top. Mr. Lucas might have been a creep, but he was on the Regional Performance Choir Board. He made a point of knowing the judges. He got his team an advantage by any means possible."

I wasn't sure what was creepier—Greg Lucas hitting on Chessie or her admiration for his schmoozing skills.

"It sounds like you know a lot about Mr. Lucas."

She shrugged. "I guess."

"Could you tell me about him?" Her eyes filled with suspicion, and I rushed to say, "I guess I feel bad that I don't even know if he has a wife or kids. After all, I was the one who found him dead. You know?"

Chessie's mouth formed a surprised circle. Clearly, she didn't know. After a moment, she said, "He got divorced last year. Everyone on the competition circuit was talking about it. His wife said he was having an affair. I'm betting it was with one of the judges from the Midwest Invitational. His choir had huge pitch issues, and they still took first. Now that he's dead, we might actually have a shot at winning." She sighed. "Too bad."

"Too bad what?"

"We could win if we had a real coach." She gave me a

saccharine smile. "Instead, we're stuck with you." With that, she flounced back into the house and slammed the door behind her.

———

With no camp the next day, I was free to rethink my strategy for getting the kids on my side. Chessie hadn't been impressed by my willingness to help her boyfriend. Maybe once he was sprung, she'd feel differently.

I got dressed and headed down to the kitchen, hoping to find Aunt Millie. Otherwise, I might not eat. The last two days, Millie had left the house before I headed for sustenance. Both days, I'd found Killer sitting in front of the refrigerator. The minute I tried to go for the milk, he growled and snapped. Food wasn't worth losing an arm for. Especially not Aunt Millie's food.

Thank goodness my aunt was in the kitchen. Killer was nowhere in sight. Aunt Millie turned her perfectly lacquered head and smiled over her coffee cup.

I poured myself a large mug of coffee, snagged a bagel from the cupboard, and sat down at the counter. "I took your advice."

"That's wonderful." Millie's eyes gleamed. "Jackie Mitchell swears you'll meet the man of your dreams if you just give the service a chance."

I groaned. "Not that advice." Aunt Millie had been happily unmarried all of her life, but that didn't dampen her enthusiasm for matchmaking.

"Oh. You're getting highlights."

"No. My student, Eric Metz, asked me to tell his girlfriend that he was okay. I did and decided to ask her some questions about the murdered director."

"Did you learn anything?"

"Turns out Greg Lucas had an affair and got divorced." I took a swig of coffee to fortify myself and added, "My star performer also thinks my presence sabotages any chance the team has at winning this year."

Millie put her cup on the counter with a thud. "Your student clearly doesn't know who she's dealing with."

"She might be right," I admitted. I'd come to that conclusion before falling asleep. "Greg Lucas was a decent director, but his real skill was networking with the show choir judges."

Networking was not one of my strengths, something my agent constantly pointed out to me. Talent was a great thing, but only if someone in a position of authority noticed it. I didn't want to be noticed because of who I knew. I wanted to make it to the top because of my talent, which was probably part of the reason I was directing show choir instead of touring Europe.

Aunt Millie shrugged off my concern. "You're new. The judges won't expect you to know their kids' names and take them to dinner. I bet they'll be watching your team more closely because a director they don't know is in charge. In my book, that's an advantage."

"I hope you're right."

"It's my experience that people who make lots of friends also make lots of enemies." Millie gulped down the rest of her coffee and straightened her glasses. "An angry ex-wife is probably the tip of the iceberg. I have to run to a meeting. See you at dinner. I saw a new recipe on television that I'm dying to try."

Oh goody. Something to look forward to.

My phone rang as I popped the last of the bagel into my mouth. Larry. I chewed, swallowed, and answered the phone just as it went to voice mail. Damn. I hit redial.

"Paige. Good, I'm glad I caught you." Larry sounded a bit tired but upbeat. "Some of us are getting together to plot strategy. Greg's death is a tragedy, but it does open up the field for this year's competitions. We don't want to miss that opportunity."

I assured Larry I would meet them at ten. Hanging up, I couldn't help but wonder if the murderer had just that opportunity in mind while hitting Greg on the head with a microphone and wrapping the cord around his neck.

———

An hour later I parallel parked my blue Cobalt in front of Armanti's Bakery and Coffee shop. The place was located on the corner of Lake and Main, right in the heart of the recently refurbished downtown Prospect Glen. The shops, eateries, and public buildings were all a combination of red brick and white paint with large oak wood signs. Except for Armanti's. Its door was green, the shutters were painted red, and the sign blinked a combination of red, green, and white.

The inside was a lot like the outside—all Italian. Statues, paintings, Italian flags, and maps covered every inch of wall space. A large fountain that looked a lot like a converted birdbath sat in the middle of the café. Larry waved at me from a table in the back. I waved and headed over to join him and a beaming Felicia.

"Paige, I'm so glad you could make it," she gushed as I sat down. "Larry told me you spent some time in Italy, so I suggested we come here. I thought the atmosphere would make you feel more at ease."

How anyone could feel at ease with naked stone cherub butts pointed at them was beyond me. Still, I appreciated the gesture if not the décor.

"Why don't you get yourself some coffee or a snack while

we wait for our fourth to arrive? The raspberry scones are worth the extra round at the gym. Trust me."

"Someone else is coming?" I asked. The three of us were the only ones who had represented Prospect Glen High at show choir camp.

"Our drama teacher, Devlyn O'Shea." Larry leaned back in his chair and rubbed his eyes. He looked exhausted. "He choreographs all the musicals. We thought he might be able to help with the show choir this year."

I tried not to take that as a knock on my choreographing abilities and failed. Plastering a smile on my face, I excused myself from the table and got a large latte with extra whipped cream and a cinnamon roll. I was bolstering my bruised ego with sugar and fat. Sue me.

Taking a hit of coffee, I headed back across the room. Larry was gesturing wildly. Felicia's eyes flashed as she said something back. Larry's neck turned bright red. This was not a happy conversation. Felicia opened her mouth to say something else and spotted me. "The cinnamon rolls here are fabulous. Good choice."

I sat down and looked from Larry to Felicia. He was looking like someone had drop-kicked his puppy. She was giving me a cheesy smile. Something was up.

"What's the problem?" I asked.

Felicia looked down at her hands. Larry's ears turned redder than his neck. "I was just telling Felicia about Eric. She was upset we couldn't do more to help him."

"Did you get in touch with his parents?"

"They're driving back."

Maine had to be at least twelve hundred miles away from our small Chicago suburb. I did the mental math. With stops for food and gas, Eric's parents might be here by tomorrow. "Is Eric still in jail?"

"I think the detective was going to let him go home." Larry shrugged, then smiled as he spotted someone behind me. I turned to see a dark-haired man walking through the front door. The man was dressed in gray slacks, a powder-blue-and-violet-striped shirt, and white suspenders. Despite the plethora of pastel, he managed to ooze sex appeal. The guy looked around the room, smiled, and walked over to our table. Wow. Maybe allowing the drama teacher to help me choreograph wasn't such a bad idea after all.

"Sorry I'm late, kids," he said, standing to my left. I looked up at him and smiled. His features were too angular to be called traditionally handsome, and his nose was slanted a bit to the left. He also had a bruise over his left eye. Yet, something about the way the pieces fit together made him the most attractive guy I'd met in years.

"Hi. I'm Paige." Was I witty or what?

"Devlyn." The man walked around the table to take the seat opposite mine. "How are you holding up? I heard you were the unfortunate soul who found Greg's body."

Finding a dead body wasn't the claim to fame I was looking for, so I just nodded and asked, "Did you know Greg?"

"I choreographed North Shore High School's musical last year. Greg was the music director."

"Devlyn did an amazing job." Felicia put her hand on Devlyn's arm and giggled. "I have no idea how you taught those kids to dance like that in only seven weeks."

Damn. Devlyn had to be the guy Felicia was dating.

Or maybe not. He gently shrugged off her hand and leaned back in his chair. "It's easy to teach kids who are willing to put in the work. I'm excited to work with our show choir. Music in Motion is a great group."

I blinked, then remembered. Music in Motion was the name of the top show choir. My show choir.

"And this year we have a real chance at taking first," Larry declared. "Which is why we're all here. Let's talk strategy."

An hour later, we had a list of songs—all songs I'd already decided on—ready to go. Devlyn proved to be an unexpected ally. Whenever Larry or Felicia suggested a song, he'd take one look at my face and launch into a reason why it was (a) overdone, (b) not quite right, or (c) a surefire audience killer. I ate my cinnamon bun, ordered another cup of coffee, and let Devlyn fight my battles for me.

"This is the first time in years we have a real shot at winning." Larry's eyes gleamed as he leaned forward. "We just need to hold auditions for the one open slot, and we'll be ready to go."

"What open slot?" Auditions had taken place in the spring before I was hired, and all the kids on the cast list were at camp this week.

Larry let out a sad sigh. "Eric's position needs to be filled."

"Why?"

Felicia looked at me as though I'd lost my mind. "He's in jail. I don't think the police will let him out to compete."

Duh. Still. "Replacing him before he's even charged makes it look like we think he's guilty."

Felicia and Larry looked concerned but resolved.

Devlyn looked pissed. "Paige is right. I know Eric. He didn't murder Greg. Kicking him out of the choir before school even starts will send the wrong message."

Larry tilted his head and closed his eyes while he considered Devlyn's advice. Nodding, he opened his eyes and said, "I don't want to lose Eric. He's the best tenor we have, and he's a good kid. But the district rules say a student has to be in school on the first week of class to participate in extracurricular activities for that semester." He crumpled up his cup and sighed. "I don't see any way around the rules. If Eric is still in jail by then, we'll have to replace him."

Shoulders drooping, Larry got up and stalked over to the garbage can. He pitched his cup and disappeared out the front door.

"Is he right?" I looked to Devlyn for confirmation.

He let out a dramatic sigh. "I'm afraid so. A couple years back, we had a lot of students showing up for class several weeks into the school year because of late summer vacations. The school board created that rule to crack down on the problem."

"They won't make an exception," Felicia added. "And even if he's not in jail, the school board might not let him attend school. They have the right to remove disruptive influences from the classroom. A potential murderer would definitely be disruptive."

Well, crap.

Felicia gave my hand a squeeze. "I know it's hard, but you need to start thinking about a replacement. The fall concert is only eight weeks away. Parents, alums, and our school board will be expecting your best. If they don't see it . . ." She shrugged. "I'm sure you have nothing to worry about."

Um, yikes.

Felicia smiled at Devlyn and dug into her purse. "I have to go, but here's that number I promised you. Richard is smart, sexy, and an incredible artist. The two of you would be great together."

The cinnamon bun sat like lead in my stomach. As far as I could tell, Eric had to get himself cleared of all charges or his senior year, perhaps his entire future, was screwed. And to top it off, the sexiest man I'd met in years just turned out to be gay. This day couldn't get any worse.

Chapter 5

I was wrong.

"What do you think?" Aunt Millie beamed.

Two black poodles, a pair of pugs, and a brown-and-white border collie sat motionless in the middle of Millie's perfectly decorated living room. They watched me with their beady glass eyes as I tried not to panic.

My aunt didn't notice. "Aren't they fabulous?"

Fabulous? No. Horrific? Hell yes.

Killer cowered against the cream-colored sofa and whined. For the first time Killer and I were in agreement. These things were scary.

"They certainly look lifelike." It was the best I could come up with. Taxidermied dogs complete with sparkly collars and permanent-pressed fur weren't my thing.

Millie patted the top of the border collie's head. The collie was in a seated position looking upward as though waiting for a treat. "Romeo was a champion show dog. Took best of breed at twenty-four shows and best in show seven times."

Oh God. Romeo had been one of Millie's dogs when I was in high school. Romeo loved car rides, playing fetch, and me. And now he was stuffed with sawdust.

"Where did they come from?" The thought of Millie digging up Romeo and friends was more than my nerves could take.

Killer whined again. I couldn't blame him. Seeing what would become of me after I died would creep me out, too.

Millie leaned over and scratched him. "I've had all my dogs in cold storage along with my furs. I figured it was time to trot them out. They liven up the place, don't you think?"

My aunt really didn't want to know what I thought. "I remember Romeo and Bonnie and Clyde." The two pugs had loved running in circles when I came home from college to visit. "But who are the poodles?"

"Those are LouAnne Gill's dogs. She loved the idea of keeping her friends with her after they passed, but she got heart palpitations when they were delivered to the house. I had to rescue them before LouAnne threw them in the garbage. You don't throw two grand champion dogs away like that."

I would argue that you don't sit them in your living room to collect dust, either, but what did I know?

Aunt Millie squinted behind her pink glasses. "Now, I need to find the best rooms to put them in. Do you want to help?"

My cell rang. I dove into my purse for it and flipped it open as Millie picked up one of the poodles.

"Hi, Paige," Devlyn's rich voice greeted me. "You left in such a hurry. I wanted to make sure everything was okay."

The combo of Eric's impending doom, Devlyn's preferred

dating choice, and the tacky décor had me up and out of the coffee shop moments after Felicia's departure. "Thinking about Eric got me down," I said, watching my aunt haul the poodle up the stairs to the second floor. "But I'm fine. Honest."

"Glad to hear it. So, I was wondering if you'd like to get together today. We could start setting the choreography. The more we do, the less chance there is of Larry trying to help. His help might not be the kind we're looking for."

"You don't like Larry?"

He chuckled. "Larry's a great guy, but have you seen him dance?"

"Gotcha." I laughed and felt the need to confess, "Dance isn't my strongest area, either."

My aunt trotted down the stairs without the poodle as Devlyn said, "I've seen some of the shows you were in. Trust me, you'll do just fine. So what do you say? Do you have some time this afternoon?"

My aunt picked up the second poodle and headed for the kitchen as I asked, "Can you do it now?"

———

I walked into the Prospect Glen High School choir room trying to ignore the icky feeling in my stomach. Just down the hall was the auditorium. A place filled with dead-guy cooties.

"Are you sure you're okay?" Devlyn appeared from the storage closet. He'd changed clothes. Now he was wearing a fitted pink T-shirt and a pair of off-white workout shorts. In one hand, he held a CD player. A top hat was in the other.

I nodded, trying not to notice how sexy Devlyn looked in pink. "I thought the cops had shut down the school."

"They did." Devlyn plugged the CD player into the back

wall. "After searching the entire building, they decided the only thing off-limits is the auditorium—including the backstage, the dressing rooms, and my office." He grimaced. "I'm hoping the fingerprint dust cleans up easily. They let me take a quick look, and you wouldn't believe the mess they made."

"They fingerprinted your office?"

"And the piano, the microphone cord, and the door handles. I doubt they find anything useful, though. Hundreds of kids and a bunch of teachers touch those things every semester, and the janitorial staff doesn't get paid well enough to polish doors."

Fair point.

Putting down my bag, I pulled out the CD I'd burned of this year's music choices. "You said you worked with Greg, right?"

He took the CD and nodded.

"I don't mean to be nosy, but you don't seem that upset by his death. No one does." Except me and poor Eric.

Devlyn clenched his jaw. "Greg Lucas was a hard man to work with. He was an even harder man to like. I'm not surprised someone wanted him dead."

Yowzah. "Anyone you can think of that might top the list?"

He smiled. "Are you investigating?"

"No." Not really. Maybe. "I'm concerned about Eric. There must be better suspects out there than a seventeen-year-old high school student."

"I can name four or five off the top of my head."

"Like who?" I asked with a touch more intensity than I'd meant to.

Devlyn laughed. "Honey, you need a hobby."

"Humor me."

His smile dropped. He stepped back, perched a hand on his hip, and cocked his head to one side while studying me. I fought the urge to squirm. Finally, he said, "Okay, I'll play along. There's the ex-wife, Dana. She was seriously put out when a judge gave Greg joint custody of their son. Dana showed up at *West Side Story* rehearsal at least once a week in a rage over something, threatening to kill Greg. Catfight city."

Dana Lucas sounded like a great suspect, although I'd hate to think what would happen to the son if she'd done it. "Who else?"

"North Shore High's football coach, Curtis Bennett, would also be a top contender."

"Why would the football coach have a problem with a choir director?" If Greg taught marching band, I would almost understand.

Leaning against the wall, Devlyn gave me a grim smile. "Somehow Greg got the star wide receiver to give up playing football to sing in the show choir. The football coach was pissed."

"Losing a football player isn't a reason to commit murder."

He arched an eyebrow at me. "Tell me that after you've met Coach Bennett."

I decided to add the coach to my mental list. "Anyone else?"

"How much time do you have?" Devlyn popped the CD into the player and hit play. The intro to "Ease on Down the Road" echoed through the room. "Larry is an obvious choice. So are a number of female students who hit on Greg and were turned down. Greg was an alley cat who liked the thrill of the hunt. Aggressive women didn't do it for him. Come on."

He sauntered past the piano to an empty space in the room and executed a perfect double turn. Holding out his hand, he said, "This is what I was thinking for this number. Let's dance." He strutted, turned, and added some hip-hop-style stomping.

I shook my head. "They won't be able to sing. This is show choir. If they can't sing while they're dancing, what's the point? How about something like . . ." I did a couple of tap flaps and stomps in between some poses all the while followed by Devlyn's intense gaze. The fact I didn't trip over my own feet under his watchful eyes was cause for celebration.

"I like the tap, but the steps aren't flashy enough." Devlyn tried a couple variations of what I had just done. "We need minimal-effort glitz with a few lifts or harder moves thrown in to wow the judges. Right?"

"Right."

"Okay. Let's do it."

Holy crap. Devlyn was a machine. Once we got a combination we liked, he insisted I repeat it several times while singing, just to make sure I could. I reminded him that my breathing technique was better than that of the average high school singer. He just shrugged and said I'd teach them to do it. I appreciated his confidence in me. Too bad he didn't realize the entire choir thought I was a joke.

Aunt Millie had always told me that women don't sweat, they glow. She was nuts. Sweat poured off my face and trickled down my back. It was Devlyn who glowed. His skin just glistened with a touch of moisture, making his muscles look even more sculpted than they had before.

He grabbed my arm and twirled me up against his chest. "Want to try a lift?" he asked.

No. I wasn't the cute, one-hundred-pounds-sopping-wet ballerina type. Opera singers didn't have to be rail thin to succeed. Still, while my head insisted I say no, the rest of me was enamored with the way Devlyn's body felt pressed up against my back. The man was gay. That alone should limit the attraction. Right?

Wrong.

Growing up, I always wanted whatever I couldn't have. As a toddler I wanted matches. My preteen self wanted purple hair and Julia Roberts's nose (which Aunt Millie was willing to help with, but my parents nixed), and as a teen I wanted any good-looking guy who happened to be in a solid relationship or was otherwise unavailable. My aunt told me that this was my youthful self's way of helping me avoid getting knocked up and that I would grow out of it. I thought I had.

Until now.

"Are you ready?" Devlyn's voice was deep and sexy in my ear. I tried to pretend he was my brother. Or my mortician second cousin whose only topic of conversation was making dead people look lifelike. Talk about a turnoff. "I'm going to lift you up onto my shoulder. One. Two."

Wait. What?

"Three."

Devlyn put his hands on my waist and lifted. I went up and felt his hands start to slip against my sweaty sides as he tried to prop me onto his shoulder. For a moment the world went into slow motion as my backside brushed his collarbone, then started to descend.

Thunk.

Yeouch! My hip and knee hit the tile, sending a wave of pain through my right side. That was going to leave a mark. At least my hands had stopped my face from colliding with the ground. Otherwise, I would have needed that long-wished-for nose job.

"Oh God, Paige. Are you okay?" Devlyn looked down at me from above.

I frowned. "Why aren't you on the ground with me?"

He gaped, then laughed. "Because I wasn't the one up in the air."

"Whose fault is that?"

"Mine." Still chuckling, he held out a hand. "Next time I promise I'll fall first so you have something soft to land on."

Oh goody. Something to look forward to.

I took his hand and let him haul me to my feet. My whole body ached. To top it off, the sweat on my skin had attracted every dust mite on the linoleum floor. For the first time I was thankful Devlyn wasn't attracted to women. My current state made the Bride of Frankenstein look like a cover model.

"Why don't we call it quits for the day?" Devlyn walked over to the CD player and killed the music. "We can finish blocking the ending tomorrow after camp. Larry said it was going to be an abbreviated schedule considering everything that's happened."

Made sense to me. It was hard to preach about jazz hands and Vaseline smiles after a murder.

"Hey," I said. "You never finished your list of murder suspects. You named the ex-wife, the coach, and Larry, but you said you could name at least four or five."

Devlyn walked over to a gray duffel bag near the door and pulled out a towel. "I'll finish the list if you tell me why you're so certain Eric didn't do it. You've known him for all of three days."

Technically four, but who was counting? "Eric doesn't strike me as the murdering type." He was more like the playing-video-games-while-eating-greasy-pizza kind.

"I saw Eric when I stopped by my office on Tuesday night. He looked pretty angry."

"Angry enough to strangle someone with a microphone cord?"

Devlyn shrugged. "The cops asked the same thing. I told them that teenagers get angry. They stomp and scream and sometimes they punch things. Then they move on."

"So who wouldn't move on? Who else was angry enough with Greg Lucas to kill him?"

"You really want to know?"

I nodded.

Devlyn wiped the back of his neck with a towel. Then he shoved the towel into his workout bag and winked. "Me."

Chapter 6

He was joking. He had to be. Right?

I asked myself that question at least a dozen times on the ride back to Millie's place. No person in his right mind would willingly offer himself up as a murder suspect. Then again, what person in his right mind actually murdered someone? I didn't know what to think.

The only thing I was certain of was my need for a shower. I bounded up the living room steps to the second story before Killer could come find me, grabbed a clean set of clothes from my bedroom, and headed for the bathroom. Peeling off my sweaty shirt, shorts, and underwear, I dropped them on the floor, hit the light switch, and took a step toward the shower.

Eek!

Sitting next to the toilet, looking at me with its mouth half open, was a lifeless black poodle. I grabbed a towel and wrapped it around my torso. Yeah, I was being silly. The dog's beady blue glass eyes couldn't see me. But they were enough to wig me out.

I tied the towel tight around me, grabbed my clothes both clean and dirty, and went in search of another bathroom. This week had been stressful enough. Having a lifelike poodle watch me shower was more than my blood pressure could take.

Once I was clean, I went to my frilly green-and-white bedroom to check my cell messages. I lived in hope that my manager would call with an offer to take me away from all this. Nothing. I booted up my laptop. Damn. He hadn't e-mailed me, either.

I sat back in the ornately decorated wood chair and sighed. If I'd gotten the role with the Lyric Opera, I probably would have heard by now. My heart sank. Until another opportunity presented itself, I'd have to suck it up and do the best job I could with the hand I was dealt.

Snagging my purse off the floor, I pulled a piece of paper out of the side pocket and unfolded it. Ex-wife, Dana Lucas. Football coach, Curtis Bennett. My boss, Larry DeWeese. My three suspects. Grabbing a pen, I added Eric Metz and Devlyn O'Shea. I didn't think either one of them killed Greg Lucas, but keeping them in mind couldn't hurt.

Turning to my laptop, I typed *Greg Lucas* and *North Shore High* into the search box and hit enter. I saw several articles dated today about his murder, all giving sketchy details as to the circumstances. Larry was quoted in all of them saying Greg was a talented educator who would be missed. I wondered whether Larry's nose had grown while spouting that eulogy. One of the articles ran a picture of Greg, his wife, and their son, Jacob. I clicked onto Facebook and did a search for Dana Lucas. Bingo. Her work history was set for public viewing—yoga and Zumba instructor at the Women's Wellness Center.

I called the center. Yes, Dana Lucas was teaching there. She had a beginning and an advanced yoga class scheduled for the afternoon. Would I be interested in taking one of them? The beginner class was scheduled for five thirty. That gave me an hour and fifteen minutes to get there. I wasn't sure what I would get out of meeting the former Mrs. Lucas besides a workout, but I figured going wouldn't hurt. I signed myself up and typed "Coach Curtis Bennett" into the search box.

Wow. The guy got a lot of ink in the local papers. Probably because his team won. A lot. Scratch that. They used to win. For the past three years, Coach Bennett's luck with talented teams seemed to have run dry. Last year the team won two games, and one article reported some boosters were saying the coach should step aside. If I were the coach, I'd be pissed. Maybe he wasn't such a bad suspect after all.

Directions to the workout center in hand, I grabbed my purse and headed downstairs. After getting a soda, I left Aunt Millie a note letting her know I'd be late for dinner. Then I headed out the door. The class didn't start for an hour, but I had a stop I wanted to make first.

———

Detective Mike Kaiser took one look at me being led into the squad room and shook his head. I thanked my escorting officer and strolled over to the back corner desk where the detective was seated. Today the room was filled with cops in uniform writing reports, sucking down coffee, talking loudly, and occasionally lobbing balled-up pieces of paper into wastepaper baskets. This was my idea of what a police station should look like.

The detective leaned back in his chair. "So, to what do I owe the pleasure?"

"Do you still have Eric Metz in custody?" I asked.

"Did you bring a cake and nail file with you?"

I smiled. "I'm not much of a baker."

He laughed. "Too bad. Most of the guys around here have a sweet tooth."

"I'll keep that in mind if ever I get picked up for jay-walking."

Detective Mike leaned forward. "I took Eric home last night with strict instructions not to leave town. His parents promised to bring him in for questioning when they get back. Does that work for you?"

I wanted to do a happy dance, but my muscles were too sore. Instead I said, "I'm glad to hear it. Eric's a good kid."

"A week of teaching at show choir camp gave you that insight?"

I chose to ignore the snide emphasis the detective placed on "show choir." Face it, I felt the same way. "Musical extracurricular activities draw a group of dedicated, artistic kids. Eric is one of them."

"He's also a kid who threatened to kill my murder victim." Detective Kaiser's smile disappeared. "I have to take that seriously."

"I understand, Detective," I said. "I just want to make sure you're not overlooking the multitude of other people with motive to kill Greg."

"I told you to call me Mike. What other people are you talking about?" His eyes narrowed. "You didn't have any suggestions when you were here last night."

"You told me to keep my ears open, so I did." I rattled off my suspects, leaving Devlyn off the list. The more I thought about it, the more I was certain he was pulling my chain. "What do you think?"

Detective Mike gave me a smug smile. "I've already talked to the ex-wife. Nothing there. The coach is an interesting theory, but no one else mentioned him. And your boss seems to have an alibi. Your student is my best option so far, but I appreciate your initiative even if you're off the mark. Not bad for a complete amateur." The phone on his desk rang. "I have to take this. Feel free to let me know if you have any more theories."

By the time I got out to the parking lot, I was feeling as steamed as the inside of my car. As a college student, I'd heard "you have incredible potential" almost weekly from my vocal music instructors. At first, the praise thrilled me. Then it just pissed me off. I wanted to be fabulous, not just have the potential to be fabulous. So being called a complete amateur irked me. At this moment, I didn't want to be any kind of amateur. I wanted to prove to Detective "Call-Me-Mike" Kaiser that he was wrong about Eric and about me.

Stepping on the gas, I tooled over to the Women's Wellness Center for my yoga class, determined to succeed where Detective Kaiser had failed.

The Women's Wellness Center took up half of a ritzy-looking strip mall at the south end of suburban Glenview. One step into the frigid, arctic air-conditioned building, and I knew I'd never want to come back. All the women in the place were wearing designer spandex on their perfectly toned bodies. I looked down at my red shorts and white tank and considered hightailing it out the door.

"Are you here for a class?" A perky blonde in a black-and-pink-zebra-striped leotard tapped me on the shoulder. She was standing directly in front of the door, blocking my escape.

"I signed up for Dana Lucas's beginning yoga class, but I forgot my workout clothes."

The blonde giggled. "That's the best part about being in an all-female gym. We don't have to impress anyone with what we're wearing. Comfort is our top priority."

A dark-haired woman walked by in a thong leotard. At least I assumed it was a thong. The thong itself had gone where the sun doesn't shine, giving her what had to be the world's worst wedgie. Yeah, comfort was king around here.

"Come on." The blonde grabbed my arm with her perfectly manicured nails and pulled me deeper into the building. "I'll help you find Dana. Her room is just down the hall."

I followed along beside the girl as she continued to yammer. "We've had several cancellations for today's class, so you'll be getting a lot of personalized attention. Here we are."

We stopped in front of an open door. The blonde gave me an encouraging shove into the room. I stumbled in, and three pairs of eyes turned toward me. Two of the women smiled. One glared and stalked to the back of the room.

"Hi," I said to the two friendly women. "My name's Paige. I'm new."

A petite fiftysomething woman with painted-on eyebrows smiled at me. "I'm Marta. I'm definitely *not* new." She shot a glance over at the woman at the back of the room and lowered her voice. "If Dana starts to yell at you, just pretend to pull a muscle. She'll back off."

"That's Dana?" Wow. Greg must have liked to live on the edge if he cheated on her. The woman was at least six feet tall with broad shoulders, short spiky blonde hair, and biceps Arnold Schwarzenegger would kill for.

The other woman brushed back a tendril of brown hair and nodded. "Dana's really a nice person, but she takes her yoga classes a bit too seriously."

"A bit?" Marta snorted. "She's a Nazi. You'd think the future of the world depended on the perfection of my tree pose."

I had to ask. "Then why do you come to class?"

Marta's penciled eyebrows knitted together. "Dana's been having a hard time. I know what that's like. Her ex has been jerking her around on child support and a bunch of other things. Been there. Done that."

"She's lucky to have friends like you to confide in." With friends like this, Dana certainly didn't need enemies. I hoped my own friends wouldn't spill my secrets to strangers or at least hold out until they got a decent bribe. Performers were always short of cash. I wouldn't blame them for wanting to pay the rent.

The second woman cringed. "We're not friends, exactly. We're just the only people who still come to class. Now that she's told us . . . things . . ." She swallowed hard as Marta gave her a stern look. "Well, it makes it hard to leave."

The two women looked relieved when Dana yelled, "It's five thirty. Find a mat and take a seat."

The other two women walked over to their mats. Oops. I looked up at Dana. "I don't have one. Sorry."

She rolled her eyes and pointed toward the front of the room. "You can use one of those."

I walked over to the mats. My nose twitched. I leaned closer to the mats and sniffed. Dried sweat. Yuck. I didn't want to sit on someone else's sweat, but I didn't have much of a choice. Not if I wanted to get the dirt on Dana. The two other students had alluded to a secret, and I really wanted to know what that secret was. Cringing, I picked a mat out of the bottom of the pile (telling myself most mat borrowers took the ones off the top) and took it back to the center of the room.

I'd always heard it said that yoga helped a person find peace and harmony. Whoever said that lied. There was nothing harmonious about this class. We each sat on a floor mat as Dana stalked around the room like a lion ready to attack. The minute our butts hit the ground, she yelled, "Let's stretch out those backs. We'll start with pelvic tilts. Bend your knees. Feet and hands flat on the floor. Now tilt."

I slowly tilted my pelvis up and stretched my back. Wow. That felt really . . . Dana stared down at me from her immense height. "Your feet aren't flat."

"They aren't?"

"No," she growled. "Here. This is flat."

Dana stepped down on both of my feet and looked down at me. "Now tilt."

Yeouch.

We tilted. We also did cat stretches and some kind of lunges and stood like trees. All while Dana barked orders about deep breathing and relaxation. By the time she announced the end of class, I needed more than deep breathing. I needed a drink.

The two other students rolled up their mats and disappeared out the door in record time. Dana looked like she wanted to stop them, but she took one look at me and shook her head. Clearly, whatever she wanted to discuss wasn't for my ears.

"Thanks for the class," I said, rolling up my mat. "Do you ever do private classes? My high school choir students would enjoy this." Not.

She blinked. "You teach high school choir?"

"Actually, I teach show choir." I watched her eyes widen. "I'm new to the school, and a yoga class might be a good bonding experience with the kids. We had a crisis at our camp this week. I found one of the directors . . ." I looked down at my feet as if overcome with emotion and sniffled. Ugh. The stench of caked-on sweat hit me upside the nose, and my eyes began to water. I needed another shower. Pronto.

Dana took a step forward and touched my arm. "You found Gregory Lucas?"

I looked up at her confused expression and nodded. "Was he a friend of yours?"

"He was my ex-husband." With a clear and bitter emphasis on ex. Interesting.

I put my hand to my chest and gasped. Hurray for acting classes. "You were married to Greg Lucas? I'm so sorry for your loss."

"You didn't know Gregory very well, did you?"

I shook my head.

She choked out a laugh. "Trust me when I say Gregory's death isn't much of a loss. At least, not to me. I'm sure there are a bunch of women out there who don't feel the same." She tried to act as though she didn't care, but the way her nails were digging into her palms gave her away. This was a woman on the edge.

I tried to come up with an appropriate response. Nope. Nothing. I was at a loss.

Dana took several deep breaths (way deeper than the ones she taught in class) and sighed. "That must sound unfeeling. Really, I'm not. Our son was grief stricken when Gregory left us. I've been dealing with the fallout ever since."

"That must be hard."

"You have no idea."

"How's your son dealing with Greg's death?" I waited for Dana to bludgeon me for overstepping my boundaries, but she just sighed.

"He's devastated, but he'll get through it. Actually, a dead father is easier to live with than one who doesn't care." She straightened her shoulders and gave me a chilling smile. "Whoever bashed in Gregory's head with that microphone did us a huge favor."

Eek.

It wasn't until I climbed into my car that it hit me. The papers hadn't reported the head wound, but Dana knew all about it. I wanted to know how.

Chapter 7

"Did you tell Dana Lucas that her husband died from a microphone to the head?"

Detective Kaiser looked up at me, a Big Mac stuffed between his lips. He extracted the sandwich from his mouth and frowned. "How did you know to find me here?"

I sat down across from him at the very back corner red-and-white table and smiled. "The guy manning the station's front desk said you went out for dinner. I remembered you had a McDonald's bag yesterday when I ran into you, so I thought I'd take a chance." The fast-food restaurant was located a half block from the police station, which made it an obvious, albeit unhealthy, choice.

The detective chuckled. "I'm impressed. Of course, you could have just called me. You wouldn't have had to waste time going to the station."

"I'll remember that for next time."

He took a bite of his burger, and my stomach growled.

The smell of sizzling meat made me remember I hadn't eaten yet. Trying to ignore the supersized fries on the table in front of me, I asked, "Did you tell Dana that her husband got whacked with a microphone?"

"Giving out details of a crime scene to potential suspects isn't part of my daily routine." The detective took a drink of soda, grabbed a couple of fries, and raised an eyebrow. "Why are you asking?"

"Dana told me that whoever hit her husband over the head with a microphone did her a favor. I didn't realize it until after I got in my car that she knew about the microphone. That's important, right?"

"What were you doing talking to Dana Lucas?"

I was so enamored of the smell of French fries I almost missed the sharp edge in Detective Kaiser's voice. "I took a yoga class. Dana was the instructor." Both true statements. No fibbing here.

"You had no idea Dana would be teaching the class?"

Okay. I hated lying if I didn't have to. It was a weird quirk that I fully intended to get rid of at some point. So, instead of saying no, I asked, "You don't believe in coincidence?"

He smiled. "Not when it comes to you."

"You just met me. Aren't police detectives supposed to assemble all the facts before passing judgment?"

"I'm making an exception in your case." He popped another French fry. "So, tell me exactly what you said. I need to know if Dana is going to show up at the station and press stalking charges."

"I didn't stalk her." The detective didn't look convinced so I added, "Dana would never think I stalked her. I took her class, mentioned I was a show choir teacher, and she jumped at the chance to talk about Greg."

Detective Kaiser noticed me eyeing his fries and pushed a few my way. I picked one up and sighed as the salty grease hit my taste buds.

"Did the rest of the class hear your conversation?"

I shook my head and munched on another fry. "There were only two other women there. The minute class ended they booked it out of there. They said they didn't like taking the class, but they were afraid to drop out because of some secret Dana shared with them."

Swallowing my last fry, I realized I needed a drink. Not waiting to be asked, the detective pushed his beverage toward me. I took a hit. Sprite. Blech. My mother always made me drink the stuff when I had the stomach flu. The memory tainted the soda forever. But it was better than nothing. "Thanks."

The detective popped the last piece of hamburger into his mouth and motioned for me to continue.

"Anyway, I think she must have told them she was plotting a murder. What else would scare them into doing yoga classes with a teacher who causes hyperventilation?"

"Their cellulite?"

"I'm serious."

He laughed. "So am I. My ex-wife would suffer through anything if you told her she had cellulite."

"You were married?"

He picked up his soda with a smile. "Surprised someone would marry me?"

"You don't strike me as the commitment kind. Guess sometimes you can't judge people from your first impression of them." I smiled. "Maybe you should talk to Dana again in case you got the wrong impression of her."

He sighed. "Look, I hate to ruin your fun, but Dana has

an alibi for the time period in which we believe Greg Lucas was murdered. She's in the clear."

"Why didn't you tell me that ten minutes ago?" Heat raced to my cheeks. I took a couple more fries to battle the embarrassment.

He grinned. "This was the most entertaining dinner I've had in months. I'll be back here again tomorrow. Feel free to join me. I'll even buy you your own fries." He picked up his tray with the remains of his meal and headed for the trash can.

I trailed after him. "So, you were just humoring me?"

"Not exactly." The amusement disappeared. He looked around the mostly empty restaurant to make sure no one was paying attention. "I do find it interesting that Dana knew about the microphone and the head wound. We haven't made that public. I'll have a follow-up conversation with the former Mrs. Lucas just to make sure that T is crossed. Those are the kinds of things that help the defense's case."

"Hey," I asked as he turned toward the door. "Who was Dana's alibi for the time of the murder?"

He rolled his eyes. "This is a police investigation. We don't share names of alibi witnesses with the public."

Fair point. Only, I had a strange idea, and I wanted to know if I was right. The detective pushed the door open and headed out into the sticky, hot air with me close behind. "Detective Kaiser, can I ask one more question? Then I promise I'll leave you alone."

He turned and smiled. "I told you to call me Mike."

"Okay, Mike." I took a deep breath and asked, "Was Dana's alibi named Marta?" If she was, it was my bet Dana didn't have an alibi at all.

Mike didn't answer. He just smiled, turned, and walked

out the door without giving me a clue as to whether I was right or wrong. Which meant one thing. I had to find out on my own.

———

"How are you going to find that out?" Aunt Millie gave my unmoving fork a stern look. I didn't have the nerve to confess I'd already eaten a double cheeseburger, so I shoveled up some dried chicken coated in lumpy gravy. When my fork touched my mouth, Aunt Millie added, "You can't just ask Dana who her alibi is. She'll find that suspicious."

Aunt Millie's phone rang. The minute she looked at the screen, I spit the forkful into my napkin. I would have given it to Killer, but he was nowhere to be found. Too bad. He thought lint was tasty.

"I haven't figured out that part yet. Got any suggestions?"

Millie closed her eyes, giving me an opportunity to shove more food off my plate. "Does this Dana belong to any country clubs?"

"I don't know, why?"

"There are no secrets at a country club. Trust me. I've been naked in enough steam rooms with those ladies to know what I'm talking about."

Eeeew.

"I'll make some calls tonight. Yoga is big with a lot of my friends. I'm betting at least a couple of them will know her." Aunt Millie pushed her almost untouched plate away. "In the meantime, what other suspects do you have?"

I blinked. "You don't think Dana Lucas did it?"

"I think I didn't become Mary Kay's top seller in the Midwest region by pursuing only one option."

"This isn't cosmetic sales."

"No." Her eyes met mine. "This is about a boy's life. If

you really want to help get him out of jail and back onto your show choir roster, you have to look at all the possibilities."

Okay, she had me there.

"The next name on my list is Curtis Bennett. He coaches football at North Shore High." Unless I wanted to masquerade as the world's oldest and dumbest cheerleader, casually chatting him up was going to be difficult.

Aunt Millie picked up her phone and started pushing buttons. Her texting ability would make most teens envious. I knew better than to ask what she was doing. She wouldn't answer until she was good and ready. To pass the time, I picked up our plates, dumped the contents into the garbage, and loaded them in the dishwasher. By the time I sat back down, Aunt Millie was beaming. "Bobby Davidson is going to meet you for drinks at Gulliver's Tavern in an hour."

"Who is Bobby Davidson, and why am I going on a date with him?"

"You're having drinks, dear. This isn't a date."

I stared Millie down. My aunt has used similar lines on me in the past. The last time I fell for it the guy had flowers in one hand and a box of lactose-free chocolates in the other. Thank goodness the guy was not only lactose intolerant, he was allergic to the flowers. After a half hour of violently sneezing himself off the bar stool, he called it quits.

Millie frowned at me. "Bobby Davidson is a North Shore High School alum and president of the football boosters. He's always hocking raffle tickets at bridge club. If you want to know about North Shore football, Bobby's your guy. Now, are you going to meet him or should I text him back?"

"I'll meet him." After all, I didn't have a better idea. Besides, it sounded like my aunt was trying to help me solve a problem instead of fixating on my love life. I wanted to encourage that behavior.

After another shower, which I really needed, I headed off to meet Aunt Millie's friend. Gulliver's Tavern was an old Victorian house converted into a bar and grill. The bar was located in what must have been the original living room. A handful of patrons were sitting at high wooden tables. Six televisions on various parts of the walls were streaming golf, preseason football highlights, and women's lacrosse to anyone interested. I looked around, trying to pick out Bobby. A big, bald-headed guy with brown furry eyebrows waved from a stool at the bar. Aunt Millie's description had made the guy sound like 007. Aunt Millie needed her glasses checked.

I walked over and held out my hand. "Mr. Davidson?"

He smiled. "Call me Bobby. What can I get you to drink?"

"A rum and Diet Coke, but the drinks are on me. It's the least I can do after you dropped everything to meet with me."

"Your aunt has helped my family more times than I can count. I owe her." He finished off his beer and asked the bartender for another. His eyes shifted to the television over the bar. After a moment, his attention came back to me. "Millie said you needed information on Coach Bennett. What do you want to know?"

Good question. "I heard he had a problem with the choir teacher at the school."

"You could say that." Bobby took a hit of his beer. "You could also say he threatened to rip out Greg Lucas's tongue and wrap it around his throat."

Yowzah. "Really?"

He nodded. "I was there dropping off raffle tickets when Coach got an e-mail from his prize running back. The kid was dropping the team and joining the show choir."

"And Coach Bennett was upset?"

"Coach looked like he was having a heart attack. He got up out of his chair and charged down the hall. I thought he was sick, so I followed him all the way to the choir room. Coach took one look at that director's smug face and lunged. I had to pry his hands off Greg Lucas's throat."

Wow. I sucked down half my drink. "Did anyone report this to the cops?"

"Nah. School was out. No kids were around. Greg decided to let it go."

"You think he should have pressed charges?"

"I think he couldn't press charges." Bobby put his beer down on the bar with a thud. "I asked around about Greg after that incident. People had a lot to say."

"Like what?"

"He had a reputation for taking things that didn't belong to him. If you know what I mean." He winked. "More than one person lodged a complaint, but his program is strong so the board looked the other way. It's not a surprise some people took matters into their own hands."

"Murder is kind of extreme, don't you think?"

"I wasn't referring to Greg's murder, although I wouldn't be surprised to hear some jealous husband or pissed-off girlfriend was responsible." Bobby leaned an elbow on the bar. "I did a little asking around before coming here tonight. Greg's had a couple of *accidents* recently."

I sucked down the rest of my drink and ordered another. "What kind of accidents?"

"Some were no big deal—like air being let out of his tires. But Greg getting hit by a car got people talking."

Holy crap. "Somebody ran over Greg?"

"They tried to. Greg mostly got out of the way, but he had a sprained ankle and a couple of bruises."

"Did anyone get a good look at the car or the driver?"

"Not that they mentioned to me." He laughed. "Your aunt told me you sang opera for a living. Was she pulling my leg?"

"I'm taking a break from performing to teach for a while." The bartender brought me another drink, and I took a large gulp. The rum helped mask the bitter taste my career, or lack of it, had left in my mouth. I stood up, pulled out some cash, and laid it on the bar. "I appreciate the information."

Bobby frowned at my money then shrugged. "My pleasure. Can I ask you a question?"

I sat back down.

"Would you mind if I passed your number along to my son? I think the two of you might get along."

Damn. Not knowing how to say hell no politely, I said, "The next time you see him feel free to give him my number."

Bobby smiled. "I'll walk it down to him tonight when I get home. His apartment is in our basement."

Chapter 8

My aunt was nowhere to be found when I arrived home. I grabbed a soda, stretched out my aching dance muscles, and went to veg out in front of the television in the living room. The two stuffed pugs were seated in front of the TV as though waiting for me to turn it on. I had three choices: watch television with Bonnie and Clyde, relocate the critters, or go to bed. After the week I'd had, moving dead bodies— even stuffed, furry ones—wasn't appealing.

Turning on my heel, I trekked upstairs to my bedroom, thinking about what I'd learned tonight. Lots of people disliked Greg Lucas. At least one of those people had tried to hit him with a car, and another threatened to strangle him. I was pretty sure Detective Mike knew about the first one, but Greg hadn't pressed charges on the second.

I pulled out the card Detective Mike had given me and dialed. Voice mail. "Hi, Detective. I was just wondering if you had heard that North Shore High School's football coach threatened to kill Greg Lucas. If not, you might want to look into it. Have a good night."

I hung up and got into my pajamas. It was only ten o'clock. Feeling like a loser with no life, I climbed into bed and went to sleep.

I jolted awake as something cold and wet touched the back of my neck. My eyes flew open, and I squeaked out a scream as I hurdled out of bed toward the light switch.

Light poured into the room. From the middle of the queen-sized bed, Killer raised his fluffy white head and blinked at me.

"Out." I pointed to the door.

Killer whined and put his head down on the bed.

"I mean it."

Killer roller over and put his paws up in the air. Had this been another dog, I would have been charmed into giving up half my bed. But this was a dog that pushed me down stairs and growled when I tried to pet him. I wasn't about to be lulled into a false sense of security.

"I'll be back," I told Killer as I headed out the door and down the hall to Aunt Millie's room. Aunt Millie had a special dog bed in her room for Killer. It was white and pink with a canopy. As far as I knew, Killer had never missed a night sleeping in that silly bed. Maybe Millie had closed the door by accident, leaving Killer stranded on the other side.

Nope. The door was half opened. Aunt Millie's snoring hit me the minute I poked my head in. Killer's bed sat waiting for him in the corner. Standing guard next to the bed was Romeo, the former champion border collie.

I tiptoed back to my room and looked at Killer, who had moved to the left of the bed, making more room for me. He whined again.

"Okay." I turned off the light and climbed back into bed. "You can stay. But remember one thing—I bite back."

Aunt Millie kept the air-conditioning set at an arctic sixty-four degrees, and Killer hogged the covers. The combo made me wake up shivering more than once, which meant I was bleary-eyed the next morning. I was also sore and bruised. Dancing, falling, and yoga had taken their toll.

After a muscle-soothing shower, I pulled on a pair of jeans and a turquoise tank. The jeans weren't very summery, but they hid the enormous black and blue mark spreading across my left leg. By the time I walked into the school's field house, I'd had enough caffeine to feel almost normal.

The number of kids present was a third of what had been here Monday through Wednesday. Not surprising. With a microphone-wielding murderer still on the loose, I'd keep my kid home, too.

I spotted Felicia and Larry at the back of the field house along with some of the other directors. Trying not to limp, I walked over to join them. Eric, Chessie, and a couple of my other students were clustered twenty feet away. I smiled at Eric. I considered his not being in jail a good sign.

Standing in between Larry and Felicia, I looked around the group. Nobody looked happy. "What's going on?"

Larry frowned. "We're discussing whether Eric Metz should be allowed to participate today."

"I thought we settled this discussion yesterday."

"We did," Felicia said in dramatic whisper. "Not everyone agrees with us."

The directors all started talking at once. It was hard to keep track of what each of them said, but the message was clear. They were determined. Eric had to go.

"Hey," I yelled. One of the perks of being a professionally

trained opera singer is the ability to project my voice. When I want to, I can be very loud. Today, I had serious motivation to scream like a banshee. I firmly believed Eric was innocent. He was also the key to my success as a director. He was going to stay.

The directors all turned toward me, and I lowered my voice to a more reasonable level. "The police haven't arrested Eric because he's not the *only* suspect in this case. I've talked to the lead detective, and he's pursing several other suspects."

"Really?" Felicia's eyes widened. "Do you know who?"

Casper. The Ghost of Christmas Past. The Loch Ness Monster.

I smiled. "I have no idea. You'll have to ask him." Felicia frowned. The rest of the directors looked confused. "Look, Greg was alone when he was murdered. Don't you think everyone will be safe if we stay in one large group?"

They all looked at one another. When no one objected, Larry clapped his hands together and said, "Okay. Since today is only going to be two hours, I suggest we get to work."

Larry went over to break the good news to Eric and company. The rest of the directors went to find their students, leaving me alone with Felicia.

She grabbed my arm and whispered, "Who are the police investigating? It's Larry, isn't it? He's been acting really strange the past two days. Almost as if he's in a fog. I bet the guilt is eating him alive."

Felicia looked like most people I see reading the *National Enquirer*, equal parts delighted and horrified. I shook my head. "I honestly don't know who the police are looking at. Detective Kaiser said he couldn't share the details of his investigation." Felicia looked skeptical, and I almost said,

"Cross my heart and hope to die." Being back in high school made me want to regress.

Thank goodness a director yelled over the microphone for the kids to take the floor before Felicia could grill me any further. I dumped my bag on one of the bleachers as music began to pump through the loudspeaker. It was time to sing and dance.

A little over an hour later, the kids had executed hundreds of jazz squares to hits like "Don't Stop Believin'," "Ain't No Mountain High Enough," and "Jump, Jive an' Wail" while the parents sitting in the stands cheered them on. I'd liked those songs well enough before camp started this week. If I never heard them again after this, I wouldn't be sorry.

Still sweating and panting, the kids were asked to take a seat in the stands so we could talk to them about what had happened to Mr. Lucas. This was supposed to provide "closure." It also lent itself to bored expressions and a lot of texting. Both had nothing to do with the subject matter and more with the presentation. The director doing the talking made murder as exciting as watching paint dry. A neat trick.

When the guy was done, the kids milled around the field house saying their good-byes before heading for the door. I walked over to the far left corner, where Eric was changing his shoes.

"How are you holding up?"

Eric looked up at me and smiled. "Better than the last time you saw me."

Cheesy show choir tunes beat jail any day.

"Did your parents come home?"

"They got into town this morning. Detective Kaiser said I have to be at the station this afternoon ready to talk." He tucked his thumbs into his jeans pockets and struck an uncaring pose. Too bad his eyes gave him away. My heart went out to him. The kid was terrified.

"It sucks you have to go through this. Just so you know, I've been asking around. Mr. Lucas upset a lot of people, and Detective Kaiser is aware of that."

Eric swallowed hard. "I hope you're right."

"Eric, are you ready to go?" Chessie sashayed up to Eric and put a possessive hand on his arm. "My mom will freak if I'm not home on time. She thinks the boogeyman is going to get me."

I smiled at her. "Your dancing looked very polished, Chessie."

Her eyes flicked over to me. "Gee, thanks. That means a whole lot coming from someone like you." The sarcastic tone said the opposite. "Come on, Eric." Hoisting her pink dance bag onto her shoulder, Chessie strutted toward the exit, not even glancing back to see whether Eric was following. More than likely, he always did.

Eric looked down at his shoes. "Sorry about that."

"I'm getting the feeling Chessie doesn't like me."

"It's not that she doesn't like you," he hurried to reassure me. "She said you were really cool to go to bat with the cops for me. It's just—"

"What?"

"Well, she wants a coach who can help us win. Sorry." Eric grabbed his gym bag and trudged after Chessie.

"Kids can be a tough crowd to win over." Devlyn's voice reached over my shoulder. I turned, and he smiled. "Don't worry. Once your choir sees the moves we're working on, they'll love you. Trust me."

"Chessie Bock hates me."

"She hates losing. There's a difference." He sat down on the ground and crossed his legs. Today Devlyn was wearing a lime-green-and-yellow shirt and light blue jeans. He patted the space on the floor next to him, and I planted my butt on the ground. "Paige, you have a lot to learn about teenagers, but you've come to the right place."

"High school?"

"Me." He grinned. "I've been teaching them for twelve years. I've learned that once you win their trust, they will walk off a cliff for you. Until then, you just have to keep trying. You've already got them halfway by helping Eric. It won't take a lot to push them over to your side."

"Like proving he's innocent?"

Devlyn let out a deep, sexy laugh. "That would probably do it. But just in case you aren't the next Sherlock Holmes, we should probably polish Plan B. What do you think?" He hopped to his feet and held out a hand.

I really wanted to go home to Aunt Millie's and climb back into bed. Instead, I took Devlyn's hand and let him hoist me to my feet. "Let's do it."

It took me a minute to figure out where I'd stashed my bag. We were halfway to the choir room when we heard a singsong voice call out, "Devlyn, wait up." The clip-clop of high heels and the high-pitched perky voice announced Felicia's presence before the rest of her appeared around the corner. "If I didn't know better, I would think you were trying to avoid me." Felicia waited for Devlyn to deny it. He just gave her a mysterious half smile. Undeterred, she continued, "I talked to Richard this morning, and he said you haven't called him. Don't put it off too long. Someone else will snap him up."

"Then I'll be happy Richard is happy." Devlyn perched a hand on his hip and let out a huge sigh. "Actually, I met someone interesting yesterday, and you know me. I'm a one-love-interest-at-a-time kind of guy."

"I wish more men had that problem. In my experience it seems to be the more the merrier."

Devlyn put his arm around her and squeezed. "Honey, you deserve better than that."

Felicia sighed. "You have no idea how long it took for me to figure that out. Ah well. Tell your new man he's a lucky guy. I have costumes to sew. Bye."

Once she was gone, it was time to get to work. We danced through everything we'd already choreographed, made a few changes, and finally got to the big finish. Yesterday, that involved me mopping the floor with my butt. I wasn't inclined to repeat the experience.

"We need a lift at the end," Devlyn insisted.

I tried to ignore how sexy his damp hair looked. "Breaking bones is not going to help me win over the kids."

"The lift isn't that hard. We just had a minor mishap. New partners have an adjustment period. Yesterday was ours."

"You call falling on my behind an adjustment?"

He pushed a lock of dark hair off his forehead and flashed a wide grin. "Yeah. That's exactly what I call it. Are you ready to try it again? If I drop you, I promise this time I'll break your fall."

Devlyn's smile was flirty and teasing. Thank God he was gay or womankind would be in serious trouble. I was going to cave, but not without getting something I wanted. "I'll do it on one condition. You tell me why you listed yourself as a suspect in Greg's murder."

He chuckled. When I didn't, he stopped laughing. "Are you serious?" I waited. Finally, he blew out air and said, "Okay. Greg and I didn't have the best relationship. I thought his directing style was a little too focused on the girls."

"He hit on them?" My stomach clenched. I already knew Greg hit on Chessie, but hearing it was still a shock.

"Technically, he never crossed that line. At least not in public." Devlyn clenched his jaw. "He was always showing the kid playing Tony how to hold Maria. I called him on it after rehearsal one day. He denied it and decked me. The next day he acted as though we'd never had that conversation."

"Did he leave the girl alone?"

Devlyn's face was grim. "He did, which annoyed the hell out of her. She looked like she wanted to scratch my eyes out."

"The girl wanted the attention?" I never knew when a guy was hitting on me, so I assumed the girl was comparably oblivious.

Devlyn barked out a bitter laugh. "I hate to be the one to tell you this, but lots of teenage girls think they want that kind of attention. They wear sexy clothes, ask for individual practice sessions, and text 'thank you' messages. I'm sure Greg got more than his fair share of messages telling him how much they owed him for his hard work."

Things had changed a lot since I was in high school. Or maybe they hadn't, and I just never noticed. Both thoughts were more than a little disturbing.

"Why didn't you report Greg?"

"Rehearsals were public. Lots of people were watching, and no one else reported it for the same reason I didn't. I might have been wrong. A report of that kind of behavior is the kiss of death for a teacher's career. I've known more than one teacher who was falsely accused, proved he didn't do it, and still couldn't get another teaching job."

Scary. "So your confrontation with Greg is the reason you could be a suspect?"

"Well, I did say I'd kill him if he ever did anything like that again. Threatening death tends to put a person in the suspect column."

True enough, but in this case I was pretty sure I could cross Devlyn off the list.

He held out his hand and asked, "So, do you think I'm a killer? If not, you owe me a lift."

I wasn't one to welch on a deal. The first lift wasn't successful, but neither of us landed on the floor. Things were looking up. The next was better. The third time was the charm. I landed on his shoulder, keeping my chest high and my weight balanced. Devlyn's left hand sat on my hip. He placed his right hand on my knee to keep me stable. Only now that I was up here, I wasn't sure how he planned on getting me down. All one hundred and thirty-three pounds of me was going to get heavy—fast.

"Ready." Devlyn sounded out of breath. Crap. His hands grabbed my hips, and I tried to hop off his shoulder. He must not have been expecting that choice. His hands slipped, and I started to plummet. My arms flailed as the ground neared. Devlyn wrapped his arms around my chest, which pulled him off balance, and together we went crashing to the floor. He was good to his word and cushioned my fall. This time he ended up on the linoleum with me seated in his lap.

"My fault," he panted into my ear. "We should have talked about a dismount before we did the lift."

"That would have been helpful." I shifted my weight on his legs in an attempt to get up. He in turn tightened his grip around my waist. I instinctively leaned into his chest and put my head against his shoulder, enjoying the contact. Then I twisted around to look at him. He smiled at me, and his eyes met mine. I saw a spark of amusement and something else. His hand brushed my cheek, and he leaned down and kissed my nose.

"Ready to try again?" he asked.

I sighed. For a moment I'd almost forgotten the man was gay. Maybe Aunt Millie was right. I needed a date.

"Let's do it," I said, climbing to my feet. "If I don't do the lift perfect during our demonstration, the kids will eat me alive."

The next three lift attempts went off without a hitch. We ran the entire number one more time before deciding to call it quits.

Devlyn turned off the music and grabbed a towel from his bag. "What are you doing after this? More murder investigation?"

"I plan to go home, check the bathroom for dogs, and then take a shower." Devlyn raised an eyebrow, and I laughed. "Don't ask. You really don't want to know."

He shrugged. "Do you want to schedule some time to choreograph the rest of the music? My weekend is open."

"What about your new love interest?"

"I'm still not sure the feeling is mutual, so I'm taking it slow." He reached into his bag and pulled out a business card. "Here. Call me if you have some free time. I'll even buy you dinner."

"I might just take you up on that."

His smile widened. "That's what I hoped you'd say. Come on. I'll walk you to your car."

The sun felt great on my skin as we strolled to the faculty parking lot. When we got to my car, I reached into my bag for my keys and pulled out a folded piece of paper. Huh. Aunt Millie must have left me a note this morning. I opened the paper, and my stomach clenched. It was a printout of a review of a production I'd starred in. I didn't have to read the paper to remember the reviewer said, *Ms. Marshall would have done the audience a favor if she had died before the curtain opened.*

Aunt Millie definitely didn't leave this. Whoever did had scribbled a message on the bottom of the page.

Take a hint and get off the stage. Or else.

Chapter 9

Devlyn called the cops. I stared at the paper for several seconds before putting it back in the bag and getting out my own phone. Conveniently, Detective Kaiser was the last number I'd called. I hit redial expecting to get voice mail, but Mike himself answered.

Taking a deep breath, I explained what I'd found in my bag. Then added, "Another teacher has called the police, but since it happened here at the school, I thought you'd want to know." I sounded logical and calm, which was a miracle. My stomach hurt, my heart thudded in my chest, and I heard a dull roaring in my head.

I waited for the detective to tell me not to worry about the note. That it was a prank. Instead, he said, "I'll be there in ten minutes."

Seven minutes later, a black Ford Mustang pulled into the lot with Detective Kaiser behind the wheel. He climbed out as a black-and-white Prospect Glen police cruiser and two uniformed officers arrived.

Detective Kaiser waved at the officers, who stayed in their car, then walked over to me. He was wearing jeans with a white dress shirt, black tie, and gray sports coat. "You've had an interesting couple of days."

The detective held out his hand. I looked down at the paper and cringed. Sharing the worst review of my life made me want to throw up. Or maybe it was being threatened that made me feel that way. At the moment it was hard to tell.

I put the paper in his hand and leaned against my car. Devlyn put his arm around me and gave me a hug. I leaned against him, grateful for his support.

The detective looked up from the paper and raised an eyebrow. "When did you get this?"

"I don't know." Which scared me more than the note itself. "I went to get my keys out of my bag and found the note. I'm pretty sure it wasn't there this morning when I got here. Someone must have slipped it into the bag after I arrived."

"Was your bag locked in your office?"

Office? What office? "I sat it on one of the bleachers in the field house during camp. Once camp was over, I took it with me to the choir room until Devlyn and I were done working."

"So, your bag was out in the open."

I nodded.

He sighed. "You probably shouldn't do that. It's a good way to lose your wallet."

Or get threatened. I got the message.

Detective Mike pointed to the guys in the squad car, and they climbed out. "Officer James and Officer Mesching are going to take your statement while I chat with Mr. O'Shea. Technically, this doesn't fall under my job description, but I still want to talk to you after they're finished. Just in case."

The two officers took my statement, put the note in a plastic bag, and gave me a copy of the report. Neither of them seemed to think they'd find the person behind it, but they promised to do their best.

When they were gone, Devlyn asked, "Are you okay? You look pale."

Probably because I was feeling faint. "I'm fine. I didn't realize anyone around here knew about that review."

"The Internet makes those kinds of things easy to find," Detective Mike said with a shrug.

Devlyn gave my hand a squeeze. "Don't worry about people seeing that review. I saw that show. The reviewer was an idiot." He looked at the detective. "I've got to run, but the detective promised me he'd make sure you got home safely. Call me later so we can plan dinner this weekend. You keep your chin up."

I squeezed his hand back and watched him climb into his red BMW and drive off.

"Nice guy." Detective Kaiser leaned against my car. "Have you known him for long?"

"I met him yesterday."

"Did you see him near your bag this morning?"

"He was standing next to me when . . ." I stared at the detective. "You think Devlyn planted that review?"

"I don't know what I think. That's why I ask lots of questions." He pushed away from the car and frowned. "Sounds like you've been asking a lot of questions, too."

"You told me to," I reminded him. Or maybe Aunt Millie suggested I do it. I couldn't remember.

"I told you to keep your ears open and let me know if you heard anything I'd find interesting. Stirring up trouble wasn't exactly what I had in mind."

"So you think my questions and the note are related?"

"If they aren't, it's a big coincidence."

"And you don't like coincidences."

"I'm a cop. I'm genetically predisposed to dislike them." He shrugged out of his jacket and rolled up his shirtsleeves. I was impressed he'd worn the jacket for that long in the eighty-degree weather. "You didn't answer my question. Was Mr. O'Shea around your bag when you left it unattended?"

I started to say no, then remembered. "He was standing in front of the bleachers after camp today. My bag was about a row behind him."

"So he could have slipped the paper in your bag without you noticing."

"He could have, but he didn't."

"How can you be so sure? You've known Devlyn O'Shea for twenty-four hours." Detective Kaiser shook his head and gave me a stern look. "I've been asking around. The man had a beef with the victim, and his office is near the murder site. If he knows you've been asking questions about the murder, he might have good reason to try and scare you off."

When the detective put it that way, I understood his point even if I couldn't make myself believe it. Since I wasn't going to change his mind, I decided to change the subject. "Did you get my message about the football coach?"

He smiled. "I did."

"And? What do you think?"

"I think you've got too much free time on your hands." He looked at his watch. "It's time to get you home. I have an interview to conduct back at the station."

"Detective, are you going to arrest Eric?" If he was, I wanted to know. It was going to totally ruin my day.

A muscle in his jaw twitched. "How do you know I'm meeting with Eric?"

"He mentioned it after this morning's camp session."

I could see the detective trying to find fault with that. He must not have since he said, "I try not to arrest people unless I'm certain I have all the pieces in place. And remember, I asked you to call me Mike."

Right.

After climbing into my car, I headed back to Aunt Millie's with Mike's Mustang trailing behind me. I pulled into Millie's crowded driveway, and Mike honked twice before pulling away.

Millie's incredibly long drive was a parking lot filled with expensive, recently washed and waxed cars. It looked like Millie was having a party—which, knowing my aunt, was entirely possible. I backed out my car, parked it on the street in case I needed to make a quick getaway, and hiked up the drive to the front door.

A wave of sound hit me the minute I stepped into the arctic air. For a minute I thought I'd walked into the monkey house at Brookfield Zoo. I crept toward the noises into the living room and froze in the doorway. At least a dozen diamond-wearing women were munching on sandwiches, sipping wine spritzers, and getting facials. Monkeys would have been better.

"There you are, Paige. We've been waiting for you." Millie hurried over to me as fast as her pink pencil skirt and four-inch heels would allow. She grabbed my arm before I could beat a retreat. "Everyone, this is my niece." A bunch of heads swung toward me. Millie leaned toward me and whispered, "All of them belong to Dana Lucas's country club. If we ply them with enough pampering and liquor, they'll tell us every detail down to the style of her bikini wax."

I was going to pretend I didn't hear that, and if any of

these women decided to talk about their own bikini waxes, I was going to dive out a window. I couldn't afford the therapy bills.

"Why do they think they're all here?" I asked.

Millie smiled. "I'm holding a spa day with Mary Kay products. By the time today is over, the women will give us the dirt on Dana and buy thousands of dollars in products."

Leave it to my aunt to find a way to turn spying into a marketing plan. There was a reason she was the number one sales associate in the Midwest. This was it.

"Get a sandwich and a glass of wine and mingle." My aunt grabbed my hand, pulled me to the middle of the living room, and headed off to help one of her "clients." I looked around the room, trying to decide what to do. Three women were sitting on the couch and two on the love seat. Seven other guests with green-and-white goo on their faces sat in chairs while two twentysomething stylists hovered over them. All the women were impeccably dressed in tailored shorts and matching tops. The Stepford wives had come to life.

My stomach growled, which made my decision for me. I headed toward the dining room, where a lady with brown teased hair and an unfortunate choice of bright blue eye shadow was busy piling mini sandwiches and raw vegetables on plates.

I grabbed one of Millie's silver-and-white china plates and said, "Hi. I'm Millie's niece, Paige." Not the best opening, but it's what I had.

The woman pulled a carrot stick out of her mouth and gave me a tentative smile. "Millie talks about you all the time. I'm Eliza."

The woman sounded like she'd performed CPR on a helium tank. "It's nice to meet my aunt's friends. Do you belong to her country club?"

"No. My husband and I belong to the Glen. I met your aunt at a dog show two years ago. My Binkie competed against Killer for Best in Show." Eliza put down her plate and reached for her wallet. Moments later, I was viewing professionally retouched pictures of Eliza's wire fox terrier, Binkie. Binkie running. Binkie sitting. Binkie wearing a sparkling blue-and-white tiara. The little white-and-brown face was cute, but after the first ten photos I stopped paying attention.

Thank God Eliza was so busy telling me about Binkie that I didn't need to comment. That left me free to eat the other three sandwiches on my plate and grab two more. If it weren't for her high-pitched, squeaky voice, the situation would have been ideal. The sound was great for calling dogs but bad for digestion.

Once the photo array was stowed, I changed the subject. "You look like you work out. Does your club have good facilities?"

"Oh yes. Although, running with Binkie is all the exercise I really need. But I do enjoy yoga. My instructor had to cancel this week, which was sad. I find yoga very relaxing."

"I took a yoga class last night. I wouldn't say I found it relaxing."

A voice from behind laughed. "That's because you don't take it from Madame Zandri. She's part yoga instructor and part psychic."

I turned. A tall woman with bleached blonde hair and black eyebrows stood in the doorway. She was wearing torn jeans and a faded green tank top. Most surprising, she looked to be at least thirty years younger than the rest of the guests.

Eliza sniffed. "Madame Zandri is a lovely teacher. I know several of her private students who say they have out-of-body experiences when doing yoga with her."

The mystery woman grinned. "You'd have an out-of-body experience, too, if you inhaled Madame Zandri's incense." She turned to me and added, "She burns homegrown marijuana."

"I think it's time for my facial." Eliza frowned at the newcomer as she marched into the living room.

As soon as she was out of earshot, I asked, "Does Madame Zandri really burn marijuana?"

"Yep." She sauntered into the room and grabbed a chocolate chip cookie off the table. "She also uses her homegrown incense during tarot readings."

"Sounds like more fun than I had. Hi. My name is Paige."

She smiled as she shook my hand. "Sherrie Bush. Did you take your yoga class at the club?"

"No. Although, I believe Dana Lucas also teaches at the Glen."

"Dana?" Sherrie laughed. "No wonder a drug-induced haze sounds good. Dana used to be a pretty good teacher. Then her marriage went bust. I guess she couldn't take out the aggression on her husband so she started using her students." Sherrie finished her cookie and grabbed another.

I snagged an oatmeal raisin and started munching. From the next room Aunt Millie's voice announced it was pedicure time. "Do you want to get your toes done?"

We both looked down at her feet. Sherrie was wearing black-and-red high-tops with frayed laces. In several places, I could see the white of her socks peeking through the worn fabric. My clunky white sneakers looked downright stylish in comparison.

"Never mind." I laughed. Then I switched to my topic of choice. "Dana's aggression explains the low attendance at her class yesterday."

"Her ex-husband getting whacked probably made her

students a little leery, too." Sherrie chomped down on her cookie. "He was murdered a couple nights ago."

"I heard." That sounded better than saying, "Yeah, I was the one who found him." "I'd like to think her students would make a point of coming to class to express their sympathy."

Sherri laughed. "The new Dana doesn't encourage sympathy."

"Did the old Dana?"

Leaning against the table, Sherrie chewed on her cookie and thought about the question. "The old Dana was softer. More interested in helping people. She never yelled or raised her voice, and her classes were challenging, but only because she pushed you to get better control of your body. Going to her classes was the only good thing about having a club membership until her husband two-timed her. I hope the guy I saw her with coming out of the club on Wednesday night treats her better."

"Guy?" What guy? Greg Lucas was either killed on Wednesday evening or early Thursday morning.

Sherrie raised an eyebrow and studied me for a minute. Finally, she said, "The guy was a little shorter than Dana with brownish hair. I would have thought she would have been done with guys shorter than her after Greg, but I guess the rest of him was different enough to make her take a risk."

"Different how?"

She smiled. "He was kind of scrawny and cute in an I-need-to-spend-time-in-the-sun kind of way. He even opened the car door for her. Greg would never have done that. Heck, if this guy wasn't driving a Dodge Neon, I might have fought for him. A girl has to have her standards."

Sherrie grabbed a glass of wine off the table and downed it. "Time to get my eyebrows plucked. I promised my mother."

She sauntered back into the living room, leaving me

alone and choking on my oatmeal cookie. Sherrie had just described Larry from the tip of his pasty white toes all the way to his budget car. What the hell was he doing at the Glen Country Club with his arch-nemesis's ex-wife? Something told me that whatever Larry was doing, it couldn't be good.

Chapter 10

I was conflicted. The nosy part of me wanted to rush out the door, hop in my car, and find out what Larry was doing fraternizing with the yoga Nazi. The wimpy side wanted to stay indoors and hide from whoever was slipping veiled threats in my dance bag.

Wimpy sucked. I opted for nosy. But when I marched into the living room, I ran smack into a cloud of cloying perfume. My eyes began to water, and my nose twitched as women sprayed their wrists with Aunt Millie's latest and greatest products. From the way the women in the middle of the room were teetering on their heels and slurring their words, I guessed they'd hit the free bar a bit too hard. Either that or Mary Kay's new line of fragrances could be used as biochemical weapons. One spray and terrorists would start singing "Kumbaya." Awesome.

I crept around the country club ladies, hoping no one would notice. Until I tripped on a pair of purple-and-gold heels and went crashing to the floor. Crap. All heads turned in my direction. A blonde woman with no shoes and a smear of red lipstick on her cheek gasped and hurried over. Swaying slightly as she walked, she reached me and held out a hand. "I'm sorry. I have no idea how my shoes got over there."

The woman grabbed my arm and tugged me to my feet. The minute I let go of her hand, she went flying four steps backward, tripped over the edge of the love seat, and went hurtling into the lap of a sleeping white-haired lady. The sleeping woman woke with a yelp and smacked the blonde with her purse.

The blonde shrieked. "How dare you?" And grabbed the purse with her newly manicured fingers. She cocked back her arm and prepared to let the purse fly when the tiny Eliza snatched the bag from her and smacked her from behind.

"Don't you dare hit Melinda," she hollered as the blonde grabbed a pillow off the love seat, glared at Eliza, and gave the pillow a fling.

The blonde had terrible aim. The pillow flew wide to the right and took out two dark-haired women in tennis attire. The blonde shrieked again and grabbed another pillow. Not to be outdone, Eliza took off her shoe. As footwear and foamed fabric flew, I headed for the exit. I closed the door on the sounds of primal screams and shattering glass.

I hurried down the drive, weaving in between the Lexus SUVs, and pulled out my cell. Aunt Millie answered her phone on the third ring. "Where did you go?" she yelled. Somewhere in the background I heard a groan.

"I got a lead from Sherrie and decided to check it out."

"Kathleen, put down the vase this minute," Millie yelled.

I looked back at the house and sighed. Leaving Aunt Millie to deal with the fallout felt icky. "Do you need me to come back and help? It sounds like things got out of hand."

"Don't worry about me, dear. The day I can't handle a bunch of inebriated women is the day I die. Besides, once I get enough coffee in them, they'll feel so guilty they'll triple their orders. You go run down your lead and save that boy. I'll take care of the rest." I heard another crash, and Millie disconnected.

I still felt bad about ditching my aunt with the drunken debutantes, but I knew better than to interfere with Millie when she in Mary Kay sales mode. And she was right. The minute the women realized they'd trashed her living room, they'd get out their credit cards and charge them to the limit. By the time the day was done, Millie would probably earn another pink car.

Cranking the air in my car, I dialed Larry. I hoped he'd have time to get together and chat. Damn. Voice mail. I opted not to leave a message, hung up the phone and hit the gas. No way was I going back into Aunt Millie's house until the coast was clear. The clock on my dashboard read 3:14 P.M. The school would still be open. Maybe Larry was putting the finishing touches on his lesson plans.

Football practice was still going on in the field to the left of the school, which meant at least one door to the school would be unlocked. Larry had given me a key to the choir room and another to his office, but I wasn't entrusted with a key to the front door—yet. Guess they were waiting to see if I could resist the urge to steal the erasers.

The side door near the practice field was open. I walked down to the Fine Arts wing, trying not to look as out of place as I felt. My high school experience hadn't been terrible. In fact, compared to those of a lot of my friends, my high school life had been downright wonderful. I'd gotten better than average grades, scored leads in the musicals, and even got elected to prom court my senior year. Still, despite the fond memories, returning to high school in any capacity wasn't something to which I'd ever aspired. And yet, here I was cruising the halls and championing one of the students I had never wanted to teach. Life was strange.

The choir room door was locked. I knocked just in case Larry was inside. Nothing. I got out my shiny new key and twisted it in the lock.

No one was inside. The adjoining office was also dark. Drat. Still, now that I was here, familiarizing myself with the space wouldn't hurt. Perhaps I'd poke around some desk drawers, flip through whatever papers I could find—all in order to understand Larry's organizational system, of course. And if I found something incriminating, well, I couldn't help it.

I went over my reasoning twice to make sure I could spout it back to someone if I was discovered. As a performer, I liked knowing my lines. Certain I could bluff with the best of them, I crossed the room and began pawing through the stacks of paper on the piano. Lots of bad choral arrangements. I resisted the urge to hide the worst of them and looked in the piano bench. Larry's metronome and conductor's baton sat inside along with several ancient-looking cough drops. The rest of the room was filled with equally professional items. Not exactly a surprise, but under the circumstances, disappointing.

That left the office.

I got out my other key, took several deep breaths, and let myself in. Hitting the light, I stepped into the room. Just standing in the small, cluttered space made my muscles tense. Two filing cabinets and an upright piano were positioned against one wall. A large metal desk sat on the opposite side of the room. A desktop computer sat on the desk, along with enough paper to throw a ticker tape parade. On the wall were photos of kids in glittery costumes smiling wide at the camera. In the middle of each group of kids was Larry.

That's when it hit me. This was Larry's personal space. Yeah, I was allowed to use it, too, but as a guest. This felt like breaking and entering. For the first time in my life, I was probably doing something more illegal than photocopying music. Illegal was bad. Then again, so was being threatened for trying to help a teenage boy prove his innocence.

Shoving my doubts aside, I headed for the filing cabinets. Locked. Good. One less thing to feel guilty about invading. I sat down at the desk and flipped on the computer. While I was waiting for it to boot, I scanned the desk calendar. In perfect penmanship, Larry had written in all the official school events. Every football game, dance, and choral concert for the upcoming year was accounted for.

I sifted through the stacks of loose papers. Class lists, music theory worksheets, Illinois Music Educators Association memos, and a bunch of pamphlets for the Symphony Center and other professional Chicago choral groups were piled on the desk. I even found a folder containing handwritten notes about dance steps to the clichéd show choir songs Larry suggested yesterday.

Yikes. The steps weren't just basic, they were boring. I wasn't an expert on these competitions, but from the videos I'd seen, any choir doing these steps would be blown out of the water. Judging by the notes in the margin, Larry knew this as well. This combined with his desperation to win might have made Larry snap.

Shoved in the back of the dance steps folder was an overdraft notice from Larry's bank. He probably didn't even know it was in there. It was dated a week ago. Poor Larry was more financially strapped than I was, which was saying something.

I put the papers aside, turned to the computer, and clicked through a bunch of folders. Nothing terribly exciting. A couple of folders labeled *Grades* and followed by a class number were password protected. I clicked on Larry's e-mail and a password screen appeared. For kicks, I tried a couple of musical terms.

Denied.

I didn't know Larry well enough to make a real attempt at cracking his password. With Aunt Millie it was easy. Plug in the name of one of her dead dogs, and you were in. My former roommate was even easier. Her theatrical memory skills were impeccable. Her daily memory was sketchy at best so she kept a list of her passwords taped to the bottom of her desk drawer.

I scooted the chair back a few inches and stared at the desk drawers. Larry wouldn't do something that silly. Would he? I pulled out the side drawers. Lots of paper clips, rubber bands, highlighters, and sticky notes. I even found a few grade books and binders, but nothing had passwords written on them. I tugged on the middle drawer. Locked. Since picking locks wasn't my specialty, I was going to have to call it quits. Unless . . .

Pushing the chair all the way back, I got on my hands and knees and crawled under the desk. Ick. The janitorial staff definitely needed to vacuum. Sneezing, I flipped onto my back and looked up. Taped to the bottom of the desk was a Post-it Note. The tape was also yellow, giving the impression that Post-it had been there a long time. On it were written combinations of letters and numbers. Each combination ended with the numbers 2003.

Huh. I scribbled the numbers onto a new Post-it, backed out of my position under the desk, and sat back down on the chair. Armed with passwords, I started typing.

None of them worked. I looked back down at the combinations. Could 2003 be the year Larry taped the Post-it to the bottom of the desk? If so, maybe he changed the passwords every year. I tried all four with this year's numbers at the end. Nope. Damn. Well, maybe he forgot to change the password when the calendar changed this year. Nope. I scrolled back another year.

Open sesame! My heart skipped several beats as the graphic changed. I was in.

Larry's e-mail appeared on the screen. Right off the bat I decided not to touch any of the new ones since I wasn't positive I'd be able to return them to their currently unread state. I scrolled past the ten bolded, unread e-mails and focused on the others in the inbox. I saw e-mails on music orders, textbooks, and riser setup. Riveting. Nothing suspicious.

Clicking on the save folder, I selected the most recent message dated almost two weeks ago from a KRIS42. I skimmed it and sat up straight in the chair. *Ok. I'll do it for $1,500 cash. Tell me when you need it done.*

The sender didn't sign his name, and his e-mail address didn't provide any hints. I scrolled down the saved e-mails. The only other one from KRIS42 was sent a week before the one I'd just read. I clicked it. *If you want me to kill, it'll be $4,000.*

The back of my neck started to sweat. Larry's e-mails to KRIS42 weren't included on KRIS42's replies. I might be jumping to conclusions, but the amount of money combined with the word kill had warning bells going off in my head.

Hands shaking, I clicked on the sent box. I saw e-mails

dating back months, but nothing sent to KRIS42. They had been deleted. I clicked on the deleted folder. Nothing there. Computer geeks somewhere might be able to recover the e-mails Larry sent, but I was at a loss. Which really made me wonder. From the looks of things, Larry never deleted his sent e-mails or cleared out his e-mail trash can. Yet, he deleted these specific e-mails. Why would a person do that unless he had something to hide?

I jumped at the sound of footsteps coming down the hallway. Heart racing, I closed down the e-mail program and logged off the computer. The footsteps were getting closer. I hit the off button, hurried out of the office, and closed the door behind me just as the choir room door swung open.

Felicia walked in, spotted me, and smiled. I shoved my hands in my pockets so Felicia wouldn't see them shaking. Next time I broke and entered, I needed to bring a lookout.

"Hey, Paige. Have you seen Larry?" Felicia shoved some papers into her purse and frowned. "We were supposed to meet to go over a few ideas for his choir's costumes."

Larry's choir had double the number of kids as mine. They competed in a different division and only went to half the competitions, which meant they only got to spend a fraction of the overall costume budget. Making thirty kids look fabulous on almost no money took skill and a lot of creativity.

Felicia sniffed at the air, took a step closer, and sniffed at me. Her nose crinkled, and she let out a high-pitched sneeze. I sniffed at my shirt. Oh God. I smelled like a funeral parlor.

"My aunt was having a Mary Kay demonstration. I guess I got too close to the perfume," I explained. Then I directed the conversation back to less embarrassing ground. "I haven't seen Larry."

Felicia sneezed again and frowned. "He's not answering his phone. I was sure I'd find him here." She walked toward the office, and I prayed to God I'd remembered to turn off the light. I turned around and let out a whoosh of air. The lights were off.

"I tried to call him, too," I admitted. Then I got an idea. Felicia seemed to keep up with the gossip. Maybe she could answer some questions for me. "Maybe he's with his new girlfriend."

Felicia frowned, and her eyes narrowed. "Larry has a girlfriend?" Three more sneezes. "Who is it?" Felicia didn't like being left off the gossip train.

"I thought you might know. Someone mentioned Larry was escorting a tall blonde to his car the other night."

Felicia shook her head. "I'm betting she's just a friend. Larry has a hard time making the first move. He needs the woman to do it for him." Her phone beeped. She flipped it open and laughed. "Larry is sitting at Starbucks waiting for me to show up. I mentioned we could grab coffee while we talk. He must have forgotten I said for us to meet here. Oh well. No harm. Do you want to come with?"

Hell no. After finding those e-mails, I wanted to stay as far away from Larry DeWeese as possible. Only, unless Detective Mike stumbled across the e-mails I just read, the truth about them and the identity of the mysterious KRIS42 wouldn't come out anytime soon. It sucked that I couldn't just hand the messages to the detective. But stolen evidence wouldn't be admissible, and I'd end up cooling my heels in an ill-fitting jumpsuit for breaking and entering. Orange was definitely not my color. What I needed was real proof that Larry offed Greg. And I figured the only person who had that proof was Larry himself. Which is why I said, "I'd love to go."

Larry was sitting at a small table in the back of the Starbucks when we arrived. He waved at Felicia and gave me a pleasant, albeit confused smile. "I didn't know you were going to be here, Paige, or I would have gotten you a drink."

An iced coffee was sitting on the table. Felicia picked it up and winked at Larry. "Isn't he the best? If only I dated men that were half as wonderful."

Larry blushed.

"Felicia and I ran into each other." I pulled out the chair across from Larry and took a seat. "She asked me to come along."

"Do you want a coffee? I'm happy to get one f-f-for you." The only other time I'd heard Larry stutter was when Greg was antagonizing him. What was causing Larry's emotional lather this time—my presence or Felicia's flattery?

I turned down the offer for caffeine. I was jumpy enough without adding a stimulant to my bloodstream. "Let's talk costumes."

We did, which made me wish I'd accepted the coffee offer. The discussion over whether rhinestones or sequins sparkled more was enough to make me fall into a coma. Larry and Felicia finally decided to bedazzle the costumes and moved on. Hallelujah.

After another half hour of costume chat, Felicia tucked her notes away and finished her coffee. "This is going to be a fabulous year. I can feel it." She leaned over and kissed Larry on the cheek. Larry looked like he was ready to pass out as Felicia giggled, "Oh, I probably shouldn't have done that. Your girlfriend might think I'm trying to move in on her man."

"G-g-girlfriend?" Larry swallowed, and his eyes darted around like a man trying to escape. "I never said I had a girlfriend."

Felicia smiled. "You didn't have to. Someone spotted you and your blonde companion getting into your car the other night." She winked at me.

"A b-b-blonde?" Larry's eyes opened wide, and he shook his head. "Oh, her. She's helping me with a financial issue."

Felicia sighed. "I was hoping one of us was starting to get lucky in love. Oh well. I guess we just keep trying." She sneezed and looked at her watch. "Speaking of getting lucky, I should go home and change for my date. I'll see you two on Tuesday morning." She pushed back her chair, and all male eyes in the place, especially Larry's, watched her hips as she swished out the door.

"So," I said, trying to get Larry's attention. "I hope the financial situation isn't serious. My aunt had a run-in with the IRS a couple years ago, and it wasn't fun." In truth, Aunt Millie had loved every minute of being audited. The IRS auditor was the one who hated the process, including meeting Killer. Millie had every deduction backed up with color-coded receipts. Too bad the auditor didn't know when to cut his losses. He ended up losing the case, his job, and part of his sports coat in the process. Killer had a fondness for polyester.

Larry shook his head. "It's nothing s-s-serious. You can forget about it."

Yeah, right. I gave Larry my best nonthreatening smile and said, "Hey, I've been meaning to ask. Do you know Dana Lucas?"

Larry went still. "Dana Lucas?"

I pretended not to notice the color draining from Larry's face. "I met her yesterday at the gym. She wasn't all that upset that her husband was dead."

"Th-they got d-d-d-divorced for a reason."

"I know, but . . ." I bit my lip and tried to look conflicted.

Larry leaned forward. "But what?"

Ha! So much for the teacher that gave me a B on my acting final in college. "Detective Kaiser asked us to report anything out of the ordinary. Don't you think this qualifies?"

"No." He swallowed hard. "I think pointing fingers at people would make us look bad. I have to go. See you on Tuesday. It's the first day of school so don't be late." He pushed out his chair and stalked to the door.

The minute Larry hit the sidewalk, he got out his phone and started dialing. I grabbed my purse and got to the door in time to hear him say, "I'll meet you in ten minutes."

Hmm.

I got in my car and watched as a Larry walked down the block to his. A few minutes later, I was cruising several car lengths behind his silver Dodge Neon as it wove through Friday afternoon traffic. If Larry was meeting Dana, I wanted to be there to see it.

Chapter 11

Larry pulled onto a residential street and parked in the driveway of a two-story white brick house. The house looked expensive. After seeing his financial statements, I figured Larry would be more the no-frills renter type. I parked on the street several well-manicured lawns away and waited. A few minutes later, a cherry red Jeep pulled in behind Larry's Neon, and Dana Lucas climbed out.

Score one for intuition.

Dana walked up to the front door with an agitated Larry trailing behind her. She unlocked the door, and the two disappeared inside.

Huh. Now what?

My watch ticked off the seconds as a man walked his German shepherd down the sidewalk. A squirrel scampered up and down the tree to my left four times, and a bird crapped on my windshield. Other than that, nothing happened. How was I supposed to learn anything by sitting out here watching the grass grow? Stakeouts in movies always looked way more exciting than this.

I was considering heading home when something knocked on the passenger window. I turned and screamed as a face stared back at me. Then I realized the face belonged to Detective Mike, and I wanted to cry. Going to jail for stalking was going to really suck.

Sweat ran down Mike's face as he pointed to the lock on the passenger door, and I hit the switch. A few seconds later, he slid into the passenger's seat with contented sigh. "Your air-conditioning works a lot better than mine."

I blinked. I was waiting to be arrested or at the very least yelled at. The conversation about car efficiency threw me.

Mike shifted in his seat and smiled. "So do I need to ask what you're doing here?"

I could be honest or try to be cute. "Right now I'm allowing you to use my air-conditioning."

"Which is the reason I'm considering not hauling you in for obstructing justice."

Yikes. Cute wasn't working. I switched to honest. "Someone told me Larry and Dana have been spending time together. I thought that was strange, so I decided to check it out."

He half laughed, half sighed. I wasn't sure if that was a good response, but it was better than anger.

"You could have called me instead of playing private investigator. Larry could have spotted you tailing him."

"How did you know I followed Larry?"

"I watched you do it. I'm parked right over there." He pointed to where his car sat—directly across the street from me.

Oops. I'd been so focused on Larry's car, I never noticed Mike's Mustang. Note to self—next time watch the entire street. "Why are you sitting here watching Dana's house? I thought you told me she wasn't a suspect."

"I said she had an alibi."

"What's the difference?"

"I said one. The other one you inferred."

A fair if annoying point. "So you don't believe Dana's alibi?"

"I didn't say that."

"Why else would you be here?"

He grinned. "Maybe I just want to annoy you."

If that was the case, it was working. I looked back at Dana's house, trying to ignore Mike's eyes boring into the back of my head. The wind made the leaves on the tree flutter. A dog barked in the distance. As far as I could tell, a stakeout was a fancy term for intense boredom.

"Do you go on stakeouts a lot?" I asked.

Mike chuckled. "This isn't a stakeout."

"It's not?" We were in a car watching a house currently occupied by suspects. It felt like a stakeout to me.

"No. You're going to go home and take a shower." He sniffed at the air and shook his head. "You smell like my grandmother. While you do that, I'm going to go knock on the door. Have a good night."

He closed the passenger door, waved at me, and walked up to Dana's oak door. A few seconds later, Dana opened the door and the detective disappeared inside.

I sniffed at my clothing and sighed. Driving with the windows open had helped air out the worst of the smell, but I needed a shower and a wardrobe change to get rid of the rest. Only, I couldn't bring myself to leave. Now that Mike was in the house, things might get interesting.

Nope. Still boring. I watched a fly bang his head against the window in a futile effort to escape the heat. After what felt like hours—but my clock had the nerve to claim was only fifteen minutes—Mike walked out the front door. His eyes narrowed as he spotted me.

He looked back at the house. Dana was watching from the doorway. He frowned at me, got in his Mustang, and pulled away. A minute later my phone rang.

"Wait until Dana goes back in the house, then drive away. I'll meet you at McDonald's in ten minutes."

The call disconnected.

I watched the Mustang disappear down the street and waited for Dana to duck back inside. She didn't. Instead, she glanced back inside the house, then stepped outside. Dana paced up and down the driveway, pulled a pack of cigarettes out of her back pocket, and lit up. Smoking and yoga. Huh.

My phone rang again.

"Where are you?"

Dana let out a puff of smoke and turned. Now she was facing my direction. Crap. I scooted down in my seat to make myself less noticeable.

"Paige. What are you doing?"

"Trying not to be seen," I whispered.

"Dana's still outside?"

I peered over my steering wheel. Dana was puffing hard on her cigarette. "She's smoking. I'm keeping low so she can't see me."

There was a pause. "Is your car still running?"

"Yeah." Air-conditioning required it.

"Don't you think it looks suspicious for a car to be running without anyone sitting inside?" He disconnected.

Good point. Damn. I'd have to remember that for the next stakeout.

Thank goodness Dana didn't seem to care. She puffed,

dropped the cigarette butt on the grass, and lit up another. I resisted the urge to run out and step on the cigarette butt. Dana clearly hadn't paid attention to Smokey the Bear.

A few puffs into Dana's second cigarette, a red-faced, heavy-breathing Larry darted out of the house as if a team of angry football players was chasing him. He dashed past Dana and opened his car door. Dana shut the door before he could get in and yelled something. I was too far away to hear what it was. Damn it. Next time I'd park closer.

Larry shook his head no. Dana yelled something else as Larry looked up and down the street. Clearly, he was worried someone would see them. I fought the urge to wave.

Arms flailing, Dana stomped around. She put her hands on her hips and stared Larry down. He hung his head, dug into his pocket, and handed something to her. Turning on her heel, Dana pocketed the item and stalked up to the house. She locked the front door, headed to her car, and zoomed away. Larry zipped off moments later.

I counted to twenty before leaving my parking space, just in case. Five minutes later, I pulled into the McDonald's parking lot next to Detective Kaiser's muscle car.

He was sitting at a table near the door. I smiled at him. He didn't smile back, but he did hand me a supersized order of fries. I took that as a good sign and sat down.

The minute I had fries in my mouth, Mike said, "After the threatening note today, I would have thought you'd stay out of trouble."

Clearly, he didn't know me that well. As a matter of fact, I'd almost managed to forget about the threatening note. Watching the country club women in the middle of a cage match was distracting. Now that he'd reminded me, my stomach clenched and I put down the fries.

"The note was most likely a prank. Don't you think?" I willed Mike to say yes. A killer sending me notes was definitely in the undesirable category.

"If you hadn't been poking your nose into a murder investigation, I'd say yes." He picked up some of my discarded fries and started munching. "I checked the Internet. The review isn't easy to find, but it's there. Anyone motivated enough to dig for dirt on you would have found it."

Nice to know my failures would be on the Internet for decades to come. For some reason, I felt the need to say, "I got a lot of good reviews, too."

He smiled. "Those were easier to find. I guess I should come hear you sing sometime. Most of the reviews say you're fantastic. Which makes me wonder—why are you annoying me instead of singing onstage somewhere?"

Good question. One I'd love to know the answer to myself. "Just waiting for the right opportunity." Now I was depressed and freaked. Time to change the subject. "So what did Dana say when you went inside?"

I didn't really expect him to tell me, but I lived in hope. Besides, asking was better than talking about my performing career. Or lack of.

Mike grabbed a couple of fries and leaned back in the white-and-red chair. "Dana was surprised to see me."

"I'll bet. What about Larry?"

"I didn't see him."

"He was there." We'd both watched him go in.

"Not according to Dana. She said a neighbor was parking his car in the driveway."

Ha! I waited for Mike to tell me I was right. Dana had just lied to the police. Larry was hiding from a police detective. That had to make them both prime suspects. Eric was off the hook. I grinned. "And?"

Mike took a hit of his enormous soda. "She answered a couple questions and walked me to the door. End of story."

I blinked. "But she lied to you. The car belongs to Larry. He was probably hiding in one of the closets so you wouldn't catch them together. Why didn't you arrest them?"

"For the same reason I haven't arrested Eric Metz. I like to have real evidence before I charge someone with murder. So far, I know Dana Lucas and your boss have something to hide. Most people do. It's my job to figure out what that something is."

The something probably had to do with the item Larry handed over to Dana. Or maybe the e-mails and Larry's lack of financial planning. There were lots of possibilities. Too bad I couldn't share some of them without getting accessorized with handcuffs. This investigating gig was hard work.

Mike grabbed a few more fries and stood up. "Now, I want you to go home and stay there. Let me do my job. I promise I won't lock up your student unless I'm certain he's guilty. Fair enough?"

My mouth was full of fries. Politeness prevented me from answering, which was pretty handy since I wasn't about to agree. I really wanted to know what Larry and Dana were up to. If Mike figured it out, the chances of him sharing that information were slim to none.

Mike started to walk away, then turned back. "Oh. I don't have to tell you this, but I'm guessing you're smart enough to figure it out. The house we were at today doesn't belong to Dana Lucas. It belonged to her ex-husband, Greg."

———

Pulling into Millie's driveway, I realized I hadn't asked Mike whether he'd checked out Coach Bennett. Not a surprise considering the detective's parting words. Knowing Larry and Dana were skulking around Greg's house looking for God only knew what was creepy.

Bracing myself for the worst, I walked into Millie's living room. All signs of the country club chaos had been removed, including the couch and love seat. Casualties of the cosmetics war. Millie, herself, was also missing. She wasn't in her office, the den, or upstairs. I found a note from her on the kitchen counter: *I'm on a date. Don't wait up. Love, Millie. P.S. Check the machine.*

I grabbed a soda and an apple from the fridge before Killer showed up. Then, crunching into my dinner, I hit play on the machine.

"Hi, Paige." The overly chipper voice of my manager, Rick, filled the room, and my heart gave a hopeful skip. "I just got a call about a part that is perfect for you. We have to act fast, but I think this might be the break we've been waiting for. With any luck you'll be singing in Europe next week."

Chapter 12

I did a happy little dance in the middle of the kitchen floor. Even Killer's appearance couldn't deter my elation. My career was going to take off, and show choir would soon be a thing of the past. I felt a tug of disappointment at not being able to show the kids, especially Chessie, the fabulous choreography Devlyn and I came up with. Maybe I'd have time to attend one or two rehearsals next week and help get the ball rolling.

I hopped up on a kitchen stool and took a swig of soda as Killer glared at me from his place in front of the fridge. I stuck my tongue out at him, and he growled. Fingers shaking, I pulled my phone out of my purse and hit Rick's number.

"Hey, Paige. I was hoping you got my message. What do you think?"

"I think Europe sounds great. What's the gig?"

Silence.

Uh-oh. My heart dropped into my intestines. When there

was good news to be had, Rick loved the sound of his own voice.

"Here's the thing. An artistic director in Germany is looking for a Musetta for his *La Bohème*. I told him you'd be perfect, and he's willing to take a look. Auditions are next week in Berlin. You'll have to pay your own travel, but the exposure you'd get from the role would more than make up for it."

I'd heard that before. "Why can't we just send them a tape?" The fortune I'd paid for a professionally constructed video was part of the reason I was bunking at my aunt's house.

"The director's seen your tape. He thinks you're wonderful, and he wants to see you and a few other girls live before he casts the role."

"How many other girls?"

More silence. I waited for the other shoe to drop.

"Fifteen that I know of. But you're the only American on the list." Like that was supposed to make me feel better. I had a one in fifteen chance or worse of getting the role.

"How much does the role pay?"

"This isn't about the money. Reviewers from across Europe will see this show. You can't pay for this kind of exposure."

Actually, I'd paid for this kind of exposure before. Every time I was promised a low-paying but high-profile gig would put me on the road to success. The only success thus far had been on my credit card company's side.

I rested my head on the kitchen counter and asked, "When's the audition?"

The audition was in ten days, but I had to let Rick know if I was attending in four. My aunt would lend me the money if I asked, but if I didn't get the role, my job, as crappy as it was, would be gone. At twenty-five I would have jumped at this chance. At thirty I was hard-pressed to find the same kind of enthusiasm for a potential lost cause. Feeling incredibly adult and more than a little depressed, I said, "I can't afford the trip. Could you try and get them to keep me in the running based on my tape?"

"I had a feeling you'd say that." Rick gave a dramatic sigh. "I'll see what I can do, and don't worry. If this doesn't work out, I'll come up with something else. You're too talented to sit on the shelf for long."

He hung up, and I headed to the freezer. I needed chocolate ice cream. Now.

"Grrr." Killer stood up. I reached for the door, and he bared his teeth. Ice cream wasn't worth losing a limb for.

"You win," I told him. "But you're sleeping in the hallway tonight."

I went upstairs and took a hot shower, hoping to ease the tension knotted in my shoulders. It didn't work, but at least I lost the lingering smell of dying orchids. That was something. I sat on the edge of my bed and called a few friends, hoping they could make my conversation with Rick less depressing. Each call went directly to voice mail. What else could I expect? It was Friday night. My friends were either performing in a show or at one. Knowing I wasn't made me feel worse.

I'm not the type that does depression well. I don't like watching copious amounts of television. I don't drink alone, and currently I couldn't get to the fridge to consume empty calories. Without Aunt Millie around, I was going to go stir crazy with only my own company to entertain me. What I needed was a distraction.

I plopped in front of my laptop. I now knew where Greg Lucas lived. That made me wonder. Where did Dana and her son live? After a couple taps on the keyboard, I found their address. It was a few blocks away from Greg's house. When he was alive, the proximity must have made visiting his son convenient. Now it meant easy breaking and entering for his ex-wife.

I plugged Larry's name into the white pages and doodled on a piece of paper while I waited. Aha. Larry lived in a house a couple of towns over. Writing down the address, I added one more name into the search engine—Coach Curtis Bennett. Grabbing my purse, I made a beeline for the door. Maybe a drive would take my mind off my problems. And if I happened to spot something interesting outside any of my current suspects' houses, so much the better.

━━━━━

Dana Lucas's place was first on my list since she lived the closest. It was only six o'clock. That meant the sun was still shining, which gave me a great view of the two-story yellow house. No cars were in the blacktopped driveway, and no lights were shining inside the house. Not a creature was stirring. The rest of the neighborhood was equally as quiet. Oh well. On to the next location.

Twenty minutes later I was cruising a street desperately in need of repaving. The extreme Midwest weather changes had taken their toll. I spotted Larry's car in the driveway of a gray ranch and parked just down the street to observe. Half an hour into my surveillance, a rusting yellow Chevy Cavalier with a Papa John's pizza delivery light on top pulled into the driveway. A less-than-enthusiastic-looking boy climbed out with a pizza-warmer bag and trudged to the front door. A few minutes later, the door swung open. Larry signed what I was guessing was a credit card slip, then took two pizza boxes from the kid and disappeared back inside.

Either Larry was expecting company or he was working on fighting off a depression of his own. Ten more minutes passed, and no one showed. Larry was consuming pizza on his own, and unless he had to make a soda run, he was staying in for the rest of the night. Time to hit the road.

North Shore High School's football coach lived the farthest away. Probably a good choice when working with overly testosteroned and immature boys. Living close raised the odds of your house getting toilet-papered after every football game. It took years and hundreds of rolls of toilet paper for my high school's football coach to figure that out.

It was only seven thirty, so I still had natural light to observe Coach Bennett's natural habitat. Two middle-school-aged boys shot hoops in the blue colonial's driveway. A couple of Schwinns lay on their sides in the grass to their left. A petite brunette woman with a watering can appeared from around back, said something to the boys, and walked over to water the red, white, and blue petunias hanging from baskets on the front porch. The woman had to be Mrs. Bennett.

A FOR SALE sign in a yard two doors down gave me an idea. I hopped out of my car and walked down the sidewalk, pretending to be checking out the up-for-sale property. From the height of the grass and the number of weeds, I was guessing the place wasn't occupied. After a couple minutes of staring at the house, I slowly strolled down the sidewalk as if taking in the neighborhood. Mrs. Bennett put down her watering can and walked down the driveway with a wave.

Score.

I waved back and walked over to her. "Hi. My name is Paige. Would you happen to know anything about the house for sale? I left a message for the Realtor, but I haven't gotten a call back." Yeah. I lied. Practice was making me better at it.

She looked over at the overgrown house with a small frown. "The Millers relocated about six months ago. The inside is beautiful. Sharon just finished having the kitchen redone when her husband got transferred to the West Coast."

"That's good to hear," I said with a cheerleader smile. "The outside had me a little concerned."

"I've been worried about that." Mrs. Bennett sighed. "I should have my husband mow the lawn when he's home for more than a few minutes."

"Sounds like he travels a lot."

She laughed. "He's a high school football coach, which means I'm basically a single parent from August to November. After all these years, you'd think I'd be used to it. But some weeks are harder than others. Especially this one." Her smile disappeared. "One of the teachers at my husband's school died."

"I'm so sorry. Was he sick?"

"No." Her eyes grew wide, and she looked behind her as if checking to see whether the boys could hear. "He was murdered."

I made what I hoped was an appropriate gasp of shock. "That's terrible."

"I know, and it happened in a high school, which makes it even worse."

"Were you close with the victim?"

"My husband couldn't stand the man," Mrs. Bennett admitted. "But it's still a shock that someone killed him."

A silver minivan pulled up in the driveway, and the kids playing ball waved at the hulk of a man who got out. He had a buzz cut, hairy thighs, and shoes the size of small boats. One of the boys raced up to the man and demonstrated a couple of fancy dribbles. Not to be outdone, the other kid snagged the ball and shot a basket. Nothing but net. Two points.

Mrs. Bennett sighed. "Our sons love basketball. My husband wishes they shared his fondness for football, but what can you do? You can't force kids to follow in your footsteps."

My dad learned that the hard way. He's a minister on Sundays and a dairy farmer on the other days. My brother headed west to program computers. And me . . . well, in Dad's mind, dreams of performing onstage were akin to running away with the circus. Truth be told, he would have been more comfortable with the circus. The smell of animal poop was something he understood.

After shooting a couple of hoops, Coach Bennett turned and headed in our direction. The closer he came, the bigger he got. The incredible hulk had nothing on this guy.

"Is everything okay?" he asked his wife while looking down at me from his over-six-foot height.

His wife smiled. "Paige was in the neighborhood looking at the Miller's house. She's been having trouble getting a hold of the Realtor, so I was answering a few of her questions about the place. I even thought you could have the boys help cut the yard. Having a house empty on the street after Greg's murder makes me nervous."

"He wasn't murdered here," Coach Bennett assured me.

"Your wife mentioned it happened at your high school."

"Not my school." When the coach put a hand on his wife's shoulder, I couldn't help noticing how big his hands were. The man could easily choke someone to death with them. Gulp. I took a step back. If I had to make a quick getaway, I needed as much of a head start as I could get.

The coach didn't seem to notice my concern. He just laughed. "Thank God Greg got whacked at Prospect Glen, otherwise the cops would be all over me."

"Greg and Curtis had a misunderstanding not too long ago." Mrs. Bennett gave her husband a nervous smile.

"Misunderstanding my ass," the coach bellowed. For the first time I noticed a slight slur to his speech and the shine in his eyes. The hulk was hammered. "The man was screwing my program. He convinced my best player he'd have a better chance of getting a college scholarship if he pranced around like a fairy and wore makeup."

As someone who did both the prancing and the makeup wearing, I took exception to that.

Judging by her tense frown, his wife did, too. "Not everyone wants to play football for the rest of their life, dear."

"Drew Roane was going to help us get to state this year." Coach Bennett took a step away from his wife and raised his voice. "Now that Greg Lucas is out of the way, the kid will come back to the team where he belongs. I've talked to the kid's father. Drew will be at practice tomorrow morning even if his father has to drag him by his frilly little dance tights."

"Sounds like Greg's death was the best thing that could happen for you." Not the smartest thing for me to say, but I couldn't help it. Drew deserved a chance to make his own choices about his after-school activities. I had high school friends still going to therapy because their fathers forced them out of the arts and into the macho male-child mold.

Coach Bennett's eyes narrowed. "Are you saying I had something to do with that jerk's death?"

"No." At least, not to his face. I was pissed. I wasn't stupid. "I was making an observation. Your football team will be a lot better because of the murder."

"My football team was great to begin with. I can coach anyone. Do you hear me?" His hands clenched and unclenched at his sides as his eyes bugged out. He took a step forward and swayed dangerously on his feet.

Out of the corner of my eye I watched Mrs. Bennett's face go white. Clearly, she hadn't considered the possibility of her husband's involvement in his colleague's murder. By the way her lip was trembling, I'd say she now believed he could have done it.

As a matter of fact, so did I. It was time to get out of here.

"I've taken up enough of your time," I said, backing away. "Have a nice evening." I bolted back to my car and motored into the fading light.

Pretending to real estate shop and being nosy had worked up an appetite. I drove through at McDonald's and picked myself up my version of a balanced, healthy meal—a salad and an apple pie. Driving back home, I debated whether to call Detective Mike and let him know about my encounter with Coach Bennett.

By the time I pulled into Millie's driveway, daylight had ended. I'd also eaten the apple pie and decided against sharing the details of my evening until I had something more substantial to report to Mike than the coach's serious rage issues. McDonald's bag in hand, I trucked up to the front door. The door swung open before I could put the key in and a figure in black came racing out.

Directly at me.

Chapter 13

Heart thudding, I squeaked and jumped back. My arms windmilled, and I toppled into the bushes as the person in black raced past me down the steps. By the time I disentangled myself from the shrubbery, the person was gone.

I raced inside and hit the lights, hoping they would scare anyone else who might be lurking inside. Going into the house felt dangerous, but I had to. Aunt Millie might be in there.

"Aunt Millie?" I yelled, racing through the living room toward the kitchen. Millie was tough, but the intruder might have had a weapon. Millie had to be okay. She just had to. "Hello?"

Flipping on the lights in the kitchen, I let my eyes slide over the room. No Millie. I pulled a knife out from the butcher block and went to search the rest of the house, turning lights on as I went. Millie wasn't in any of the downstairs rooms. Taking the stairs two at a time, I started searching the bedrooms. No. No. No.

A sound at the end of the hall made me suck in air. Somebody was in my room. I felt for the cell phone in my jeans pocket and heard the sound again. Oh God. Someone was whimpering. Millie.

My feet started moving before my brain could stop them. I raised the knife, hoping to God I wouldn't have to use it, and pushed open my bedroom door. I kept my back to the wall as I hit the light switch and blinked as the room sprang into Technicolor.

Oh no. Killer lay on the floor. A dark streak of red colored the top of his pompon head. He looked up at me and whimpered. The sound broke my heart.

Tears stung the back of my eyes, and I knelt down next to him. I may not love the vicious little beast, but I didn't want him to die and end up as part of Millie's petrified pet collection.

I stroked Killer's neck, and he tried to lick my hand. Either that or he was trying to bite it. Either way, I took the movement as a good sign. There was a gash on Killer's head. I ran to the bathroom, ignored the poodle watching my every move, and grabbed a wet washcloth. Back in the bedroom, I dabbed Killer's wound and tried to get a better look.

The bleeding had stopped, but a huge bump was already forming on Killer's head. I dialed Millie's number. She was giggling at someone in the background when she answered. The merriment stopped the minute I told her what had happened to Killer. She promised to call the vet and come right home. She disconnected, and I called Detective Mike. I was pretty sure investigating home invasion wasn't part of his homicide detective job, but I was completely freaked and I didn't want to talk to a stranger. Mike sounded confused as I told my story, but he promised to be right over.

Knowing backup was on the way made me feel better,

but my legs were still wobbly as I fetched a bowl of water for my patient. The minutes dragged by as I waited for help to arrive. Finally, I heard footsteps downstairs and my aunt yell, "Paige? Where are you?"

Killer perked up at the sound of Millie's voice and tried to stand. I held him down and yelled, "We're in my bedroom."

Feet pounded up the stairs and down the hall. I heard Millie gasp from the doorway as she saw me on the floor holding Killer's head in my lap. Dr. Wilson from next door was right behind her. Millie must have called him from the car. I wished I had thought of that. The man wasn't a vet, but he knew how to treat open wounds.

Killer's tail thumped against the carpet, and he tried to get to his feet. Millie knelt on the floor and gently pushed Killer down as he licked her face and whined. My aunt sniffled and wrapped her arms around me in a death-grip hug.

"Thank God you're not hurt," she said as she squeezed even tighter. I felt like I was going to pop. After another hard hug, she turned and gave the doctor a pleading look. "Is Killer going to be okay?"

I stood up and sat on the bed so Dr. Wilson had room to examine Killer. The apple pie I'd eaten rolled in my stomach. If Dr. Wilson gave Killer a bad prognosis, I was going to hurl.

The short, balding doctor looked at Millie and said, "Your boy took a knock to the head. The cut isn't deep, which is good. I'd recommend taking him into an emergency clinic to get some X-rays. Head wounds can be tricky."

Millie wrapped Killer in a blanket, and the three of us awkwardly carried the dog down the hall. When I was a kid, I thought poodles were always cute and little. Killer weighed a ton. It took everything I had not to drop him as I felt my way step by step down the stairs. Once we got him out the door and onto the stoop, Millie hurried over to her pink convertible and pulled it up to the door. Dr. Wilson settled Killer in the backseat just as Detective Mike's Mustang pulled into the driveway.

Millie revved her engine. "I'll call you from the clinic. We'll probably be there a while before I know anything. Lock all the doors and don't wait up." And she zoomed off.

"Rough night?" Detective Mike slammed his car door and walked over to where I was standing on the front step.

The kindness and concern in the detective's tone made my eyes start to burn and my throat itch. I didn't want to cry, but the stress of the evening combined with genuine caring was making that hard.

Through a constricting throat, I said, "Coming home to an intruder and an injured dog isn't part of my normal Friday-night ritual."

"Can't imagine it is." The detective pulled out his cop book and nodded toward the house. "Let's go inside so you can tell me about it."

Dr. Wilson gave Mike his contact information and went home. Mike and I went inside. I was going to sit in the living room until I remembered the lack of furniture. Instead, I made a beeline for the kitchen because that's where the caffeine was. Heading for the fridge, I took one look at the empty space in front of it where Killer typically stood guard, and my lip started to tremble. I reached for the fridge door and a tear escaped down my cheek. Then another.

I walked to the kitchen table, took a seat, and buried my head in my hands as I started to cry. Killer was in the doggie hospital fighting for his life. Aunt Millie would be heartbroken if he died. Hell, I'd be heartbroken.

A hand touched my shoulder and gave it a squeeze. That

made me cry even harder. Finally, after a lot of tears and hiccups, I took a shuttering breath and raised my head.

Mike looked down at me with a small smile. "Feel better?"

Not particularly. Now instead of just sad and freaked, I could add embarrassed to the list. Yippee.

"Sorry about that," I said with as much dignity as I could muster. My breathing was still high and uneven, and my hand was streaked with mascara from wiping the tears off my face. It was hard to have dignity when you looked like a zebra.

Mike sat across from me. "Why don't you tell me what happened tonight."

So, I did just that. I started with walking up to the front door and ended with Killer riding off in Millie's hot pink makeshift ambulance.

When I was done, Mike looked down at his notes and frowned. "Did you forget to lock the front door when you left this evening?"

I chewed my bottom lip. "No. I'm sure I locked it."

Mike pushed his chair back, walked over to the back door, and turned the handle. Locked. "The front door didn't show signs of forced entry. Are there any other exits besides this one?"

I walked him into the Spartan living room where the French doors were currently allowing bugs and any other critters to move right in. Bonnie and Clyde sat in the middle of the room ready to greet them. "These doors were closed when I left the house."

"Were they locked?"

Good question. "I didn't check before I left. Aunt Millie normally leaves them locked, but she had some furniture removed today. The pieces might have been taken out through those doors."

Mike examined both doors, took a couple pictures with his phone, and then closed the doors to keep the marauding mosquitoes out. "No forced entry. I'm guessing they were unlocked, but I'll double-check with your aunt."

I gave Mike a lot of credit for not mentioning the two lifeless pugs sitting in the middle of the living room floor. The man had focus. We went upstairs to my bedroom, and I let Mike go in first. I'd already seen my quota of blood for the day.

"Yours?" Mike pointed toward the bed, where I'd ditched the knife I'd been packing.

I nodded. He laughed. Then Mike looked down at the floor and stopped laughing. Putting on a glove, he leaned down to pick up something off the floor. In his hand was an ornate, cast-iron bookend of a wolf hound that looked suspiciously like an oversized rat. It was also the weapon used to put Killer out of commission.

Mike bagged the bookend and walked around the rest of the room taking pictures. "Is anything missing in here?"

"I don't know." I hadn't even thought to look. Walking around the bloodstain on the white carpeting, I took inventory of the room. Shoes were in the closet. What little jewelry I had was still in its box on the dresser. Everything looked in its place.

Wait. Maybe I was being paranoid, but it looked like my laptop had been moved. And hadn't there been more paper in the wicker garbage can when I left?

I flipped open the laptop. Nothing looked broken. Leaning over, I rummaged through the garbage. Earlier, while waiting for the Internet to kick out dirt on my suspects, I'd doodled the list of suspect names on a piece of paper along with a bunch of hearts, flowers, and other shapes. I'd pitched the paper on my way out the door. The paper was now gone.

"What's wrong?"

If I told Mike about the missing paper, he'd want to know what was on it. He wasn't going to be happy with the answer. But not telling him would limit his ability to find the person who almost killed Killer.

"There's a piece of paper missing from the garbage." I felt stupid saying it. I mean, only wackos monitor their garbage.

Mike raised an eyebrow. Yep, now he thought I was an OCD nut. "How do you know that?"

I explained my doodling earlier and tried to ignore the way the vein in his neck started to throb. "Look at it this way, whoever broke in here and took the piece of paper must be worried about my looking into the murder," I said, trying to direct his attention toward solving the crime instead of throttling me.

"And that's a good thing?"

Only if it distracted him from yelling at me. "Maybe. This could help you track down the real killer. That's got to be better than scaring the crap out of a teenager who didn't do anything wrong."

Mike's eyes narrowed, and he crossed his arms over his chest. The movement shifted his sports coat, and I could see his gun peeping out from underneath the gray fabric. Gulp. The man had been so nice to me that I had forgotten he even had a gun.

He stared me down, and I decided to backpedal. "I know you have to question Eric. It's your job."

"You're right."

"And there are a few pieces of evidence that point toward Eric."

"Right again." He smiled.

I breathed a sigh of relief. "You also know he isn't the only one out there with a motive. Dana and Larry are acting suspicious, and Coach Bennett has a huge temper when he drinks. You should have seen him tonight when—"

Oops. I clapped a hand over my mouth, but it was too late. Mike unfurled his arms and slowly walked toward me. "You saw Coach Bennett tonight?"

Not trusting myself to speak ever again, I nodded.

"Where?"

"Outside his house."

The vein in Mike's neck looked like it was going to burst. "What the hell were you doing outside of the North Shore High School football coach's house?"

Sighing, I admitted, "I was pretending to look for real estate. The house two doors down is for sale. Mrs. Bennett was really helpful answering questions about the place."

Mike's cheek twitched. "You talked to the coach's wife?"

Nodding, I said, "The coach showed up while we were talking." When Mike didn't explode, I walked him through the coach's drunken discussion of the murder and his violent reaction before I left.

To his credit, Mike didn't yell. He just shook his head and said, "You might want to rethink accusing someone of murder the next time you try something like this."

"Next time?"

"The way I see it, the only way to stop you is to arrest you."

Eek.

"Which I'm not ready to do."

Phew.

"Yet." He gave me a grim smile. "Just promise me you'll stay inside tonight with the doors locked. We'll worry about tomorrow when it comes."

Mike walked around the house one last time making sure doors and windows were locked as he went. He gave me a warning to stay indoors, and then folded himself in his car and drove off.

I turned the lock on the front door and went into the kitchen for a snack. Halfway through my second bag of microwave popcorn, Millie called. Killer was in X-ray. The vet thought he was going to be okay, but they'd know more after the pictures were taken. Regardless, Killer would be staying at the clinic overnight and so would Millie. That left me alone in the house.

On a normal day, alone was good. Alone meant I could sing at the top of my lungs, hog the remote, and run around in my underwear. Well, I never did the last one, but I liked knowing it was an option. Today, alone felt scary. I didn't want the remote or a *Risky Business* moment. I wanted company.

It was almost ten o'clock. Most of my friends wouldn't get home from their performances until close to midnight. I pulled the faculty contact list out of my bag and scanned it. Devlyn was my first choice, but calling a guy, even a gay one, and asking him to sleep over felt wrong. Asking Larry to keep me company fell into the Hell No category. That left Felicia. She said she was on a date tonight, but it couldn't hurt to give her a jingle. Just in case.

Felicia picked up on the first ring. I explained that an intruder had broken into the house and that my aunt had gone to the emergency vet with the dog, leaving me alone. Biting the edge of my nail, I asked if she would be willing to stay the night.

"I would be happy to. Just give me a few minutes to throw some things in an overnight bag and I'll be right there."

Yippee. For the first time since I was fifteen years old, I was having a slumber party. Only, this one was designed so I could actually sleep. How strange was that?

Chapter 14

I went into the living room to wait for Felicia. The pugs looked up at me as if excited about the party. Too bad they weren't going to be participating. Hoisting an immobile dog under each arm, I tromped up the stairs and deposited them next to the border collie in my aunt's bedroom. I then snagged the poodle from my bathroom and added it to the doggie eternal-slumber party. Only one more poodle to go. I looked in the two guest bedrooms and baths. Nope. Not in the living room, dining room, or in the kitchen. I was about to check Millie's office when the doorbell rang. Felicia was here, and she was dressed to kill in a tight black miniskirt, a shiny fitted red tank, and matching red stilettos.

The minute she walked in the door, she dumped her very large overnight bag on the floor, wrapped her arms around me, and squeezed. "You poor thing. First you walked in on Greg, and now this. I'm just glad you called me."

"Thanks for coming." I extricated myself from her arms

and took a step back. "Are you sure you don't mind staying over?"

"Not at all." She grinned. "This gives us a real chance to get to know each other before school starts. Things have been so crazy with . . . well, everything this week. A girls' night is just what the doctor ordered." She picked up her purple overnight bag. "Where do you want me to sleep? I can change out of these clothes, and the two of us can order a pizza. Do you like hot peppers and pepperoni?"

My stomach did a happy dance. Felicia was a girl after my own heart.

I showed Felicia to one of the guest rooms and called the pizza place. Having the pizza delivery on speed dial was the one good thing that came out of Aunt Millie's cooking adventures. Twenty minutes later, Felicia strolled into the kitchen wearing gray shorts, a white T-shirt, and no makeup. She had lost the heels and was now sporting fuzzy black sequined slippers.

I grabbed a bottle of white wine from the fridge, popped the cork, and poured two glasses—figuring, if Felicia didn't want hers, I'd drink it. After the last couple days, I needed to take the edge off.

Felicia hopped onto a stool and took a sip of her wine. "Thanks. I really needed that."

"Bad date?" I slid onto the stool next to her and took a large gulp of Chardonnay.

She shrugged. "I think I'm doomed to be attracted to the wrong type of man."

"Broke?"

"Married." She sighed. "The guy tonight claimed he was divorced."

"How do you know he's not?"

She drained her wine. "Trust me. After all the men I've

dated, I know. The wedding ring tan is a dead giveaway. So is the out-of-the-way date location. Romantic back table my ass. The guy isn't being romantic. He just doesn't want to get caught." I filled her glass, and she smiled. "I guess this one was better than the last one. It's easier to get rid of a guy after one date. Once you've been dating a while, it takes a lot more to shake him loose."

The doorbell rang, and I went to get the pizza. I tipped the delivery boy, grabbed the very warm, somewhat greasy box, and went back to the kitchen. Felicia grabbed her glass and walked over to the kitchen table as I headed for some plates. I heard the sound of a chair moving on the hardwood floor, then a bloodcurdling scream.

———

I grabbed a knife out of the butcher block and spun around, ready to do battle with an unwanted intruder. Only there wasn't anything there.

Still, Felicia kept shrieking. "Get it off! Get it off!" She pushed her chair back so hard the chair tipped backward, sending her to the floor. That got her screaming even harder. Legs flailing, she struggled to her knees. I hurried over to help her up. She took one look at the knife in my hand and went white.

Oops. I put down the knife and hauled her up. "Are you okay?"

Her frown said no, but she nodded her head yes as she backed away from the table and plastered herself against a wall.

"What freaked you out?"

"I think there's something alive down there." She pointed to underneath the table, and I squatted to take a look.

Oh God. I shook my head and groaned. Sadly, the thing

was most definitely not alive. Sitting under the table, as if waiting for scraps, was the missing taxidermied poodle.

"The good news is there is nothing alive under here," I said, trying not to feel ridiculous. How do you explain a lifeless animal camping out under your kitchen table? "My aunt really loves her pets, and well . . ." I was at a loss for words so I kneeled down and hauled the poodle out into the open.

Felicia's eyes opened wide as she and the glass-eyed dog stared at each other. She clapped a hand over her mouth, and her shoulders started to shake. Giggling, she asked, "Your aunt had her dog stuffed?"

"Technically, this isn't even her dog. But most of the ones upstairs are."

"There are more?"

I nodded.

Felicia let out a surprised, spitting laugh. When she recovered, she asked, "How many?"

As far as embarrassing moments went, this ranked up there with the time a college date took me to the zoo and a llama spit in my face. The llama managed to lodge a loogie in the top of my hair, which I learned about after walking through most of the zoo looking for a bathroom. I gave my date credit for not laughing at me. The rest of the people in the park weren't as kind.

Cringing, I looked at Felicia and slowly held up four fingers.

"Can I see them?"

I tried to decide whether she was just humoring me. Nope. Felicia looked fascinated. Maybe this wasn't as bad as the llama after all. I smiled and asked, "Can we eat pizza first?"

After six slices of pizza (they were small, I swear), Felicia and I tromped up the stairs in search of Millie's prize petrified pooches. Felicia swayed going up the stairs. She had finished the rest of the bottle of Chardonnay and started in on a bottle of Bordeaux. Felicia was feeling no pain.

I hit the light switch in Aunt Millie's room and put the stray poodle on the floor with the rest of the clan. I'd unconsciously arranged them so they were in a circle facing one another. If I got a deck of cards and a couple of visors, they would look like the *Dogs Playing Poker* picture my college boyfriend had hanging on his wall.

Felicia snorted. "I should have thought about taxidermy for my last boyfriend. The glassy eyes would have been a good look for him."

Yikes. "Stuffing someone with sawdust is a pretty stiff price to pay for adultery." Although not the worst idea I'd ever heard.

"Maybe." She frowned and sat down on the edge of Millie's bed. "You probably don't have the same guy problems I do."

She was right. I didn't have a guy so there were no problems to be had. Of course, Aunt Millie thought that was the problem. "Is it a problem that I'm attracted to gay men?"

Her eyes lit up. "Devlyn?"

I sat down next to her on the chartreuse bedspread. "Is it obvious?"

"Not at all. I just know the feeling. He's sweet and considerate and sexy as hell. I tried to jump him at a faculty party when I first started working at Prospect Glen three years ago. Then he introduced me to his boyfriend, Phillip." She sighed. "I should have known better. All the good guys are gay or taken."

"I've only known Devlyn for two days, but he seems like a great friend."

She smiled. "He is. Nobody worries more about my bad dating habits than Devlyn. He wants the whole world to be happy."

"That's the vibe I got." After the violence and threats of the past couple of days, it was nice to have my impressions confirmed. "Funny, but he actually said the cops should be considering him as a suspect in Greg Lucas's murder."

"Makes sense to me." Felicia nodded her head so hard she almost fell over.

I caught her and returned her to a seated position. "Devlyn doesn't seem like the type to hate anyone enough to kill them."

"You know the saying about the fine line between love and hate?" she whispered. "It's true."

I blinked. "Devlyn and Greg?" Ewwww. The thought made the pizza in my stomach roll.

"You never saw Greg in action. He always knew just what to say to make men and women want to please him. Why else do you think Devlyn agreed to work on North Shore's musical last year?"

"Money?" That's why I was doing the show choir thing.

She shook her head. "I know love when I see it. Devlyn wanted to please Greg because he loved him. Greg used that love to get what he wanted and then threw it away. Being hurt like that can make a person do things they never thought themselves capable of."

"Do you actually think Devlyn killed Greg?"

"I don't know. He could have. His office is right next to the theater. It would have been easy for him to do." She chewed on her bottom lip. "But Larry's been acting really strange, too, and he and Greg have hated each other since their college days."

"Larry and Greg went to college together?"

"Greg told me they met their freshman year and were best friends." Felicia yawned. "They even created a singing group together that won a bunch of awards. Hard to believe, right? Like I said—a fine line between love and hate."

A liquored-up Felicia was a fount of knowledge. I wanted to keep asking questions, but her eyes were getting droopy so I walked her to the guest room instead and said good night. Then I checked all the locks to make sure they were latched, while wondering whether Devlyn could really be a murderer. If he had the kind of feelings for Greg that Felicia claimed, he might actually have a motive.

Heading back to my own bedroom, I checked my phone for messages. Maybe Millie had called again or maybe Detective Mike. Nothing. Drat. Out of the corner of my eye, I spotted the kitchen knife still sitting on the desk and moved it to the end table just in case. Then I turned off the light, trying not to feel strangely unsettled that Killer wasn't hogging the covers.

———

I was on my third cup of very strong coffee when Aunt Millie slowly walked through the kitchen door. Her makeup was freshly done, helping her look like she'd had a good night's rest. I wasn't fooled. I could see shadows underneath the expertly applied concealer. Aunt Millie had a tough night.

Swallowing hard, I asked, "Is Killer all right?"

She looked at me and smiled. "He's fine. They want to watch him for a few more hours. I'll bring him home this afternoon."

My heart did a happy dance as I crossed the room to give Aunt Millie a hug. Then, knowing she needed it, I grabbed the coffeepot and poured her a cup. "Did you get any sleep last night?"

"More than I thought I would." She sat down at the kitchen table with a sigh. "I was going to call you when I got the news, but it was after one. I didn't want to wake you."

That wouldn't have been a problem. Even with Felicia in the house, I jumped at noises until well after two.

Aunt Millie sipped at her coffee and leaned back in the chair. She stretched her feet out and frowned. "Where's Leopold?"

"Who?"

"LouAnne's poodle, Leopold. Oh my God." She sat up straight in her chair. "The intruder must have taken him." Millie pulled out her BlackBerry and started dialing.

"Who are you calling?"

"The police. They have to know there's a dognapper on the loose."

I stopped her before she hit send. "The intruder didn't take Leopold. I didn't want to spend the night alone, so I asked a friend to come over. Leopold startled her."

"That's a relief." Millie clapped a hand over her chest. "Who's the friend?"

"Me." Felicia walked through the door and headed for the coffeepot. I'd left a bottle of aspirin on the counter just in case she needed it. From the way she was holding her head, I was guessing she did. She shook a couple aspirin out of the bottle and washed them down with coffee. Turning, she smiled at Aunt Millie. "I'm sorry to hear about your dog. Is he going to be okay?"

"He is." Millie straightened her shoulders and no longer looked tired as she beamed. "I was just telling Paige that he'll be coming home later today."

Felicia added four spoonfuls of sugar to her coffee and took a hit. "I'm happy to hear that. Head wounds can be really dangerous."

"That's what the vet said. Killer is lucky he's got such a hard head, and Paige is lucky to have a friend like you to stay with her after last night's ordeal."

"It was nothing." Felicia waved her off. "Actually, she did me a favor. I was looking for a way to ditch my date early. Paige gave me a great excuse." She looked down at her watch and sighed. "I have to get going if I'm going to get my workout in this morning. Call me later and let me know if the police have any leads about your intruder."

After I walked Felicia out to her car, I went back to the kitchen. Millie had her head on the table. Her eyes were closed, and she was snoring softly. For the first time in a long while, I could see all sixty-four years etched on her face. The strain of almost losing Killer had taken its toll. Seeing my aunt looking so tired and fragile made the fear I'd been carrying since last night disappear. Now I was pissed.

I marched into the living room and called Detective Mike on my cell, hoping he had information about the murder, the break-in, or both. The way he barked his name when answering fueled my anger. It wasn't a rational reaction, but I didn't particularly care.

Skipping the niceties, I asked, "Do you have any leads on the break-in at my aunt's house?"

"I would have called you if I did."

Somehow I doubted that.

Mike didn't give me a chance to fire off a witty comeback. "Is your aunt home? I'd like to stop by and ask her a few questions."

I peeked back into the kitchen. Aunt Millie was still out cold. "You'll have to wait."

"The sooner I talk with her, the sooner I solve this case."

Yeah, right.

I snapped my phone shut, nudged Millie awake, and helped her up to her bedroom. Covering her with a quilt, I realized the killer breaking into Millie's house was my fault. I'd put her at risk. Maybe Mike was doing everything he could to solve the case, but he had to do things by the book. That took time. Who knew how much time I had until the killer decided to come after me and my family again? I had no other choice. I had to find Greg's murderer first.

Chapter 15

Grabbing another cup of coffee, I trudged up the stairs to my room. The bright red stain on the carpet strengthened my resolve to find the person behind Killer's attack. I took a seat at my desk and opened a game of solitaire. The mindless clicking gave me something to do while I let my brain think.

So far I'd been talking to people who would make good suspects. Unfortunately, while all of them had a motive, none of them were itching to confess. Maybe it was time to go at this a different way and start taking a better look at Greg Lucas himself. If I could figure out why he was killed, that would help me narrow down the suspect pool. Felicia mentioned that Larry and Greg were the best of friends during their college years. That seemed as good a place as any to start digging into Greg's past.

Shutting down solitaire, I opened up Facebook and typed in Larry's name. He had friended me as soon as I was hired. His posts were mostly about his allergies and his dietary habits so I rarely paid attention. Now I was interested in his school history.

Ha! Larry had attended the University of Illinois, which meant Greg had, too. I typed Larry's and Greg's names into a search engine along with the U of I and hit enter. Yikes. There were thousands of entries. A lot of guys named Larry and Greg had passed through the University of Illinois over the years. I started clicking on the entries.

Drat. None of the mentions on the first three pages featured my guys. I added music to the search and hit enter. Now there were hundreds of entries. Better, but this was still a lot like looking for a needle in a haystack. I took a swig of coffee and started scanning the entries.

Nope. Nope. Nope. Wait.

On the bottom of the fourth page was a link to a U of I alum's blog called *Barbershop and Buddies*. I clicked through and read the bio of blog owner, Jimmy Waldorf. He was a business manager by day and a barbershop singer by night. He listed lots of groups he'd sung in, including Members Only—a male a cappella group from University of Illinois. I rolled my eyes at the name.

I searched through the blog for any mention of Members Only and learned that the group had a lot of success on and off campus. They performed at schools around central Illinois, at corporate events, and at U of I music concerts. Judging by Jimmy's posts, his entire college experience was wrapped up in Members Only. Too bad for him. But good for me, because Jimmy had taken lots and lots of pictures. Twenty years had passed and hairlines had changed, but standing in the middle of the group were Larry and Greg.

Huh. Now that I'd found young Larry and Greg, I wasn't sure what to do with them.

I clicked around the blog entries trying to decide. Maybe

I could talk to Jimmy about the Members Only golden days. If Larry and Greg started their feud during college, chances were Jimmy would know about it. The blog said he was from the Chicago area. I wondered if he was still here.

I was about to look for an e-mail address when I clicked on a blog post titled "My New Job." Turns out, two months ago Jimmy became the manager of Pete's Pizza and Prizes in Crystal Lake, Illinois. My watch read eleven o'clock. Kids should be busy playing games and getting nauseated from the pizza by now. I picked up the phone and dialed.

Yes, Jimmy Waldorf was currently one of the managers there. Would I like to speak with him?

Ha! I hung up the phone and grabbed my purse. With construction and traffic, getting to Crystal Lake would take me an hour or more. I peeked in on Aunt Millie, who was still sleeping, and dialed the vet to check on Killer. The angry growling in the background assured me better than the doctor that Killer was recovering just fine. Time to hit the road.

I opened the front door and almost plowed into Devlyn. Today he sported white tennis shorts and a pink short-sleeved golf shirt with a white, pink, and gray paisley ascot draped around his neck.

"I guess I came at a bad time." He gave me a wide smile. "Looks like you're in a hurry."

Felicia's drunken musings replayed in my head. Trying not to look freaked, I asked, "How did you know where I live?"

"I'm stalking you." He laughed as I took a step backward. "Sorry. Bad joke considering the week we've had. Your address is listed in the faculty directory." His smile faded. "Hey, are you okay? You look tired."

If Devlyn was the one who broke into the house yesterday, he was doing a great job of acting clueless. Either he was an outstanding acting teacher or he was innocent.

Sighing, I admitted, "Someone broke into the house last night and injured my aunt's dog."

Devlyn's eyes widened. "Oh my God. Are you okay? Were you and your aunt at home when it happened?"

I explained the events of last night, complete with inviting Felicia over for a sleepover. "The good news is Aunt Millie's dog will be fine and the cops are working on finding the person responsible."

"And what are you doing?"

I blinked. "What do you mean?"

Devlyn crossed his arms and raised an eyebrow. "I don't know you well, but I am certain you're not the type to sit on the sidelines and wait for someone to solve your problems. Where were you headed when I showed up?"

Busted.

I blew a lock of hair off my forehead and said, "I was looking into Greg's past. I thought it might help me figure out why he was murdered. Did you know Greg and Larry were best friends in college?" Devlyn's look of horror made me laugh. "I tracked down a guy who knew them both in college. I figured I'd ask him a few questions and see if I turn up anything."

I waited for Devlyn to tell me to let the cops do the investigating. It was advice any sane person would give me. Instead, Devlyn said, "Sounds like fun. Let's go."

━━━━━

The Pete's Pizza and Prizes parking lot was packed. A techno-hip-hop-Disney remix was playing on the loudspeakers. Kids hopped up on greasy pizza and overly frosted cakes were racing around playing air hockey, video games, and

Skee-Ball. Some frazzled parents attempted to keep up with the kids while desperately shooting longing gazes at the exit. Others sat at tables with the uneaten pizza, looking like they'd been run over by really big trucks. The slogan out front next to a picture of Pete, the fire-breathing dragon, read FUN FOR THE WHOLE FAMILY.

"What party?" the freckle-faced teenage boy peering out from the mouth of a dragon costume asked. He stood next to a gate at the entrance with a pen in one claw and a checklist in another.

"We're not with one of the parties," I answered.

Dragon-boy frowned. "What do you mean? Why else would you be here?"

Good question. What sane person would come to a place like this if she didn't have to? Saying that I was here investigating a murder probably wasn't going to help my cause.

Thank goodness Devlyn had an answer. "What my wife means is that we aren't here for a party today. We're planning one for our twins and wanted to see the environment while parties were in progress. We were told by one of the managers that we could stop by."

"The manager was Jim Waldorf," I added. "He said he was working today. I'd love to talk with him if possible."

"Sure thing." The dragon kid nodded and buzzed us through the gate. "We make sure all guests allowed inside are with a party or are here because they want to plan one. This helps keep the kids safe. Jim is right over there." He pointed a claw in the direction of the dining area, and Devlyn and I headed over.

The picture on the blog should have helped me identify Jim Waldorf. It didn't. I asked a kid sporting a dragon T-shirt to point him out.

Yowzah.

The blog picture showed Jim Waldorf with wavy brown hair and two impish dimples making him look like a mischievous elf. The guy the kid pointed out was bald and looked a lot more like Santa than one of his helpers. Or maybe I just thought that because the guy was red. Bright red. Either Jim had gotten caught in a paint fight or he'd been out in the sun way too long. Ouch.

Plastering a smile on my face, I dodged a couple kids racing to spend their tokens and headed for Jim. He saw us approach, smiled, and winced. I felt bad for the guy. Sunburn sucks.

"Can I help you folks?" he asked.

Devlyn spoke before I could. "My friend and I were hoping to get information about throwing a party for my niece and her friends."

I couldn't help but be a little disappointed that Devlyn had downgraded me from wife to friend. Yes, I was pathetic.

Jim didn't notice my chagrin. He just launched into his Pete's Pizza spiel. Great games. Fabulous food. Reasonable prices. "The fall months are booking up fast. You'll want to reserve a spot soon." Jim finished his speech with a whoosh of air.

A small person ran smack into Devlyn, did a one-hundred-and-eighty-degree spin, and barreled off. Devlyn laughed. "My niece turns eight in December. Her birthday always gets buried with all the Christmas celebrations so I thought it would be nice to make it special for her this year. Now I have to convince my sister."

Wow. Devlyn could lie. I was both disconcerted and highly impressed.

Jim pulled a card out of his back pocket and handed it to Devlyn. "The holiday party rush hasn't started yet, so you can have your pick of dates. Give me a call when you get your sister's approval. My name is Jim."

Devlyn handed me the card. It was my cue to start my own lie. "What a funny coincidence," I said with a laugh. "A friend of ours just mentioned he was in a singing group with a guy named Jim Waldorf. Of course, that was in college years ago."

Jim's eyes went wide. "I sang with an a cappella group in college."

"You wouldn't have gone to U of I would you?" I said, trying to sound like I was making a joke. "I think that's where Larry and Greg went to school."

"Larry and Greg?" Jim leaned forward.

"My boss is a guy named Larry DeWeese. He's a music teacher at Prospect Glen High School. Greg Lucas is a guy he used to sing with."

The minute I dropped Larry's full name, Jim grabbed his chest and took a step backward. Or maybe he was reacting to the woman screaming at the top of her lungs near a Whac-A-Mole machine across the restaurant. Hard to tell.

Several kids began to yell and race around like mad near the screaming woman as Jim asked, "Can you wait here a minute?" Before getting our reply, he dashed into the melee. The adult screaming stopped almost at once. The kids were having too much fun to settle down as quickly.

After a few minutes, a sweating Jim trotted back over to us. "Thanks for waiting. A kid thought he dropped a sticker in the machine and tried to retrieve it, only he got his hand stuck in between the mole and the hole. His older brother was having fun bopping him with the pugil stick. Mom didn't think any of it was funny."

That Jim could say this with a serious expression was a testimony to his professionalism.

"I'm impressed you diffused the situation so quickly," Devlyn said with what sounded like genuine admiration.

Jim mopped his forehead with the back of his hand. "You get used to these kinds of things around here." He sighed, then brightened. "Thanks for sticking around. I sang with Larry and Greg in college. Those were the best years of my life. I've been trying to get the group back together for a reunion. After twenty years, those two can't be holding a grudge anymore. Can they?"

"A grudge?" What grudge?

Jim ran a hand over his angry-looking scalp. "Larry and Greg had a falling out our senior year, and the group broke up right before the final concert. I tried to get them to fix the problem, but I just made things worse."

"What caused the rift?"

He sighed. "Larry was the musical brains in the group. He composed all the original music we used and did arrangements on the cover songs. He liked to tell everyone that Greg helped with the songs, but I was in music theory with Greg. Trust me. There's no way. His arrangements for class were terrible. So when I overheard Greg talking on the phone about selling some arrangements, I congratulated Larry."

"Only Larry didn't know about the sale."

Jim looked ready to cry. "How was I to know Greg would tell people he wrote the arrangements? He was supposed to be Larry's best friend."

"Did Larry confront Greg?"

"Yeah. That's when things got out of hand. Larry called Greg a thief. Greg told Larry he was too stupid to cash in on a good thing. I stopped Larry from jumping Greg and suggested they split the money. Larry looked like he'd be willing to take half and keep the friendship, but Greg refused. He said Larry couldn't prove that he'd written the arrangements. That Larry had put Greg's name on all of them. Greg then dared Larry to sue him. Greg walked out of the room, and he and Larry never talked again. At least, not during college. Hell, they even stopped talking to me."

I felt sorry for the big lug. Clearly, losing his friends and his a cappella group had ruined Jim's senior year. Considering the Pete's Pizza career path and his Whac-A-Mole rescuing prowess, I would guess it had even ruined his life.

Devlyn clapped the guy on the shoulder, and Jim winced. Sunburn must be lurking under the green shirt, too.

"Hey," Jim's face brightened. "Do you think you could tell the guys that you talked to me and pass along my number? It would be nice to get together with them and relive the glory days."

"I'll tell Larry when I see him, but Greg . . ." Jim's eyes were filled with hope. I felt like I was telling a five-year-old that there was no Easter Bunny when I said, "Greg died a few days ago. He was murdered."

"Well, that was interesting." Devlyn glanced at me as he steered his car into traffic. "I'd say money and revenge are really good motives to commit murder."

"Maybe." Funny, but now that I'd heard Jim's story, I actually thought Larry was a less likely murder suspect. If a guy didn't bean his backstabbing friend all those years ago, why would he suddenly change his mind now? I wasn't buying the character shift. Then again, maybe Dana pushed Larry into killing her ex. Anything was possible.

Devlyn raised an eyebrow. "You don't think Larry did it?"

"I think he's a great suspect, but as my aunt says: I'm keeping my options open."

"What other options are we pursuing?"

I blinked. "We?"

Devlyn laughed. "Well, there are two of us in this car, and I did a pretty good job as wingman back there."

"I was impressed. The niece detail was a nice touch."

"Actually, that was the truth. I have a niece who would love to have a party there in December. Once I convince my sister, I'll give Jim a call and book it. I'll probably catch hell from my nephews, but I can take it."

"How many kids does your sister have?"

"Two, but my brother has four more. All boys. How about you? Any siblings?"

"One younger brother. Neither one of us are married, which is driving my mother nuts. Grandchildren are high on her priority list."

"You don't want kids?"

"I want a performance career, which means I meet guys who are either taken or gay."

He laughed. "Sounds about right. Enough about our families. Who's the next suspect on the list?"

"According to Felicia, you are," I said half teasing, half waiting to see what his reaction would be. "She said you were in love with Greg Lucas."

Devlyn's head swiveled. "She said what?" It was a good thing we were stopped at a light or Devlyn might have plowed into the car in front of us.

"Felicia said you had a thing for Greg and you were upset that those feelings weren't reciprocated."

"Was Felicia on heavy medication when she said this?"

"She had had a couple glasses of wine, but she still

seemed coherent. She was very certain that you were a victim of unrequited love and that it might have pushed you over the edge."

"I've felt a lot of different emotions about Greg over the years that could have led to murder, but love wasn't one of them." The look on Devlyn's face made me believe him.

"So, why would Felicia think you loved Greg?"

"Got me." The light turned green, and Devlyn hit the gas. "She and I talked about Greg once in a while, mostly after she got back from show choir tournaments. She was always the one who brought him up. If anyone had a thing for Greg, it was Felicia."

"Felicia was in love with Greg?"

"I don't know if I'd call it love. Felicia gravitates toward unhealthy relationships. A relationship with Greg is as unhealthy as it comes."

Dana Lucas was proof of that.

"Do you think they had an affair?" Maybe Felicia was the mystery woman who broke up Greg and Dana's marriage.

"Doubt it. Felicia would have mentioned it. Besides, Greg liked women who are too young to vote or who could do something for his choir or his career. She wouldn't have qualified."

If Felicia had feelings for Greg, watching him romance other women would have hurt. Poor thing. "What's Felicia's story? All I know about her is she teaches home economics and loves high heels."

"Felicia is a lot like you. She took the teaching job in order to pay the bills. Designing her own line of clothes is what she's really shooting for. She's been working at getting funding to put on her own show. Don't know if it will happen, but I'd like to see her succeed."

"If the show ever happens, my aunt can provide the makeup design and a large number of country club women ready to fork over their credit cards."

Devlyn concentrated on driving while I stared out the window, trying to decide what to do next. As a performer, I was used to someone else providing the stage directions. This was the first time I'd ever had to improvise. I was finding it harder than expected.

The car in front of us raced into the intersection as the light turned red, almost taking out a bicyclist in the process. The near accident made me think about Greg's near-death experience with an automobile earlier in the year. It stood to reason that, having failed to kill Greg the first time, the person behind the wheel would take another whack at him. Maybe someone caught the make and model of the hit-and-run vehicle. If so, I could compare it to my suspects' cars and hopefully find a match. To do that, I needed to see the incident report. I wasn't sure whether Detective Kaiser would be in a sharing mood, but I was about to find out.

Chapter 16

Detective Mike wasn't at the station. Not surprising since it was a Saturday. The freckle-faced cop manning the front desk looked like he still had to ask permission to borrow the family car. The nice part about his youth was he was eager to please. I told him I was looking for an accident report. The kid gave me good news. I could absolutely buy a copy of the accident report online. The bad news was I needed to know the date of the accident.

Damn. I asked if he could look up the accident for me since I knew the name of the party involved. More bad news. He'd have to call his superiors and ask. Fairly certain news of the request would eventually reach Detective Kaiser, I said thanks but no thanks and walked back to Devlyn's car.

"Now what?" Devlyn asked as he slid into the driver's seat and cranked the air.

"Now we let our fingers do the walking. Let's go back to Aunt Millie's place. I need to use my laptop."

Aunt Millie's car wasn't in the driveway when we pulled

up. Killer must be on his way home. Devlyn followed me upstairs to my room. Normally, inviting a sexy man into my boudoir made me break out into a nervous sweat. On several occasions I'd managed to knock over lamps, trip on dust bunnies, and walk into closets because I forgot where the door was located. Was I a smooth operator or what?

Thank goodness Devlyn's sexual preferences kept my nerves at bay, and my fingers were able to fly over the keyboard without tipping over the computer. After three different searches I hit pay dirt. The *Daily Herald* did a short story on a May twenty-fifth accident and named Greg Lucas as the victim. An unnamed witness was quoted. He said Greg had started to cross the street at the intersection when a black Toyota pulled out of a parallel-parking spot and accelerated quickly. The car didn't slow as it approached the red light and hit Greg as he tried to jump out of the way. The car sped around a corner and disappeared. The article asked anyone with information about the hit-and-run to call the police.

"Who do we know who owns a black Toyota?"

Devlyn peered over my shoulder. "Larry used to own a black car. He traded it in just before school let out in June."

Huh. Guess my instincts about Larry changing his behavior might be totally off. If nothing else, this was worth looking into. I shut down the computer, gave my chair a shove, and stood up. At least, I tried to. The chair's front legs tilted backward. The back ones buried into the carpet, and my upward momentum had me falling backward with the chair.

The chair hit the floor with a thud. I braced for impact, but Devlyn wrapped his arms around me before I hit. He pulled me close and smiled. "We should probably stop meeting like this."

I tried to smile back, but the heat of his body, the look

in his eyes, and the proximity of the bed made my blood start to race. I licked my lips instead. Gay. He's gay. Sweat broke out under my armpits, and my heart thudded hard. My body wasn't listening.

Trying not to make a fool out of myself, I pulled away from his arms, stumbled slightly, and finally managed to stand upright. Devlyn's lips twitched as he asked, "Are you okay?"

So much for not making myself look like a fool.

"Yeah. I guess I was in a hurry to get going." I started down the hallway so I didn't have to see if Devlyn bought the excuse.

"Where to?" he asked.

"Larry has a lot of secrets. Maybe it's time to talk to him about a few of them."

Devlyn stopped halfway down the stairs and frowned.

"You don't think talking to Larry is a good idea?"

"I think someone talking to Larry is a great idea." Devlyn slowly walked down the rest of the steps.

"But not me." I couldn't help feeling put out. Thus far, I'd ferreted out secrets and gotten the killer concerned about my nosy nature. If anyone should talk to Larry, it was me.

"Sorry, champ." Devlyn put an arm around my shoulders and ruffled my hair. "Larry hasn't known you long enough to trust you. He isn't going to spill his guts to someone he's only known for a few days."

Damn. "You have a point. He won't talk to me, but he will talk to you. Right?"

"There's only one way to find out." Devlyn whipped out his cell phone and dialed. Larry picked up right away. I could only hear one side of the conversation, but it was obvious Larry was depressed. Devlyn volunteered to take him out for a drink to cheer him up and gave me a thumbs-up to let me know Larry had agreed. Devlyn shoved the phone back in his pocket with a smile. "I'll go pick up Larry and pump him for information. Once I'm done, we can catch dinner."

"Dinner?"

He laughed and chucked me under the chin. "Yeah, dinner. I plan on telling Larry I have a date. You're it."

Huh. I wondered if I could use the same line on Aunt Millie so she'd stay out of my love life. Couldn't hurt to try.

As if on cue, the front door opened and Killer slowly trotted in, followed by Millie. Killer was sporting a pink bandage around his head, making him look like a flamboyant pirate. Not to be outdone, Millie was decked out in a hot pink shirt, pink platform sandals, and a floppy pink hat.

Millie and Killer spotted Devlyn at the same time. They both bared their teeth. Millie in friendship. Killer in attack mode. Personally, I found it hard to take Killer's threat seriously when he was dressed in pink.

My aunt looked at Devlyn and back at me. I took the hint. "Aunt Millie, this is my friend Devlyn. He's the drama teacher at Prospect Glen."

Devlyn walked over to Millie, took her outstretched hand, and kissed it. She giggled and blushed. I blinked. Three of the four individuals in the room were wearing pink. I felt like I'd missed a memo.

"I hate to leave, but I have a meeting in a few minutes." Devlyn gave Millie's hand another kiss and smiled at me. "I'll be back later for our date." And out the door he went.

Aunt Millie turned to me with a huge grin.

"Don't look at me like that," I warned. "Trust me. I'm not his type. Besides, I think he's seeing someone."

"Is he married?"

"No."

"Engaged?"

"No."

"Then he's fair game." Millie gave Killer a gentle pat on the head. "Your friend Felicia wouldn't worry about whether he had a girlfriend. If she wanted him, she'd go after him."

"You met Felicia for two minutes."

"I know the type. Come on. We have work to do before Devlyn gets back."

I hated to ask. "What kind of work?"

She smiled. "Trust me."

Thirty minutes later I had been plucked, powdered, and painted. Aunt Millie wouldn't let me look in a mirror until she was done, which scared me to death. My aunt knew makeup, but she specialized in an AARP clientele. Not exactly the look I was going for.

Millie held up a mirror, and I braced myself for the worst. Wow. I looked nice. Better than nice. My eyes had a smoky, sexy thing going on. As my phone rang, I vowed to learn the technique. Devlyn. He wasn't going to pick me up for at least another hour. Larry hadn't said anything incriminating yet, but he had just started on his third drink. Devlyn would call when he was on his way.

While Devlyn was convinced vodka had truth-serum-like capabilities, I wasn't so sure. If Larry was like me, he'd fall asleep before he could say anything remotely interesting. But knowing Devlyn was going to let me know when he was dropping Larry back home gave me an idea. Larry's house was empty. This might be a good time to stop by and look around.

I grabbed my purse and barreled out the door. Traffic was nonexistent on the way to Larry's house. Larry's lights weren't on. His silver car sat in the driveway. The minute I turned off the ignition, my heart kicked into high gear. Maybe this wasn't such a good idea after all.

Sitting in the car, I looked up and down the street. Nobody was in their yards. I couldn't blame them. It was hot and sticky outside. The lack of neighborhood activity made my heart rate slow. Besides, it wasn't like I was going to break a window or something. And if I found a key, well, that wasn't technically breaking in. Right?

Taking a deep breath, I opened my car door and stepped into the August evening sauna. Trying to look as though I belonged, I strolled up to Larry's front door and rang the bell. Yes, I knew Larry wasn't home, but the rest of the neighborhood didn't have that information. I figured, if anyone was watching out a window, I would look suspicious if I didn't try the front door first. Having the cops called on me was definitely not on the agenda.

Now that the formalities were taken care of, I headed around the house to look for a side door. Locked up tight and no fake rock to be found. The sliding glass door around back was also locked. The trip was a bust.

I went back to the front of the house and was about to head to my car when I spotted Larry's silver Neon out of the corner of my eye. I never locked my car door when I parked at Millie's house. While I needed to change that habit, I wondered if Larry did the same thing. It couldn't hurt to find out.

I tried the handle to the car door. Eureka! It opened. My heart pounded as I slid into the blistering-hot front seat. Between the stifling heat and the possibility of being seen, I knew I needed to make this search fast. Wow. Larry's desk at school was a disaster so I would have bet his car would reflect that slovenly behavior. I'd have lost. The car was spotless. No empty coffee cups. No stray gas receipts or pieces of paper. What a disappointment.

The glove compartment contained the car manual, the insurance card that expired in November, plate registration, and a pad of yellow sticky notes. I wiped the sweat from my forehead and felt around in between the seats. Nothing. Wait. My fingers brushed against something round and hard. After a couple of tries, I finally pulled the object free as a voice said, "What do you think you're doing?"

Busted. I sucked in air and tried not to hyperventilate. Forcing a smile, I turned and looked up at a frizzy black-haired older woman with a cell phone clutched in her hand. She looked like the type to have the cops, the CIA, and the FBI on speed dial. This was bad.

"Hi," I said in my most cheerful, least criminal-like voice. "I work with Larry. He's had a hard week so I came by to check on him, but he didn't answer the door."

The phone lowered a fraction of an inch. "I saw you ring the bell and go around back."

Thank God I decided to go to the front door; otherwise, the police would already have me in handcuffs. "I'm glad to know Larry has people looking out for him. Things at the school have been tough."

Her frown softened. "Larry hasn't been himself this week. He's been coming and going at all hours, and his lights have been on long after midnight. I don't think he's sleeping very well."

"I don't blame him," I said, sliding the metal object into my pants pocket. "Having someone you know murdered is hard to deal with. I only knew the victim a few days, and I'm having trouble sleeping." A large poodle and a break-in contributed to my lack of sleep, but I didn't think the block busybody needed that information.

The woman frowned again. "It's good you're a friend of Larry's, but I don't understand what you're doing in his car." This was not a woman willing to be distracted by entertaining gossip. Darn.

So I improvised. Reaching into the glove box, I pulled out the yellow sticky notes. "I wanted to leave Larry a note, and I know he always keeps paper in his car." I grabbed a pen from my purse and started scribbling.

Hi, Larry. I was worried when you left so abruptly yesterday. I hope you're okay. Paige.

When I was done, I pulled the sticky note from the pad, put the rest of the paper in the glove box, and slammed the glove box door shut. "Do you know if Larry goes in the front or the side door? I want to make sure he knows I stopped by."

The phone lowered all the way down to the woman's side, and for the first time she smiled. "He goes in the side door. Most of my neighbors never use the front door unless company comes calling."

I thanked her for the information and slid out of the stifling-hot car. Feeling the resident busybody's eyes follow my every move, I walked to the side of the house and affixed the note to the door. Leaving a note wasn't part of my original plan. Personally, I'd rather Larry not know I'd stopped by. But the one-woman neighborhood watch committee would no doubt read the note after I left.

Waving, I walked down to the street and climbed into my car. I could feel the weight of the metal object in my pants pocket. Curiosity was killing me, but I resisted the urge to pull the object out and examine it. Sitting at the curb for too long would make my new friend reexamine her decision not to call the police. With that in mind, I started the car, cranked the air, and hit the gas. The minute my car began to move, the woman hightailed it up the driveway in hot pursuit of the note I'd left.

I drove three blocks before I stopped the car, reached into my pocket, and pulled out—a pitch pipe. Not exactly a case-breaking clue. Larry was a music teacher. Owning and using a pitch pipe were requirements of the job. I'd be more surprised if he didn't have one. Oh well. Going back and returning it wasn't an option. Not unless I wanted my new best friend to watch me do it. I'd just have to slip it under some of the papers on Larry's desk and hope he didn't wonder how it got there.

Chapter 17

I shoved the pitch pipe into my pocket and headed back to Millie's. My cell rang the minute I pulled into the driveway. Devlyn had just dropped Larry off at home and was on his way.

I walked into the house, caught my reflection in the mirror, and shrieked. My hair looked like I'd plugged my finger into an electric socket, and mascara was smudged under my eyes. The humidity had taken its toll.

Racing upstairs, I brushed my hair into a ponytail and wiped the raccoon circles from my eyes. The doorbell rang as I was coming down the stairs. I could hear the telltale click of poodle nails coming in my direction, so I hurried to the door. Devlyn stood on the other side, looking a lot less happy than when he left.

"Are you ready for dinner?" he asked.

"What happened with Larry?"

He grabbed my hand and pulled. "I'll tell you at dinner.

I'm starved, and after talking to Larry I really need a drink. Come on."

Ten minutes later we were ensconced in a back booth of a local Mexican restaurant. Piñatas hung from the ceiling, and Spanish folk songs played over the loudspeaker. The waiter brought over a large basket of chips and a bowl of salsa, and greeted Devlyn by name. Then he and Devlyn began speaking in rapid Spanish. After *hola*, I was lost. I took four years of French in high school and three years of German in college. Both were great for operatic singing. Too bad their practical application in the United States sucked.

After a bunch more indecipherable conversation, the waiter headed off. "You come here often?" I asked.

"About once a week." Devlyn salted the basket of chips and shoved one into his mouth. "The food is excellent, and they make the best margaritas around. I ordered one for you. If you don't like it you, I can drink it for you."

"On the rocks or frozen?"

"On the rocks."

"Salt?"

He grinned. "You have to have salt."

The chip and spicy salsa in my mouth prevented me from arguing. Then the waiter returned with our drinks. At least, I think they were our drinks. They looked like fishbowls. When Devlyn said he needed a drink, he wasn't kidding.

Devlyn picked up his glass and saluted me before taking a large gulp. I didn't trust myself to pick the thing up, so I took a sip out of the straw. Huzzah! This place didn't skimp on the tequila. After three sips, I could feel the liquor rushing to my brain. Time for food.

We studied the menu, which was mostly in Spanish, and placed our order. I ordered tacos. That seemed safe. Devlyn ordered something I couldn't translate and waited for the server to leave. After another large hit of margarita, he said, "Larry didn't kill Greg, but he knows who did."

I choked on my chip. "He told you that?"

"Not in those words."

"What words did he use?"

Devlyn leaned back against the green vinyl-covered booth. "Larry didn't want to talk at first, but after three vodka and tonics he started to open up."

One vodka and tonic would have gotten my lips unlocked. I was a cheap date.

"I tried to get him to talk about his past friendship with Greg, but he wouldn't say a word. After another drink I got him to talk about his new car. Larry said the water pump on his old car sprung a leak and the car was overheating. Buying a new car was cheaper than fixing the old one."

I slurped down some margarita. "Was he telling the truth?"

"I didn't have my polygraph turned on." Devlyn sighed. "Yeah, I think he was telling the truth. Larry isn't a car guy. The only way he'd know that his car even had a water pump is if something happened to it." Devlyn ate a couple more chips. "But once he started talking about the car, he relaxed and started talking about Greg."

I leaned forward. "And?"

"He's not sorry Greg is dead, but he feels bad that Eric Metz is a suspect. He told me he knows something that could help Eric, but him saying anything would cause a lot of people more trouble. He isn't going to spill his guts to the police unless he has to."

I munched on a chip wondering if whatever object Larry took from Greg Lucas's house and gave to Dana Lucas was the key to Eric's future. The food arrived, cutting off all meaningful conversation. The tacos smelled heavenly, and they tasted even better. The only problem was, the minute I took a bite, the shell cracked—sending lettuce, tomatoes, and meat flying. Thank God this wasn't a real date. Taco sauce ran down my chin and stained my fingers, and I didn't care. I was in Mexican food heaven.

Devlyn laughed at me.

"What?" I asked with a half-eaten taco raised to my mouth. "I'm hungry."

"I can tell."

For the first time I looked at the contents of his plate. I saw some sort of meat covered by peppers and onions in a red sauce. "What did you order?"

He smiled. "Tongue."

"Tongue? As in that used to be in an animal's mouth?"

He nodded. "Do you want to try some?"

He said it like it was a dare. If I didn't try his food, I'd be a wimp. If I did try it, my stomach would never forgive me. I was trapped.

"I'm not going to share my food with you, so you don't have to share with me."

He smiled. "You're chicken."

"Am not." Liar. Liar.

"Prove it." He cut off a piece of the tongue and held out the fork. His eyes held mine as if daring me to refuse.

"No one has dared me to do anything like this since college." I tried to ignore the forked tongue hovering in front of me.

Devlyn didn't back down. The fork inched closer to my face. My stomach flip-flopped, and horror music played in my head. No. I was not going to succumb to pressure and eat something I didn't want. If this was a date and I really liked the guy, then maybe. But this wasn't a date, and my eating a piece of cow tongue wasn't going to get me a fabulous good night kiss.

"No, thank—"

Devlyn shoved the fork between my open lips with a laugh. My stomach heaved. An unwanted tongue was in my mouth. I had two choices, spit it out and embarrass myself in front of the other diners or swallow and make Devlyn pay later.

Cringing, I chewed. The texture was soft. I tried not to think about that as I swallowed. Huh. Not bad. Had I not known what I was eating, I might have enjoyed it. Devlyn raised an eyebrow.

"It's okay, but I like my taco better." To emphasize the point, I took a huge bite.

Devlyn brushed back a lock of hair, drawing attention to the bruise above his eye. I had noticed it yesterday, but didn't feel comfortable asking about it. Today, I'd already had part of his tongue in my mouth so I figured I was allowed to make an inquiry. Wiping the taco juice from my chin, I asked, "What's with the bruise?"

He cocked his head to one side. "What bruise?"

"The one over your left eye."

"Oh, that." His fingers brushed the offending spot, and he shrugged as he helped himself to another chip slathered with salsa. "I was moving stuff in my office and bumped into the edge of my desk. The bruise makes me look dangerous, don't you think?" He flashed an evil smile, which made me giggle. The giggle made me choke on a corn chip, and I found myself sucking down margarita to make the coughing stop.

Once I was able to talk, I steered the conversation back to my boss. "Did Larry give you any idea who he thought murdered Greg?"

"No. I thought he was going to. Then he got a text message from someone. He freaked out and said he wanted me to drive him home."

Uh-oh. The text was probably from the self-appointed neighborhood watch. I checked my cell. No missed calls. If Larry was annoyed about my visit, he probably would have said something.

I finished my meal and took another sip of my margarita, trying not to be depressed at the lack of progress in my investigation. "So the night was a bust."

"I wouldn't say that."

"Why not?" What had I missed?

He grinned. "Any night that allows me to bully someone into eating my favorite meal isn't a bust." Before I could refute that, he took out his wallet and laid cash on the table. "Come on. We still have work to do."

"What kind of work?"

"I promised to buy you dinner if we got some more choreography done." He slid out of the booth and pulled me out.

"We just ate. Isn't there a rule about not dancing until at least an hour after you finish eating?"

"That's swimming, and scientists have proven that to be a myth." He marched me to the door, only stopping once—to give our waiter a hug. I wondered if the waiter was the mysterious love interest as I climbed into Devlyn's car.

"Where are we going?" I asked. "Don't they have rules about how late faculty members can be at school before classes start?" I was pretty sure I'd read that in the handbook.

He nodded. "You're right." I smiled. "Which is why we aren't going there."

Devlyn didn't offer any other hints as to our destination. He just gave me a mysterious smile and turned his eyes to the road. I closed my eyes and tried to decide what to do next. If Larry wouldn't spill his guts to Devlyn while under the influence, he certainly wouldn't talk to me. Inspiration failed to strike as the car slowed and Devlyn turned off the ignition.

I opened my eyes. "We're at Aunt Millie's house. Why? Did you forget something?"

He laughed and opened his door. "I noticed a lack of furniture in the living room. As long as your aunt doesn't object, I figured we could work there."

I scrambled out of the car after him. The lights were dark in the house. Either Millie had gone out or she'd turned in early. After last night's adventure, I was guessing the latter. Leaving Devlyn leaning against a wall in the living room, I went upstairs to check. Millie snored loudly as I pushed open her door. The taxidermied mutts were all in the circle I'd placed them in earlier, looking very much like they were holding a séance. Killer was nowhere to be seen.

Hustling back down stairs, I shook my head at Devlyn. "She'd out cold. Guess we can't dance. Darn."

"That's a shame. The plush carpet would have been a lot softer to land on than linoleum."

"You were planning on dropping me again?"

"I like contingencies." He pushed away from the wall and walked over to me. "Got any ideas for some activities that won't wake your aunt?"

I knew Devlyn didn't intend his comment to have a sexual undertone, but I couldn't help the delicious shiver that zipped through my body. Ignoring it, I said, "Scrabble?"

He took a step closer. "I suck at spelling. Try again."

"We could watch TV."

"I guess we could do that." He edged in closer.

Suddenly, I heard bells and not the wow-I'm-excited-a-hot-guy-is-making-his-move bells. Real bells.

Devlyn took a step back and pulled his phone out of his

pocket. He hit a button and held the phone up to his ear. "Hey, Larry. Are you okay?"

From the stunned look on Devlyn's face, I would say Larry was far from okay.

The police were at Larry's house. And they had a warrant.

———

Devlyn made it to Larry's place in nine minutes. Three sets of red-and-blue lights lit up the street in front of the house, and uniformed cops with flashlights were crawling inside and around Larry's car. Larry was standing at the bottom of the driveway looking like he was going to cry. Detective Mike was standing next to him. The minute the detective saw Devlyn and me approach, he sighed. Or maybe it was just me that elicited the reaction. Hard to tell.

"Are you okay, Larry?" Devlyn asked, giving Larry's shoulder a pat. Larry had been almost incoherent on the phone. Devlyn had been able to make out the words "cops" and "warrant" and almost nothing else.

Larry shook his head and bit his lip. He looked shell-shocked. "The police showed up after you left with a warrant to search my car. Why do they need to search my car?" He held out a folded piece of paper.

Devlyn took the paper and squinted to read it by cop-car light. "I don't know."

Devlyn and Larry moved closer to one of the cop cars so Devlyn could see better.

"Fancy meeting you here."

I jumped at Detective Mike's voice. "Larry was upset by the warrant so Devlyn and I came over to check on him."

"I didn't think you and Larry were good enough friends for you to visit twice in one day."

The one-woman neighborhood watch was standing on

her front porch, viewing the festivities. No doubt she'd already reported the details of my earlier stop.

"He's my boss," I said.

"An anonymous tip claims he's also Greg Lucas's murderer and that something in his car will prove it." Detective Mike's eyes narrowed as he looked at me. Swallowing hard, I glanced down the street. My favorite neighborhood busybody was sporting a pair of binoculars. Crap. The detective knew I'd been in the car earlier.

The pitch pipe suddenly felt huge and bulky in my pocket. That couldn't be what the cops were looking for. Could it? "I didn't see anything incriminating in the car when I was here earlier." Mike gave me a flat stare so I added, "I needed to write Larry a note. He had Post-its in the glove compartment."

Mike waited for me to keep talking. I put my hands behind my back. No obstruction of justice here. After a moment, he glanced at the team of cops going through the car. One of them shook his head.

Nothing.

Detective Kaiser sighed. "The tip probably came from a kid looking to get even for a bad grade, but I needed to check it out. Do you think my date will understand why I had to cancel?"

He'd broken a date to dig through Larry's car. Huh. Definitely a reason why a woman wouldn't want to get involved with a homicide detective, no matter how attractive.

"Sure she will." I nodded my head up and down. Inside, my head shook side to side. Women hated being stood up no matter what the reason. An early relationship might survive one or two broken dates, but once the excitement of dating a police officer wore off, the cancellations would become annoying. Still, I'd already lied about the important stuff. Why stop there?

"You're lying."

"No, I'm not."

"Yes, you are. Your left eyebrow twitches when you lie."

"It does not." If it did, I was screwed.

He smiled. "Ask Mr. O'Shea. He'll tell you if I'm wrong. Gotta round up the troops and call my date. She said she'd be waiting by the phone." He turned and walked up the driveway toward the car. Touching my left eyebrow, I walked over to the other side of the street where Larry and Devlyn were sitting on the curb.

"The search was a bust. The cops are packing up and going home."

Larry squinted up at me and smiled. At least, I think it was a smile. It could have been gas.

"That's good news." Devlyn stood and put his hand out to help Larry to his feet. Larry swayed dangerously, and I grabbed his arm to steady him. "Can you help me get him inside? I don't know if he's going to make it on his own."

By the time we half carried, half dragged Larry to the front door, the cops had packed up their toys and headed home. Detective Mike gave me a jaunty wave as he climbed into his Mustang and zoomed off. I opened the front door and held it open as Devlyn navigated Larry into the living room.

The room looked as though it had been decorated with leftover dorm-room furniture. A gray futon rested in front of the picture window. A large halogen lamp sat on the beige carpet. Two white bookshelves leaned against the far wall. In between them, an enormous television perched on a shiny black stand. Next to the television was a collection of video game systems, controllers, and other accessories. The only non-dorm-room item was a mahogany piano and bench that sat in the back corner of the room.

"I think I'm going to be sick." Larry clapped a hand over his mouth and bolted toward the hallway. An unhappy-looking Devlyn followed behind.

As soon as the two disappeared, I pulled the stolen pitch pipe out of my pocket. If this was what the anonymous tipster had called the police about, I wanted to know why.

I frowned. There was nothing special as far as I could tell. It looked like every other pitch pipe I'd ever seen except the letters identifying the pitches had become a little worn. Clearly, Larry used the thing.

Wait. I flipped the pipe over and spotted some engraving on the back. The engraving had also faded with use. Walking over to the lamp, I held the pipe up to the light and leaned close in an attempt to make out the words.

Thanks, Mr. L. We'll never forget you. The class of 2003.

Huh. I'd never heard the kids refer to Larry as Mr. L. Then it hit me.

Holy shit. Mr. L wasn't Larry. Mr. L was Greg Lucas. This was the same pitch pipe Greg had with him in the choir room the day he died.

Chapter 18

My first instinct was to wipe the damn thing clean and return it to the car crevice where I found it. Maybe the nosy neighbor had gotten her fill of street patrol and was inside watching *Wheel of Fortune*. Nope. She was still on her porch clutching her binoculars. Well, hell.

I looked at the pitch pipe, trying to decide what to do next. Turning it over to the cops seemed like an obvious choice, only I'd probably end up in a cell next to Larry. Not exactly my idea of a good time. Besides, something about this anonymous tip to the cops felt wrong.

"Are you okay?"

I jumped and spun around. Devlyn was standing in the living room doorway, wiping his wet hands on his shorts. "I'm thinking."

"Sounds dangerous."

I couldn't deny that. "How's Larry?"

"Passed out cold on the bathroom floor."

"Do you think we should move him?"

Devlyn shook his head. "I tried. He refused."

Huh. I was in Larry's house, with his approval, and he was unconscious. This was investigative kismet. If God hadn't wanted me to snoop, he wouldn't have let Larry drink so much. Okay, that might have had more to do with Devlyn than God, but I was still taking it as a sign.

"What do you have in your hand?"

Oops. I looked down at the shiny object and decided to come clean. "I think this is what the cops were looking for in Larry's car."

Devlyn frowned. "Why would you think that?"

"Because I found it when I was searching Larry's car."

Devlyn's eyes narrowed. "When did you search Larry's car?" His voice sounded calm, but the hand clenching at his side told me not to be fooled.

"Since you were talking to Larry at the bar, I thought that might be a good time to swing by and check out the place. Larry's car was open so I took a look inside."

"Weren't you worried someone might see you?"

I debated telling Devlyn about the woman and her binoculars, and decided against it. Being responsible for apoplexy was probably a good way to lose a friend. "I pretended I was here to visit him. I rang the doorbell and left a sticky note on his door." I wasn't a complete amateur, right? "I didn't take a good look at the pitch pipe until now."

Devlyn took the pitch pipe from me, looking more interested in strangling me for my foray into breaking and entering than in the object itself. Until he spotted the inscription. He sucked in air, and his eyes met mine. "This belonged to Greg Lucas?"

I nodded.

"How did it end up in Larry's car?"

Good question. One I really wanted an answer to. "My

guess is that whoever killed Greg planted the pitch pipe in between Larry's car seats. Then the killer called the cops with an anonymous tip to make sure Larry got fingered for the crime." I waited for Devlyn to be impressed.

Nope. He was back to looking angry. "You stole evidence. You could be arrested for that."

"Technically, I didn't know it was evidence when I put it in my pocket." I was hoping that counted for something.

"You should have turned it over to the cops when they were here." Devlyn looked a little too close to being pushed over the edge.

"Look," I said, trying to sound calm and rational. "I promise I'll turn the pitch pipe over to the cops, but I don't want Larry to take the rap for a murder unless he actually committed it."

The tension in Devlyn's shoulders eased. He blew a lock of dark hair off his forehead and asked, "How do you plan on proving he did or didn't do it?"

I smiled. "We're in Larry's house with his permission. It couldn't hurt to take a look around while we're waiting for him to wake up."

"What are we looking for?"

Not a clue. "I guess we'll know it when we see it."

We split up so we could cover more ground. Devlyn took the clean, albeit out-of-date kitchen. Probably a good choice. Devlyn looked like he could use another drink. I headed down the hall to Larry's bedroom.

Holy cow. The room looked like the closet threw up. Clothes were strewn across the floor, on top of the hamper, and over the unmade bed. If I hadn't known better, I would have thought Larry had emptied out the closet in search of the perfect date outfit. An important piece of evidence could be lurking inside this room and no one would ever find it.

At least, not the way it looked now. The only way to search was to clean. Lucky me. Picking up my boss's underwear was definitely not on my top ten list of how to spend a Friday night.

I spotted a large black plastic laundry basket under a pile of shirts at the foot of the bed. Grabbing it, I began sorting clothes. While doing my boss's laundry was above and beyond the call of duty, it gave me a great excuse to rifle through his pockets. Larry would thank me for keeping stray cash and lip balm from being decimated by the dryer. And who knows, maybe he'd even give me a raise when I explained that I cleaned up so he could have a comfortable space to recover in.

The blacks and colors went into the basket. The whites, which were mostly undershirts and tighty whities, were kicked into a pile near the closet. The only clues in that pile were to questions I didn't want answered.

By the time I was done, I had seven dollars and twenty-six cents, three paper clips, and two packages of dental floss. Enough to make an arts-and-crafts project and get a cup or two of Starbucks coffee. Not enough to solve the case.

I found the washing machine in the utility room next to the kitchen and squashed in as much as I could. A scoop of detergent and a spin of the dial and I was headed back into Larry's much tidier bedroom.

The bed was a mess, so I tucked in the sheets and smoothed the comforter. I didn't really expect to find anything of interest in it, but I figured if Larry ever got up off the floor, he'd appreciate a freshly made bed to sleep in.

Standing next to the bed, I took stock of the room. There was a nightstand with a lamp and an alarm clock sitting on the top. A large dresser stood against the wall behind me, and a television with DVD player was mounted on the wall.

I wasn't the type to keep things stashed in my dresser, so I started with the nightstand drawer. Stephen King books. A bag of cough drops. A couple of notepads with music scribbled on them and . . . Ick. Judging by the size of the box of condoms, Larry was looking to get really lucky.

Now that I knew Larry used protection, I headed over to the dresser. Just because I didn't use my sock drawer as a safe-deposit box didn't mean other people had the same prejudice. The first drawer had T-shirts and underwear. The second had socks. Lots of socks organized by size and color. If Larry had time to organize his socks into perfect rows, he probably didn't go on enough dates to warrant the box of condoms in his nightstand. Poor guy.

I was about to close the drawer when a bump in a sock near the back of the drawer caught my attention. Aha. Stuffed inside a black sock was a cassette tape. Putting the tape in my pocket, I sat the sock on top of the dresser. As soon as I found a cassette player and listened to the tape, I'd put it back where I found it.

The next two drawers turned up nothing exciting, so I bopped back down the hall, poking my head into each room and looking for a radio with a cassette player. I found one on the bathroom counter above the rug on which Larry was currently drooling. Reaching over Larry, I snagged the player, bolted down the hall, and ran into the kitchen. Devlyn glanced up from his seat at the farm-style wooden table. Several stacks of papers were spread out in front of him.

"I think I found something." Triumphant, I placed the radio on an empty spot on the table, slid the tape in, and hit play.

There was a pop and a crackle and a bunch of murmuring voices before four-part a cappella music filled the kitchen. The male voices were strong and talented, and the song was catchy. I couldn't come up with the name of the tune, but I'd heard it before. It had a jungle beat and lyrics involving stars and skies. Last week, when researching music for my choir, I'd clicked on a lot of websites for show choirs across the country. At least half of them had this song on their "best of" highlights videos. Why would Larry have a tape of the song hidden in his sock drawer?

"I know that song. 'Stars Above.' North Shore's choir performed it last year," Devlyn said.

"Larry had the tape hidden in his sock drawer." I hit stop and popped the tape out of the radio. The cassette looked old, and the label on it looked faded. "I'm guessing that the singers on this are Larry, Greg, our friend Jim, and whoever the fourth guy was."

Devlyn gave a low whistle. "Every show choir in the country has performed that song. It's a classic. If that's the song Greg stole from Larry, he's made a fortune off it. From the bank statements and bills I've found, Larry is hurting for cash."

In any cop's book, Larry would have a fabulous motive for murder. Call me crazy, but to me Larry was looking more innocent by the second. Between the pitch pipe, the anonymous phone call, and years of Larry's willingness to be cheated without fighting back, my instincts said someone else was responsible.

Devlyn didn't feel the same way. He stood up and took the tape from my hand. "We need to turn this over to the police."

I took the tape back. "We will, but first we talk to Larry. He deserves a chance to tell us his side of the story before we sic the cops on him." Devlyn didn't look convinced, so I added, "The guy is passed out cold on the bathroom floor. The least we can do is let him sleep off the booze and take a shower before sending him off to the clink. We can meet back here in the morning after Larry's had a chance to change clothes. We'll talk to him. If we don't like what he says, we call the cops. Deal?"

"Deal. Just so you know, I hate getting up early on Sunday mornings. You're buying the coffee."

Devlyn put the bills back where he found them while I moved laundry from the washer to the dryer and stashed the tape back in its sock. We then stood in the bathroom doorway watching Larry breathe. Devlyn wanted to leave him on the floor. I wanted the guy in a good mood tomorrow when we arrived. Eight to ten hours lying on tile would make me cranky, so we each took an arm and half carried, half dragged Larry to his bed. We left the side door unlocked in case we got back before Larry had finished sleeping off his drunken stupor. Then we headed for Devlyn's car.

It was midnight when Devlyn pulled back into Millie's driveway. We decided to meet back at Larry's at seven, and Devlyn insisted on walking me to the door. After last night's front-stoop adventure, I was happy to have the company. I slid my key in the lock and turned back to say good night as Devlyn's mouth latched onto mine.

I didn't know what to do. I mean, I know how to kiss. My first kiss was back in eighth grade when I got caught under the mistletoe with Jack McGregor. His nose bumped mine twice as he tried to find my mouth, and all I remember thinking was how slimy his lips were as I did my best to kiss him back. I had no idea what I was doing, but I had to kiss him back. Everyone was watching.

Well, no one was watching this kiss, but I still didn't know what to do. Devlyn's lips were warm and firm, no Jack McGregor slime. In fact, his lips were fabulous. But I couldn't enjoy the moment. All I could do was stand there with my eyes wide open, trying to decide if I'd stepped into the *Twilight Zone*. After a few seconds, Devlyn stepped back. I blinked up at him. He gave me a teasing smile and said, "Oops. I meant to do this." He leaned back down and kissed me on the nose. "See you in the morning." The man was down the driveway and climbing into his car before I could form a coherent sentence.

What the hell was that?

Dazed, I went inside, locked the door behind me, and headed up to my room. This wasn't the first time a gay man had kissed me. Far from it. Every time I went to an audition I got pecks on the lips from the men I knew, both gay and straight. But a kiss on the doorstep after going on what could be loosely considered a date was unchartered territory. I was pretty sure Devlyn was teasing me. He had to be. Right?

By the time I went to the bathroom to change into my pajamas and brush my teeth, I'd decided Devlyn had been yanking my chain. Still, after he and I had a chat with Larry, the two of us were going to have a long talk. Just in case.

Feeling less confused, I walked into my room and sighed. Sitting in the middle of the bed was Killer. The pink bandage had slipped and was now covering his left eye, making him look decidedly rakish. He took one look at me, rolled over, and stuck his feet up in the air. I didn't have the energy or the heart to toss him out, so I nudged Killer to the left side of the bed, pushed back the covers, and turned off the light.

When I staggered out of bed the next morning, Millie and Killer were downstairs in the kitchen. Between the kiss, the pitch pipe, and the bed-hogging dog, I hadn't gotten much rest. If I didn't get my beauty sleep soon, I was going to need a facelift.

"Good morning, dear. I didn't expect you up so early.

Did your date go well?" Millie's eyes sparkled with excitement.

"Devlyn is just a friend," I reminded her as I poured a large cup of coffee in hopes of bolstering my energy.

"The best marriages start off with friendship," Millie said with a wink. "Don't forget the benefit tonight. We have to be at the Ockinickys at seven. Devlyn is welcome to join us." She finished her coffee, patted Killer on the head, and disappeared out the door.

Damn. I'd forgotten about the benefit. The Ockinickys were raising money for a local children's after-school choir and art program. Aunt Millie had promised her friends I'd sing a couple of songs to help inspire guests to give money to the cause. She thought the appearance might lead to a break in my career. I figured it meant I'd just go hungry for the night. No one ever remembered to save hors d'oeuvres for the entertainment.

The thought of food made my stomach protest. I walked over to the fridge and reached for the handle as a low growl came from behind me. Killer's nails clipped along the floor, and the growl got louder as he took a seat next to the fridge. The bandage on his head had come off. He was now sporting a buzz cut and zigzagged stitching on the top of his head.

I pulled the handle on the fridge, and Frankenpoodle growled louder and snapped. Instinctively, I took a step back. Then I got mad.

"Look," I yelled. "You got to sleep in my bed, which means I get to eat breakfast. I think that's fair. Don't you?"

I reached for the door handle again, and Killer barked twice and bared his teeth. Clearly, fair wasn't in his vocabulary. I gave him what I hoped was a withering look. "Fine.

Just remember this tonight." Turning on my heel, I stomped out the door.

Thank goodness there was a Dunkin' Donuts on the way to Larry's house. I got a large latte for me, two large regular coffees for the boys, and two dozen assorted doughnuts. If after talking to Larry, we needed to call the cops, the doughnuts wouldn't go to waste.

Devlyn hadn't yet arrived as I steered my Cobalt into Larry's driveway and parked behind his silver car. If he wanted to make a quick getaway, he'd have to do it on foot. Balancing the tray of coffee and the doughnut boxes, I headed for the unlocked side door and let myself into the house. The place was quiet. No shower or radio sounds. Larry must still be asleep.

I walked into the living room and went flying. My left foot stepped on something, I lost my balance, and my body bashed into the wall. The doughnut boxes fell to the floor, but thank God the coffee tray remained upright in my hand.

Holy crap. No wonder I tripped. The place was a mess.

Video games, CDs, and video controllers were strewn across the floor along with the futon mattress. The piano bench was upside down, and sheets of music were spread across the carpet like confetti. I put the coffee tray on top of the piano and raced into the kitchen. More destruction. Drawers were emptied. Chairs were upended. Even the garbage had been knocked over. Either Larry couldn't find the aspirin or someone had tossed his house.

Careful not to trip on debris, I hurried down the hall, looking into rooms as I passed. Larry wasn't in any of them. By the time I got to the bedroom, one thing was clear. Larry was gone, and given the large streak of blood on the bed, I was guessing he didn't go willingly.

Chapter 19

Nausea sliced through my stomach. The white sheets and blue comforter I'd smoothed and tucked last night were bunched at the end of the bed. The white pillow I last saw Larry snoring on had a dark bloodstain in the center. The fitted sheet showed drips of the same dark stain in several spots. I thought I saw drops of blood on the floor, too, but it was hard to tell with the dresser drawers overturned and Larry's other belongings ransacked.

Fingers shaking, I pulled out my phone and dialed Detective Kaiser's number.

"Yeah?" Mike sounded grumpy. He got grumpier the minute I told him where I was and where Larry wasn't. "Go outside and wait for me. Don't touch anything. I don't want you disturbing the scene any more than you have. I'll be there in fifteen minutes."

Putting the phone back in my pocket, I started to leave, then noticed the overturned sock drawer. Okay. Detective Mike told me not to touch anything, but he didn't know about the audiotape. If someone had taken the tape, Detective Mike would never know about it unless I told him.

Feeling morally bound to snoop, I sifted through the socks one by one, looking for the tape. Nothing. I looked under a few shirts and a couple pairs of pants. The tape, like Larry, was missing.

My watch told me the cops would be pulling up any minute. I hightailed it down the hall to the living room and grabbed the doughnut boxes.

"What the hell happened to this place?"

The boxes went flying as I jumped and spun around. Devlyn laughed. Then he took one look at my freaked-out face, and his laughter faded.

"What's wrong?"

"The house was like this when I arrived, and Larry is gone." My breath caught in my throat as I explained about the blood and the missing tape. "I've called Detective Kaiser. He wants us to wait outside."

Devlyn looked stunned. He gave me a quick hug and reached down to pick up the battered doughnut boxes. I grabbed the tray of coffees, and we went outside to wait for the cavalry.

Detective Kaiser arrived a few minutes later. Judging by the five o'clock shadow, the barely combed hair, and the mismatched black and brown shoes, he'd been in bed when I called. A part of me wondered whether he'd been alone or if his date had forgiven last night's cancellation. If last night hadn't warned her off, this morning's wake-up call should have done the trick.

The detective stalked toward us with a frown. "You didn't say Mr. O'Shea was here."

"You didn't ask," I shot back, feeling testy. Then I admitted, "He wasn't here when I called you. We arranged to meet here at seven, but Devlyn was a little late." More like a lot late—which just occurred to me. I wondered why.

Devlyn opened a box of doughnuts and held the box out toward Detective Mike. The detective raised an eyebrow. I would, too. The doughnuts inside were a disaster. Chocolate frosting and sprinkles coated the box lid. Several of the donuts resembled miniature Frisbees.

The detective must have been hungry. He grabbed one of the Frisbees and took a bite. Swallowing, he said, "Wait here." Then he disappeared inside. My stomach growled. Devlyn swung the box of mangled doughnuts toward me. I shook my head. A smear of raspberry filling made a couple of the doughnuts look like they belonged in a trauma ward. After seeing the bloodstains in Larry's room, the disemboweled pastries disturbed me.

I sipped at my lukewarm latte and looked down at my black sneakers, trying to ignore the guilt creeping up my spine. Larry shouldn't be missing. Had I called the cops last night like Devlyn wanted to, Larry would now be cooling his heels in a room at the Prospect Glen Police Department instead of being injured. Maybe worse.

"This isn't your fault."

I sniffled and looked up at Devlyn. "Are you psychic now?"

"You look like you're standing on a ledge looking down." He sat down on the concrete driveway and patted the ground next to him. "Have a seat before you throw yourself off the curb."

I planted my butt on the ground, and Devlyn put his arm around me. We sat there saying nothing, probably because there wasn't anything we could say. Larry was gone.

"Mr. O'Shea." Devlyn and I turned to watch Detective

Kaiser trot out of the house and toward us. His expression was unreadable as he pulled a notebook out of his back pocket. "Could you step over here for a minute please?"

Devlyn gave me another quick hug and got to his feet. A minute later the two men were huddled under a tree by the side of the house, leaving me alone with my guilt and a box of doughnuts. I broke off a piece of chocolate cake doughnut and popped it into my mouth. Huh. Not bad. The glazed and the bear claw weren't bad, either. By the time Devlyn and Detective Kaiser were done chatting, my guilt was making me feel decidedly ill. Or maybe it was the five doughnuts I'd just eaten. It was hard to tell.

"Your turn, Ms. Marshall." Detective Kaiser smiled, but his eyes were anything but happy. He crooked his finger, and I swallowed hard as the doughnuts threatened to make a reappearance.

Devlyn gave me a peck on the cheek and whispered, "I didn't mention the pitch pipe. That's up to you. Give me a call when you're done." Then, grabbing the full box of doughnuts, he headed to his car and drove away.

The detective leaned against Larry's car and asked, "What did Mr. O'Shea say to you just now?"

I considered lying and decided against it just in case the eyebrow thing was true. Instead, I went with option B: a half-truth. "He told me to call him when I was done talking to you." I scrambled to my feet and asked, "What do you think happened to Larry?"

Detective Kaiser pushed away from the car. "That's what I'm hoping you'll tell me. The house is a wreck, but there's nothing to say Larry didn't destroy the place himself before leaving."

"Why would he do that?"

"I don't think he did. But right now I don't have proof that a crime took place." He smiled. "That's where you come in."

"Me?" I fought the urge to study the ground.

"Yeah. You."

We looked at each other as the seconds ticked by. Finally, I said, "I think whoever tossed Larry's house was the same person who called in the anonymous tip about his car."

"Why would you think that?"

I sighed. Aunt Millie would probably spring for my bail. "When I was getting paper out of Larry's car, I found a pitch pipe wedged deep in between the seats. Then the neighbor showed up, and I forgot to put it back where I found it. I think someone wanted the police to find the pitch pipe. When you didn't, they came here looking for it." I braced myself for lots of yelling.

"Where is the pitch pipe now?"

I was impressed. Detective Kaiser's jaw was clenched and his eyes looked ready to pop, but his voice was low and calm. I unzipped my purse, pulled out the object in question, and dropped it into his hand. "I didn't think it was important until after you left last night. That's when I took a closer look and saw the inscription. That pitch pipe belonged to Greg Lucas, and I'm pretty sure I saw him with it the afternoon before he died."

Detective Kaiser's right eye began to twitch as he examined the object in his hands. He held the pitch pipe closer to his face to read the inscription. "You do realize I could arrest you for this, right?"

My heart skipped several beats, and I sucked in air as I waited for him to pull out the handcuffs.

Instead, he shook his head and asked, "Is there anything else I should know about?"

I chewed on my bottom lip for a moment. If purloining evidence hadn't gotten me arrested, I figured I was safe. "When I was straightening up Larry's bedroom last night, I ran across a cassette tape stashed in the back of his sock drawer. I tried to find it this morning, but it was gone."

"Did you listen to the tape?"

I nodded. "Greg and Larry were in an a cappella group in college. I'm pretty sure that was the group on the recording." Now that I had started spilling my guts, I couldn't stop. I told Detective Kaiser about Greg stealing Larry's music and passing it off as his own. I also mentioned Larry's financial problems.

When I was done with my recitation, I let out a sigh of relief. Then I looked at Detective Kaiser's face. His eyes were closed. His hands were clenched so tight his knuckles had turned white, and he was taking slow, deep breaths. Five. Four. Three. Two. One. His eyes snapped open. "What the hell were you thinking?"

I took a step back. "I was trying to help."

"Help?" He half laughed, half yelled. "I don't need this kind of help. I know how to do my job."

A smart person would have agreed, taken her doughnuts, and gone home. For some reason, I was adverse to being that smart. Taking a step forward, I said, "If it weren't for me, you wouldn't know that Greg stole Larry's music when they were in college or that the tape that was in Larry's house has been stolen."

"I still don't *know* any of that. In my line of work, proof is a requirement. You telling me it's true doesn't mean jack."

"Jim Waldorf will tell you exactly what he told me. I can call him and set up a meeting." I reached for my phone. Jim would be happy for an excuse to escape Whac-A-Mole emergencies.

"You're not going to call anyone. You are going to get in your car and drive back to your aunt's house and stay there." Detective Kaiser shoved the pitch pipe in his pocket, grabbed my arm, and started walking toward my Cobalt.

I couldn't sit around doing nothing. My conscience wouldn't let me. I put on the brakes. "What about the tape? I can help you look for it. I promise I won't cause any trouble."

"You won't cause any trouble?" His mouth twitched. Then he started to laugh. "Paige, you've been nothing but trouble since the minute I laid eyes on you. I should have my head examined for not arresting you, let alone doing this."

His hands grabbed my shoulders and pulled me close. Then he kissed me. For the second time in less than twenty-four hours I had no idea how to react. Detective Kaiser's mouth slanted over mine, demanding I get involved. It was hard not to. The man knew how to kiss. His mouth was hard and hot and a little bit teasing, and bubbles of excitement popped inside my stomach as my knees went weak.

I dropped the doughnut box to the ground and grabbed on to his shoulders. His hand ran down my back and my body hummed as he nudged me toward my car and pinned me against the driver's door. Yowzah. I could feel the hand-cuffs clipped to his belt. Suddenly, the idea of using them had a definite appeal. The smell of soap and aftershave was a major turn-on as I ran my hands through his thick, curly hair. His hands traveled down my hips. Finally, he pulled his head back.

We were both breathing hard as we stared at each other.

"What was that?" If my screwing around with his case turned him on, I wondered what turned him off.

"That was me losing my mind." His voice was gruff and annoyed, but he didn't back away.

"So now what do we do?"

He sighed and tucked a lock of blonde hair behind my ear. "We forget it happened. You're a witness in one of my cases."

"There's a rule against kissing witnesses?"

"There's a moral boundary that shouldn't be crossed. I just crossed it, and I couldn't be sorrier."

Disappointment laced with anger sliced through me. I ducked under his arm and put some distance between us. "But making out with one woman while you're dating another is morally permissible?" Getting the brush-off after being kissed pissed me off. I was being dramatically girly and a bit hypersensitive seeing as how I kissed him back even though I knew he'd been on a date, but I didn't care.

"I'm not dating anyone else." He shifted his weight and tugged at his right ear. He might as well have danced the tarantella with a sign that read LIAR, LIAR PANTS ON FIRE painted on his back.

"What about the girl from last night, Detective?"

"My name is Mike." He coughed and straightened his shoulders. "It was a first date that turned out to be a last date, which isn't really any of your business. Look, this conversation isn't getting us anywhere. I'm sorry I kissed you, and I promise it won't happen again. A man is dead, and my primary suspect is missing. I need to focus."

Mike turned on his heel, stepped on one of the fallen doughnuts, and stalked back toward the house, leaving a trail of powdered sugar in his wake. I hated that I couldn't help noticing how well his butt filled out his jeans as he walked. Damn him.

I got back in my car and steered over to Millie's. My anger grew with each passing block. How dare Mike lie to me and then insinuate I was the reason he couldn't focus well enough to catch a killer? I was willing to take the blame for the whole pitch pipe debacle, but the rest wasn't my fault. As far as I was concerned, Detective Michael Kaiser had screwed this case up on his own by going after Eric. Between Devlyn's strange good-night kiss last night and Mike's fabulous but totally infuriating kiss today, I was ready to completely swear off men. Aunt Millie would just have to cope.

I parked my car and walked down Millie's driveway to retrieve the newspaper. Maybe reading about other people's problems would take my mind off my own. If not, the television schedule would come in handy.

Today, the paper had been less than expertly flung onto the grass a couple steps to the left of the mailbox. Aunt Millie's mailbox was always the landmark I used to help people find the place. It was big and white and shaped like a poodle. An enormous glittery pink bow sat on top of the dog's head. The mailbox door was crafted to look like the pooch's mouth, and the flag was the dog's tail. Tacky didn't even begin to describe it. I was constantly amazed the neighbors didn't pay a couple kids to play mailbox baseball and take the thing out.

A piece of notebook paper was wedged under the postal pup's pompon tail, and I reached over to grab it. I unfolded the note and wished I hadn't. The note read: *You've been warned*.

Lovely. As if my day wasn't crappy enough.

Sighing, I shoved the note into my pocket and bent down to grab the paper as a loud pop rang out. A clump of dirt and grass kicked up next to me. A second later, the mailbox's pink bow went flying.

Shit! Shit! Shit!

I turned and started running toward the house as a chunk of the dog's tail bit the dust. Someone in the neighborhood had a gun, and they were shooting at me.

Chapter 20

I counted two more shots as I raced up the driveway. The front door was locked. Fishing out my keys and fumbling to unlock the door seemed like an excellent way to get pegged in the ass. Since I wasn't interested in doing an impression of a duck in a shooting gallery, I veered to the left and raced around the side of the house.

Shit. The living room doors were locked.

Heart pounding in time with my feet, I reached the oak fence Millie installed when she got Killer. I glanced over my shoulder. No one was there, but I wasn't about to take any chances. I backed up a couple steps and took a running leap at the fence. My fingers grabbed the top of the fence, and my feet desperately tried to get traction on the wooden slats as I worked to climb over the top. My arm muscles felt like they were ready to snap, but I wasn't going to give up. Giving up on this workout might result in death. And right now I was certain of only one thing: Death was bad.

My right foot found a foothold, and using my legs and

protesting arm muscles, I pulled my body up and over the fence. Oof. I landed with a thud in the middle of an ever-green bush. *Yeouch!* Needles dug into my neck as I rolled off and into a bed of fresh mulch. Ick. Ick. Ick.

I pushed up to my knees and came nose to nose with Killer. He bared his teeth and started to growl. The teeth were still big. The growl was still menacing. But I'd been shot at, I'd been scratched, and I was covered in manure-laced mulch. My ability to care about whatever was stuck up Killer's butt was minimal at best.

I scrambled to my feet, gave Killer a kiss-off look, and bolted to the back door. The minute I was inside, I reached for my cell and dialed 911. The operator answered before I had a chance to catch my breath. After saying my name for the third time and getting "Could you say it again, please?" as a response, I hung up and dialed Detective Mike. The man was a menace, but he had a gun. At this moment, that counted for a lot.

"Did you steal more evidence?" was his greeting.

The fact that he had my number memorized or pro-grammed into his phone was something I'd think about at another time. At the moment I was focused on the big pic-ture. "Someone shot at me outside Aunt Millie's house," I managed to say in between gasps for air.

"Where are you now?" The sarcasm disappeared, and the professional-cop persona took over. It made me feel bet-ter to hear someone sound in control. Control was something I was seriously lacking.

"I'm in the house."

"Is your aunt home?"

"I think so. Killer is in the backyard." Although Millie didn't come running at the sound of gunfire. Maybe she was in the shower. The idea that the shooter might have gotten to her first twisted in my stomach.

"Find her and stay away from windows until I get there."

Mike disconnected, and I followed instructions. Keeping myself as far away from windows as possible, I went in search of my aunt. I found her in one of the spare bedrooms. She was walking on her treadmill in a hot pink sports bra that pushed her ample cleavage up to her chin. The white spandex short shorts she had squeezed into were slightly transparent and at least two sizes too small. Millie didn't seem to care that they showed off her purple-and-yellow-flowered underwear as she jammed out to her iPod. The two glassy-eyed pugs sat facing the treadmill. Each was sporting a pink bandana and tiny leg warmers. I sagged against the door and smiled as my aunt noticed me.

Millie whacked the off button and pulled her earbuds out of her ears. "What have you been up to this morning?" She grabbed a towel off a white wicker chair and flashed a mischievous smile as she gave my appearance a once over. "Have you been rolling in the dirt with a sexy drama teacher?"

"Someone shot at me at the bottom of the driveway. I fell into the mulch while running away." Millie dropped the towel, and her eyes went wide with fear. I hurried to add, "Detective Kaiser is on his way over. He said to stay away from the windows until he arrives."

Millie swallowed hard and hurried over to give me a tight, sweaty hug. When she pulled back, bits of mulch had transferred onto her sweat-coated skin. "Thank God you weren't shot." She peered into my face and asked, "Are you okay?"

Clearly, my acting skills weren't up to par in a crisis. "I'm fine now. Unfortunately, your mailbox might need to be replaced."

"They shot Bitsy?"

I nodded. Millie had named the mailbox after a dog from her youth. Given the glittering of her eyes and the clenching of her jaw, I'd say she wasn't happy about losing Bitsy a second time.

Thank goodness the doorbell rang, cutting off whatever tirade Millie was about to embark on. I bolted down the stairs and looked through the peephole just in case the shooter had decided to get closer to the target. Two uniformed police officers, a tall middle-aged guy and a short just-out-of-college chick, were standing on Millie's stoop. I unlocked the door and opened it.

"Paige Marshall?" The tall, blond guy looked over my mulch-covered self with a frown.

I nodded as I stood on my tiptoes and looked for Detective Mike charging up the driveway. Mike was nowhere in sight.

"Detective Kaiser said you reported shots fired at this address. Since we were in the area, he asked us to check it out. I'm Officer Higgins. My partner is Officer Andreas."

A bubble of disappointment burst inside my chest. I'd been shot at by a homicidal maniac, and the guy who just kissed me senseless wasn't coming to make sure I was okay. Tears pricked at the back of my eyes. Yep. I was a complete schmuck.

Taking a deep breath, I gave the cops a rundown of the shooting. Didn't see anyone or anything. Too busy saving my own butt to be observant. Officer Higgins told me to stay indoors. Then he hitched up his belt and trotted down the driveway to check out the mailbox. Officer Andreas gave me what I assumed was designed to be a reassuring smile.

The freaked-out look in her eyes ruined the effect. Guess there weren't a lot of shootings in this section of town.

Officer Higgins hiked back up the driveway and went around the side of the house. After a minute he reappeared. "I need to check the backyard."

I led the two cops through the kitchen to the back door as my aunt made an appearance. She had changed out of her workout garb and was now wearing white lounging pants, a pink sequined tank, and a white satin kimono. A pink belt was wrapped tight around her waist. Too bad the flip-flops ruined the great Karate Kid motif she had going.

Officer Higgins stepped outside, and I heard a growl. Killer regarded anything he peed on to be his own personal territory. Trespassers were most definitely not welcome. Since I doubted there was a patch of grass that Killer hadn't christened, I was guessing Officer Higgins might be in trouble.

"Be careful of the dog," I yelled. "He's not good with strangers."

He wasn't good with friends, either, but I figured I didn't need to admit that in front of my aunt. She was upset enough.

My aunt walked over to the door and cooed, "Killer, baby. Come here and get a treat." Killer must have decided bacon-flavored dog biscuits were more important than protecting his personal potty because he stopped growling. He bounded into the kitchen and over to the pantry, leaving the yard to Prospect Glen's finest.

The two walked around the backyard for a while, stared at the bush I dented in my dive to safety, and came back into the house. Officer Higgins sighed. "We'll interview the neighbors. With luck, one of them saw something."

His partner looked more hopeful about that prospect than he sounded. Her eyes gleamed with unsuppressed excitement as she added, "My partner found one bullet lodged in what's left of the mailbox. We'll take that back to the station with us and have it logged into evidence."

I had a hard time sharing her enthusiasm for the recovered bullet considering it had been aimed at me.

Killer gave the officers the evil eye as they walked past him gnawing on a doughnut-shaped rawhide. Given the company, I thought the choice of chew toy was appropriate. I escorted the two back to the front door and opened it as the doorbell rang. Detective Kaiser stood, hand poised to knock, on the other side. The clenching of his jaw and the furrowed lines on his forehead made his mood clear.

Detective Mike motioned for the two cops to join him in the heat. The minute I moved my foot across the threshold, he barked, "Stay inside."

I wanted to fight him on principle. This was my house. Okay, technically it was Millie's house, but I was living in it. On top of that, I was the one who was shot at. I deserved to know what was going on. Instead, I nodded and closed the door. The fact that a maniac with a gun was taking potshots at mailboxes made the outdoors feel scary. It made standing in front of windows a bit frightening as well, so I used the peephole to satisfy my burning curiosity.

Drat. Detective Kaiser was standing on the stoop with his back toward me, effectively blocking my view. I wouldn't doubt he had taken that position on purpose, knowing I was lurking behind the door.

I paced the length of the foyer several times. Finally, I heard a knock. Before I could answer it, the door swung open and Detective Mike marched inside.

"Why did you bother to knock if you weren't going to wait for me to open the door?"

"The rules say I have to announce my presence. I did."

He shrugged off his tan sports coat, revealing a gun holstered to his side. He hadn't been wearing the gun earlier or my hands would have felt it during that kiss. I wasn't sure if I was relieved that he was packing or disturbed that he found it necessary. Probably both. "The officers gave me a report. Now I want to hear it from you. What the hell did you do to get yourself shot at?"

The insinuation that I encouraged someone to take potshots at me pissed me off. I planted my hands on my hips as a flare of righteous anger sped through me. "What did I do? I bent down to get my aunt's newspaper. Somehow I don't think the sight of my behind up in the air was enough to cause gunfire."

Detective Kaiser glanced at my backside, and I considered decking him. The action would get me jail time, but the sentence might be worth it.

His eyes met mine. "Did you stop anywhere when you came back from Mr. DeWeese's house?"

"No."

"Did you see anyone suspicious while you were driving? Maybe a car following you?"

I was too annoyed by his post-kiss brush-off to notice much of anything. "No. I drove home. Parked the car and got shot at. End of story." The fact that it was almost really the end of my story was still making me a bit light-headed. Being angry was keeping me from falling apart.

Detective Mike ran a hand through his hair and let out a loud huff just as Kung Fu Millie walked into the foyer with her sidekick, Killer. She marched up to the detective and poked her finger in the direction of his chest. "I've been waiting for you to get here. Those two kids were nice, but they have a lot to learn about being cops. They didn't even draw their guns. The shooter could have pegged them in the back before they ever got around to taking the safeties off their Smith and Wessons. Personally, I think a Smith and Wesson isn't an exciting gun choice, but selecting police side arms isn't my job."

Detective Kaiser and I gaped at Millie. The detective recovered first. "What kind of gun do you think we should be using?"

Millie smiled. "I prefer a Beretta 8000. It's easy for me to quick draw, and in my opinion the accuracy is second to none."

"You don't say?" Detective Kaiser raised an eyebrow. "I've tried a Beretta 8000. Not bad, but I would think you'd prefer the Smith and Wesson .40 compact. It's lighter weight than the Beretta. You might want to give it a whirl."

"Nah. Too light is no good. A real woman likes at least a little weight in her hands. Besides, I am biased toward Italian designers for clothes and weaponry."

"Fair enough."

Detective Kaiser didn't seem concerned by the conversation, but I was trying hard not to look freaked. My pink-adoring, cosmetics-wearing, canine-loving aunt had a gun. After this week's experiences, living in this house seemed a lot less safe.

"So, Detective," Aunt Millie said, straightening her shoulders. "I certainly hope you have a plan for catching the person who shot at my niece. You're the reason it happened in the first place. If you'd caught the person who murdered that Mr. Lucas, he or she would never have been on this street aiming a gun at Paige."

Detective Kaiser's jaw clenched. "If your niece wasn't poking her nose into police business, no one would have a reason to shoot at her."

"If a certain detective wasn't going around arresting innocent students, Paige wouldn't have had to poke her nose into anything." Millie wagged her perfectly painted fingertip. "You should try arresting the people who actually committed the crime."

Detective Kaiser's eyes narrowed, and his right hand tightened into a fist. This conversation was going downhill. Fast. And both parties had guns.

The doorbell rang, and Millie and the detective lost their WWE wrestling cage-match stares. Thank God. The detective walked to the door, looked through the peephole, and rolled his eyes. He swung open the door, and a very violet Devlyn smiled at us. He had changed clothes since earlier today and was now sporting deep purple pants, a violet dress shirt, a white vest, and two-tone gray-and-white shoes. The whole ensemble was tied together with a purple, gray, and white ascot.

Devlyn's eyes fastened on Detective Kaiser, and his smile disappeared. "Did you find Larry?" He swallowed hard.

My aunt blinked at me. "Larry, your boss? Did something happen to him?"

"He's missing," I answered.

"Missing?" Aunt Millie's eyes grew wide. "Maybe he was kidnapped by the person who shot at you."

"Someone shot at Paige?" Devlyn's voice got loud, and his eyes widened.

Detective Mike shook his head. "I haven't heard from Mr. DeWeese yet, but I've put out an unofficial alert for officers to keep an eye out for him." Then Detective Mike turned toward me and sighed. "Whoever shot at you today means business. We're going to do our best to track down the shooter. Until then, I want you to stay inside and out of trouble." With that, he brushed past a confused-looking Devlyn and headed out the door.

The minute Mike was gone, Devlyn rushed over and put

his arms around me. "Thank God you're okay." He took a step back and looked me up and down. His nose wrinkled when he spotted the mulch stains. "When did the shooting happen? Did it happen here? Why didn't you call me?"

All good questions. And I was thankful Aunt Millie was more than up to the challenge of answering them. When she was done, she volunteered to make coffee for everyone and headed off to the kitchen.

Devlyn gave me a shoulder squeeze. "I can't believe so much happened after I left you and the detective at Larry's house."

"It's still early." I tried to sound upbeat. "Who knows what other excitement today might bring."

Devlyn looked down at his two-tone velvet shoes. "Well, something *is* happening today, but I don't know if I should tell you about it." His dark eyes looked into mine. "The detective said he wanted you to stay inside where it was safe."

The detective also kissed me as if his life depended on it and then changed his mind. As far as I was concerned, the detective's opinions had some consistency issues. "What's going on today?"

"A memorial service for Greg Lucas. His ex-wife, his son, and the kids from his choir set it up. They sent out e-mail invites yesterday, but I didn't check my inbox until this morning. Do you want to go?"

On television cop shows, the killer always shows up at press conferences or funerals. The idea of being in the same room as the shooter didn't fill me with joy, but neither did sitting at home waiting for the murderer to come find me. Inactivity and I did not go well together. "When is it?"

Devlyn looked at his watch. "In a little over an hour. I can hang around and entertain your aunt while you get ready."

I agreed and bolted up the stairs. Ignoring the pugs stationed as hall sentries outside the bathroom door, I went inside and jumped into the shower. I let myself have a ten-minute crying jag as the nasty-smelling mulch and a large knot of tension melted away under the scalding hot water. As I was washing my hair for the second time, I found myself questioning my decision to leave the house.

Hearing Detective Kaiser order me to stay put made me want to do the opposite. However, now that I was less on edge, I could admit his idea had merit. I might have even agreed with the plan had it not been for the lack of progress made in tracking down the killer. Only a couple of days had passed, but in that time an innocent boy had been accused, my aunt's house had been broken into, my boss had gone missing, and someone had used me for target practice. Detective Mike and his team were working hard, but so far they weren't making any noticeable strides. Besides, I was morbidly curious as to what kind of memorial service Dana Lucas and the show choir kids would put together. Yep, I might regret the decision later, but I was going to go. Now I just had to figure out what to wear.

Forty-five minutes later, my hair was blown dry, my makeup was applied, and I was sporting a navy blue sundress. Devlyn was waiting for me in the living room with my aunt. She handed me my purse and made us both promise to be careful before shooing us out the front door and into the blistering heat.

It wasn't until Devlyn had steered his car down the block that I realized my purse felt heavier than usual. I unzipped the bag, peered inside, and let out a whoosh of air. Sitting next to my wallet and a container of orange Tic Tacs was a gun. And not just any gun. This gun was pink.

Chapter 21

"Are you okay?" Devlyn asked.

"Yes." No. I was carrying a concealed weapon. That made me far from okay. I zipped my purse shut, then cringed as the car hit a pothole. The gun didn't go off. That was good. But it was still sitting on my lap inside my purse. That was very, very bad.

Thank goodness Devlyn's eyes were firmly affixed to the road so he hadn't seen my panic or the gun. I had never even touched, let alone fired, a gun. What was Millie thinking sending me to a memorial service filled with high school kids toting the pretty-in-pink pistol? Yes, a maniac shot at me today, but even if I knew who the shooter was, I wasn't about to return the favor.

"Wow. This place is packed." Devlyn steered his car into the overflowing parking lot of the North Shore Park district building. With no spots left in the lot, we parked the car on the street almost two blocks away and hoofed it back. For a moment, I considered leaving the weapon under the seat of the car, but I couldn't do it. The idea of leaving a gun unattended made me queasy. Not that carrying one into a memorial service made me feel any better, but it seemed a tad more responsible.

The arctic air inside the building made me shiver. Signs directed us toward the park district's theater, but the music coming down the hallway would have led us to the service without them. "Amazing Grace" was being sung by a remarkably talented choir. If this was Greg Lucas's group, he'd done his job well.

The song came to an end, and the blue-and-red-polyester-robed choir started singing another. This time it was "You'll Never Walk Alone." An awkward-looking boy in a forest green shirt ambled over to say hello to Devlyn. The two of them exchanged condolences and then talked about potential colleges for the kid while I scoped out the room.

I spotted Dana Lucas standing near the stage accepting condolences from a group of teenagers. She was decked out in a tight-fitting black dress that showed off every inch of her yoga-toned body. The unhappy-looking preteen boy standing beside her had to be her son, Jacob. From this distance, he looked more like Greg than his mother in both coloring and height.

Since Devlyn was still deep in conversation, I wandered over to the left of the auditorium to get a better view of the crowd. The choir finished singing, the lights over the audience dimmed, and the crowd grew silent. A much-larger-than-life photograph of Greg Lucas was projected onto a screen on stage, and the sound of people sniffling echoed throughout the room. Dana Lucas walked onto the stage and took her place behind a wooden podium to the left of Greg's photograph. A number of mingling guests scrambled for their seats. I could see Devlyn looking around for me as he took a seat in the back with the college-bound teen and his parents. There wasn't another empty seat near Devlyn, so I decided to lean against the back wall. Scoping out the attendees was easier from a standing position. Being upright also lent itself to a quicker getaway. It was sad that both were necessary.

Dana Lucas grabbed the microphone off the podium and said, "Thank you all for coming. Everyone in this room was shocked to hear of Gregory's death. My husband was a dynamic man who loved music and teaching. His death is a blow to us all, and words cannot express how much he will be missed."

I couldn't help but notice that she referred to her relationship with Greg in present terms. No ex for this occasion. Dana dabbed her eyes with a tissue and began to catalog Greg Lucas's professional achievements. Hearing her talk about Greg taking a personal interest in his students was enough to make me gag. I looked around the room to see if anyone else was having the same issues.

Guess not. I saw lots of hand wringing and lip trembling, but no outraged expressions in the bunch. Wait. There was an angry expression. On an aisle seat to the right was football coach Curtis Bennett and his wife. Coach Bennett's lip was curled into a snarl. His wife was doing her best to look calm and somber while shooting nervous glances at her husband. Hell, if I were seated next to the man, I'd be nervous, too.

A slideshow of Greg's top moments began to flash across the big screen as Dana narrated. Greg taking his first steps. Greg going to the prom. Greg graduating from college after screwing over his best friend. Okay, I added the last part, but I was starting to feel testy about the adulterous, thieving, creepy teacher getting such accolades.

Doing my best to ignore the photos of Greg helping his female students with their dance steps, I slowly walked around the back of the theater looking for other familiar faces. I admit that part of me was looking for Larry. Despite the blood, Larry still might have left his house under his own power. If so, I was certain he would have found a way to be here.

Sadly, Larry was nowhere to be found. However, Chessie, Eric, and a bunch of my other students were seated near the front. I squinted into the darkness, trying to tell if Chessie was upset by the "Greg was God" rhetoric. Nope. If anything, she looked bored. Eric, however, looked ready to implode.

The slideshow finished, and Dana announced, "To celebrate Greg's life, his choirs have put together a very special performance for all of us. I know Greg would have been very proud to have been remembered in this way."

The lights on stage brightened, and the sound of bongo drums and calling monkeys filled the air. Kids dressed in black and silver sequins came racing onto the stage. They struck a pose as the bongos and monkey sounds changed to strings and wind instruments. Then they began to sing.

It took me a minute to figure out what they were singing. At first, I thought it was an African Gospel song. Then the choir switched to English, and I groaned as a kid in front began to sing the words to "Circle of Life" from Disney's *The Lion King*.

The soloist was talented. I was impressed he could sing through tears. That wasn't easy to do. I'd had to cry while singing for more than one show, and it took lots of practice to sing without sounding as though a frog took up residence in your throat. The kid deserved props for holding his own. So did the rest of the kids. I could see why this choir had won awards. They belted out their harmonies as they did their best to plaster on cheesy smiles. Only, instead of looking happy, they all had a deranged I've-got-a-knife-and-I-know-how-to-use-it expression. Eek.

I waited for the song to end, but suddenly the music changed keys, and the power ballad changed to the up-tempo beat of "Hakuna Matata."

The kids stomped and clapped as they sang about having no worries for the rest of their days.

The audience gaped.

Sequins sparkled in the light and tears glistened on some of the singers' faces, but the warped smiles never faded as they did their best to convince the audience to clap along. Some of the people in the front rows did. The rest of the audience wore expressions of abject horror.

After two more key changes and another verse of "Circle of Life," the music mercifully stopped. Nobody moved. The tear-stricken kids on stage stared at the audience. The audience stared back. Finally, someone in the front of the theater started to clap. The sound snapped the rest of the audience to attention, and they, too, began to applaud. Whatever composure the kids had left disappeared. Weeping girls hugged each other. Teenage boys tried to look cool and failed as their lips trembled. This was a train wreck.

I looked around to see what Devlyn thought. He wasn't in his seat. I stood on my tiptoes and scanned the room. Devlyn was nowhere in sight.

Wait. I spotted him on the other side of the theater near an exit door. He was looking around the theater for something. Probably for me. After a few more glances around the room, he disappeared through the door.

A couple of adults climbed on the stage and helped the kids off as I searched for my own exit. It was time for Devlyn and me to regroup in the hall. Out of the corner of my eye, I noticed one of the women consoling teens was Felicia. Her own face was streaked with tears, but she looked calm and in control as she led several hysterical girls into the wings.

I slipped out a side door and headed to the front of the theater where we came in. No Devlyn. I peeked around the corner to see if he was hanging out by the door he exited.

Nope. No one. Personally, I was amazed the lobby was empty. After that performance, I would have thought people would be tripping over one another to get out before anyone else decided to sing.

Not sure what else to do, I went in search of the restrooms. Devlyn did have a lot of coffee at Millie's.

The sign at the end of the red-carpeted hallway said to turn left. I was about to when I heard the sound of angry male voices coming from around the corner.

Strike that. Only one of the voices was angry, but he was pissed enough for the both of them.

"What the hell is going on? You told me this was going to work."

"You have to give it time."

Devlyn. My heart skipped as I froze in place.

"The first game of the season is next weekend against Lake Forest. I don't want my ass handed to me right out of the gate. This is horseshit."

I sucked in air as I recognized the belligerent voice. Coach Curtis Bennett.

"You have to give Drew time to get over the shock. That's the only way my plan will work."

"What shock? Greg Lucas is dead, and so is his pansy choir program. If Drew Roane doesn't start showing up to practice, my football program might be history, too."

"Trust me. Drew will be there."

"He'd better be at practice on Monday like you promised," Coach Bennett barked. He lowered his voice and added, "Otherwise, our deal is over, and I start spilling your dirty little secret. What do you think will happen to you then?"

Secret? What secret?

Uh-oh. I realized the voices had gone silent. Footsteps sounded on the carpet. They were coming in my direction. Clutching my purse, I booked down the hallway while glancing over my shoulder to make sure Devlyn or the coach didn't see me. Neither was in sight as I rounded the corner and headed back inside the theater.

Heart pounding, I leaned against the wall and tried to catch my breath. On the stage, a tall, white-haired man in a charcoal suit was talking about Greg's contributions to the music industry. At least, that was what I thought he said. My brain was fixated on what it had just heard in the hallway.

Devlyn had a secret.

Hell, Devlyn had a lot of secrets. When Devlyn mentioned Coach Bennett to me, he implied the man was someone he'd heard the gossip about but never personally dealt with. He'd lied, by misdirection if not by actual words. More important, Coach Bennett's angry words made it clear Devlyn had promised that whatever plan they'd implemented would ensure Drew Roane dropped show choir and returned to the football team. From my way of thinking, it took a lot of guts for a star athlete to turn his back on his teammates in order to sing and dance with the show choir. Greg Lucas had helped the kid make that choice, and the kid went through with it. So what could Devlyn and Coach Bennett do to convince that kind of kid to do a one-eighty and return to football?

They could kill Greg Lucas.

My knees went weak and the world in front of me spun in and out of focus as the guy at the podium announced, "That is why the Choir Boosters are creating the Gregory Lucas Scholarship. Greg Lucas may be gone, but his ability to help kids fulfill their musical potential will live on."

I barely registered the applause and cheering over the denial roaring in my head. Devlyn wasn't the killer type. Not that I'd ever associated with killers, but still. The guy danced with me. He was trying to help me win over the kids. He was nice to my aunt. He'd even kissed me.

That kiss.

My stomach clenched. Could Devlyn have kissed me in order to get close to me? My ego wanted to believe he planted one on me because he felt unbridled passion for my unique combo of personality and looks. Gay didn't mean a man couldn't be attracted to a woman. Right?

Still, it could just be the man was after something—and it wasn't my body.

Dana Lucas and her son climbed up onto the stage to shake the tall guy's hand. Over the loudspeaker, music began to play. I knew that music. It was the song on Larry's sock-drawer tape. The song Greg Lucas stole years ago, passed off as his own, and made a small fortune on.

Much of the audience started singing. Those who weren't musically inclined were smiling through their tears and swaying to the music. When the song was over, the black and silver-sparkled show choir took the stage again for one last song—"Candle in the Wind."

"Are you ready to get out of here?"

I jumped as Devlyn's voice whispered in my ear.

"Shh." Devlyn grabbed my hand and gave it a tug. When I didn't budge, he whispered, "I heard something I think is important. Come on."

My feet didn't budge, but my heart hit high gear. A large knot formed in my throat, making it hard to breathe. A potential homicidal maniac wanted to get me alone. That was bad. Worse yet, I had no good excuse for why I wouldn't go out the door with him.

"I want to hear the rest of this," I lied. And boy was I lying. The song was a bigger disaster than the *Lion King* medley.

"Really?" Devlyn wasn't fooled.

I needed a better excuse. "I thought I spotted Larry in the audience." Devlyn stopped tugging on my arm and craned his neck to canvas the room. Score. "Can you see him?" I asked. "I thought I saw him down in front." With so many people hugging and crying, getting a clear view of anyone down there was impossible. That bought me time.

The choir onstage belted out the final, off-key but very loud chord of the song as Devlyn walked a few feet to the right trying to get a better view of the fictitious Larry. As soon as the music ended, Dana took the podium once again. She thanked everyone for coming to celebrate her husband's amazing life and announced a reception would be taking place afterward in the greenroom backstage. Half the audience sprang to their feet and headed for the exit, making it harder for Devlyn to get a clear look at the crowd.

Suddenly Devlyn focused on something, and his eyes narrowed. "Did you find him?" I asked, stunned that Larry might actually be in the crowd.

Devlyn shook his head. "No, but someone else just found us. And he doesn't look happy about it." Devlyn nodded toward the other side of the theater, where a less-than-enthusiastic Detective Mike was glaring at me. He crooked his finger and waited to see if I'd come as commanded.

Normally, I wouldn't obey that kind of summons on principal, but at the moment I was looking for any excuse to get away from a potential killer. I said, "You keep looking for Larry while I go talk to the detective."

Devlyn waded into the crowd, and I bolted for the lobby. Detective Mike was waiting with his arms crossed in front of the main theater doors. The patrons leaving the theater took one look at his face and gave him a wide berth. The man was good at intimidating. Funny, but I'd never been so glad to see a pissed-off person in my entire life.

"I thought I asked you to stay home." Mike uncrossed his arms and glared.

"Actually, you ordered me to stay home."

"And?"

"And I didn't listen." I glanced at the people streaming out of the theater. Devlyn was nowhere in sight, but I was betting he'd give up his quest to find Larry soon and come looking for me. Call me crazy, but I didn't want to be found. Through the fear, I tried to smile. "However, now that I've paid my respects, I'd be happy to go back to my aunt's house. Can you give me a lift?"

Mike blinked. "You want a ride?"

"Devlyn is busy." At least I hoped he stayed busy until I got the hell out of here. "He choreographed the musical at North Shore High School so he knows a lot of kids and parents here. Some of them have been asking for college advice."

That sounded like it would take lots of time. Right? Better yet, I was telling the truth. No twitching eyebrow here—not that I believed it actually twitched.

Detective Mike stared at me. My muscles tightened with every passing second. I used ever ounce of willpower to keep from glancing at the people streaming through the theater door towards the post-memorial reception. Mike scanned the room and signaled to a guy in a dark blue suit. Immediately, the guy zigzagged through the meandering mourners over to us.

"I'm going to escort Ms. Marshall home. Keep an eye out for Larry DeWeese, and call me if you see anything suspicious." Mike turned to me. "Do you want to tell Mr. O'Shea that you're leaving?"

Not even remotely. "I'll text him." I plastered a smile on my face and started walking.

Mike's Mustang was parked in a loading zone near the front entrance. I raised an eyebrow, and he smiled as if daring me to question the morality of his parking practices. I would, but I really wanted to get out of here. Biting my lip, I climbed into the sweltering car and pulled out my phone. My sweaty fingers typed, *Being escorted home by Detective Kaiser. Keep looking for Larry. Call you later*, to Devlyn.

I hit send and leaned back as Mike cranked the air. Huh. Mike wasn't kidding when he said the air-conditioning in my Cobalt was better. The air coming out of the vents was lukewarm at best.

Mike steered the car out of the parking lot. After a few minutes of silence he asked, "So what's the real reason you were looking to get out of there?"

I opened my mouth to tell Mike about Devlyn and Coach Bennett's hallway conversation. Then I stopped. I couldn't do it. Not yet. Yes, it sounded suspicious, but something Devlyn said the other day stopped me. What if they weren't guilty? Devlyn didn't turn Greg Lucas in for hitting on a student because Greg might have been innocent. His career would have been ruined on the suspicion alone. Detective Mike wanted to catch the killer, and he wasn't above making an innocent teenage kid look like a suspect in order to do it. What would he do if I told him about Devlyn and

Coach Bennett's conversation? Did I have enough faith in my own investigatory skills to chance blowing Devlyn's career out of the water with my suspicions alone?

No. No, I didn't.

This sucked. I let out a sigh and improvised, "My near-death experience this morning made the whole celebrating the end of life thing too much for me to take."

"I can see that." Mike's eyes flicked over my face before reaffixing to the road. "Are you sure that's the only reason you wanted to leave?"

"What other reason is there?"

Detective Mike shot me a knowing glance. "Well, the two of us alone in my car seems like a pretty good reason to me."

"What?" The man wasn't making sense.

"You don't have to be embarrassed." He grinned. "I admire a woman who goes for what she wants. As a matter of fact, I want the same thing you do, especially after this morning. But I was serious when I said we can't do anything about it until this case is closed."

I went from confused to stunned to totally pissed off in two seconds flat. This arrogant son of a bitch thought I was looking for a naked tour of his backseat in addition to my ride home. In his world, being shot at was probably an aphrodisiac. In mine, it was a total buzzkill.

"You think I'm looking for a hookup?"

Mike glanced over at me, and his smile faded. "You're not?"

"I think I have more important things to worry about." I did my best to keep the sarcasm out of my voice. Mike's wince told me I failed. Oh well.

Mike drove the rest of the way to Aunt Millie's in silence. He looked uncomfortable with the situation. I wasn't. The quiet gave me time to think. Since turning Devlyn into the authorities with the information I currently had made me feel queasy, I needed an alternative plan. By the time Mike pulled up to Aunt Millie's front door, I had one.

Not quite meeting my eyes, Mike gave me the requisite "stay inside and out of trouble line" before watching me unlock the door and close it behind me. Grateful to be in real air-conditioning, I locked the door and headed upstairs to my computer. I needed proof that Devlyn was up to no good, and from what I could tell only one person could give it to me.

Football dropout Drew Roane.

Chapter 22

No cars were in the driveway at the Roane house. No one milled around the yard. I rang the bell. Yep—no one was home. I waited in my car for a while. When my butt went numb, I decided to call it quits and head home.

I walked into Millie's with a McDonald's bag filled with hamburgers and fries and jumped as Millie yelled, "There you are. I was starting to get worried. We have to do your hair and makeup or you'll never be ready in time." Millie grabbed my arm and pulled me up the stairs.

"Ready for what?"

Millie stopped. "The Ockinickys' benefit. Did you forget?"

"No." Yes. Although Millie's sparkly pink satin ensemble should have been a clue. "I didn't realize we needed to get ready this early. The benefit isn't until seven."

"But you have to be there early to rehearse with the accompanist. Didn't I tell you?"

"I don't think so." After the past few days, I wasn't sure of anything.

Millie sighed and resumed stair-climbing. "I probably didn't tell you on purpose. Marge Mitchell's son is playing for you tonight. I tried to talk Gloria Ockinicky out of it, but she didn't want to upset Marge. They're cousins."

Great.

Well, I was used to singing with less-than-gifted piano players. I used to think opera companies would employ the best accompanists because the music was often very challenging. I was wrong. A couple of years ago, after a string of bad audition experiences, I invested in some easy piano versions of my favorite opera arias and started carrying them with me to auditions—just in case. I figured if I could play them then the audition pianists could, too. My aunt's expression told me I'd best bring those songs with me tonight.

While scarfing down French fries, I struggled into panty hose and slipped into one of my favorite recital dresses—a royal blue sheath with a halter top that hugged my torso and hips then fell in graceful waves to the floor. The front was pretty. The back, or lack of one, was sexy as hell. The only problem was I had to wear heels—high ones—or else the dress dragged on the floor. Slipping into my four-inch sparkly silver stilettos, I prayed that the shooter would take a break for the night. There was no way I'd outrun my great-aunt Edna let alone bullets in these. And while I had Aunt Millie's gun, I didn't think I could actually shoot someone. Millie might, but I was hoping it wouldn't come to that.

Once Millie did her makeup and hair magic, she grinned. "Too bad the detective can't see you looking like this. He'd have extra motivation to catch the killer."

A part of me wished he could, too. If nothing else, he'd know exactly what he was missing. "Catching killers is his job. I think that should be motivation enough. Besides, I think there's a rule that police officers can't date their witnesses."

"Cops know how to bend those kinds of rules. I should know. Six or seven years ago I dated a cop. He knew exactly how to skirt the system so neither of us would get busted if we got caught without a license."

"You got caught driving without your license and didn't get a ticket?"

"I wasn't driving. I was fishing. Mick was a wildlife and forestry cop. I used to call him Smokey Bear in bed. Trust me—he knew how to make a woman feel hot."

I winced. Talk about too much information.

The Ockinickys lived one town over in an enormous white house complete with pillars, fountains, and two acres of perfectly groomed lawn, flowers, and trees. Gloria Ockinicky was nowhere to be found, so the caterers let us into the house, and Millie led me down a huge staircase into the living room.

High-top cocktail tables decorated with vases of sunflowers and votive candles were scattered throughout the room. Whatever furniture typically resided atop the shining parquet floor had been carted away. Everything except the white grand piano. The piano was beautiful. The pimply faced teenage boy seated behind it was not.

He looked up at us and scowled. "The party doesn't start until seven."

"I know," I said before a frowning Millie could reply. Being nice to the accompanist was a must. "That's why we're here early. I'm Paige Marshall. You and I are tonight's entertainment."

"Jonathan Mitchell." He shook my hand as his eyes ran up and down my body. The angry expression disappeared, replaced by a leer. "I didn't know opera singers looked like you. The ones my aunt listens to are all fat."

Generalizations like that really pissed me off. I wanted to give the kid a piece of my mind, but I satisfied myself with dropping my black binder of music on the piano with a thud. "Shall we rehearse?"

The kid was worse than bad. In fact, I doubted whether he could play chopsticks without making a mistake. After three failed attempts at the simplified introduction of "O mio babbino caro," I asked if he'd be more comfortable reading through the music without an audience. He agreed and pointed Millie and me in the direction of the kitchen. The minute my feet hit the marble tile, I sent up a prayer to the music gods that the kid had a bad case of the nerves and would get better.

"What are you going to do?" Millie asked, dodging a tuxedo-shirt wearing woman balancing a tray of wine-glasses.

The fabulous acoustics in the living room made Jonathan's practicing ring loud and clear throughout the house. Even with the chatter of the caterers and the clinking of flatware, we could hear every painful note played on the piano.

"I'm going to sing." That was my job no matter how terrible the piano playing. Taking a deep breath, I plastered a cheerful smile onto my face and marched back into the living room. My aunt didn't follow. "How's it going in here?" I asked, as if I didn't already know.

Jonathan's skin had taken on a slightly green color. He looked down at the keyboard as if it were going to bite him. "I might need a bit more time to practice."

Years might help. We had thirty minutes.

"If you don't feel comfortable playing, I can always sing a cappella."

The kid's shoulder's drooped. "My mom said I had to play."

Once the party was over, Mom and I were going to have a long chat. "Why?"

"She's been bragging to her friends that I take piano lessons, and she wants to show off what I've learned."

"How many lessons have you had?"

Jonathon's pasty skin now took on a pinkish cast. He swallowed hard. "Five."

I rolled my eyes. Mom was a nitwit. How could she possibly think five lessons qualified her kid for a beginner recital let alone playing at a benefit? Unless . . . "How many lessons does your mother think you've had?"

"Three years' worth." His freaked-out eyes met mine. "I hate piano. Dad told me I could quit, but we didn't need to tell Mom. Mom's a lawyer so she's never home."

I wanted to ask where Dad's bright ideas were when Mom was getting Jonathan this gig. The caterers laid out the food, and the bartender was finishing setting up shop in the corner of the living room. This party was about to get started, and Jonathan looked ready to puke in the middle of the pâté.

That gave me an idea. "Go home, get into bed, and pretend to be sick. If your mother asks, I'll say you have the stomach flu."

"Really?" The kid jumped up from the piano and gave me a hug. "I totally owe you one." Something told me it was no accident that his hand brushed my backside as he beat a hasty retreat.

Once Jonathan disappeared, I sat down at the piano and flipped through the music. For the most part, opera arias didn't sound right without some sort of accompaniment.

"Where did Liberace go?" Aunt Millie appeared from the kitchen, munching on a wedge of cheese.

"He wasn't feeling well."

"Having no musical ability will do that to a person." Millie polished off the cheese and grabbed a napkin off a high-top table. "Well, I'm glad you ditched the kid before his replacement arrives."

"Replacement?"

"An old boyfriend of mine is going to swing by and play a few songs for you. Trust me, the man can tickle the ivories even better than he played me. And he was damn good at both."

Huh. Maybe this guy was movie-star gorgeous. Then Millie might fixate on her own love life instead of mine. "Does your friend have a name?"

"Aldo Mangialardi."

The man in question stood five feet five inches tall, wore a powder blue tux and a white ruffled shirt, and was definitely not movie-star gorgeous. With the tiny tufts of white hair springing out from behind his ears and a thick accent, he reminded me more of an Italian hobbit than a Hollywood leading man. He also arrived thirty minutes after the party officially started. Thank God it was after our hostess fainted. She passed out upon learning her original pianist had gone home, while the kid's mother screamed at the catering staff for poisoning her talented son although no one else seemed to have a problem scarfing down the munchies. Millie and I secretly thought Gloria Ockinicky's fainting was out of relief. The twenty-foot ceilings and hardwood floors made sound travel in this place.

Aldo grabbed my aunt's hand and kissed it. The expression on his face was filled with adoration as she led him over to me. "This is my niece, Paige."

"Beauty runs in-a your family. The two of you could be sisters." He kissed my hand and left a trail of spittle in his wake.

My aunt blushed and giggled. I looked for an unsuspecting soul to wipe my hand on. Thank goodness a waiter passed by with a puff pastry and spinach appetizer and a large stack of napkins. I availed myself of both.

An hour into the party, Aldo took a seat behind the piano and played a couple tremolos to get the crowd's attention. Gloria Ockinicky walked across the room and stood next to the piano. Her black satin evening suit looked regal next to the white grand piano, and not a single ash blonde hair was out of place as she addressed the crowd. "Thank you all for coming tonight to support Education Through the Arts. Study after study finds that our youth excel in the areas of math, science, and English when they are also exposed to the visual and performing arts. Yet, year after year, the music, theater, and art programs are slashed from the public school curriculum. Your generous donations to Education Through the Arts will provide funding for these types of programs so that underprivileged youths throughout Chicago and the suburbs can work with teachers like Paige Marshall."

I blinked at the sound of my name. Aunt Millie nudged me and beamed. Gloria waved me forward, and I walked through the crowd to stand next to her. "Paige is a wonderful example of how the arts can positively impact a life." I tried not to fidget or look embarrassed as Gloria regaled the partygoers with my academic and performing résumé. She then added, "Our community is fortunate that Paige has decided to spread her love of the arts through teaching at a local high school. And we are even luckier to have her performing for us tonight."

The crowd clapped for Gloria as she stepped away from the piano. Seconds later, Aldo started to play. There was no time to contemplate Gloria's introduction or her cheerful and flattering categorization of my teaching job. I'd think about that later. Right now, it was time for me to do the one thing I knew how to do best—sing.

While Gloria had requested I sing opera arias, I decided to kick things off with a musical theater number. Upbeat, happy, and words in English were always a good idea.

The crowd tapped their toes along with "I Could Have Danced All Night" from *My Fair Lady*. Once that was over, the incredibly skilled Aldo played the opening of Bizet's famous "Habanera" from *Carmen*. The crowd didn't care that I was singing in French. They understood the sexy beat and the sultry music. I strutted around the room flirting with men then giving them Carmen's patented kiss-off.

Before the event, Gloria gave me instructions to sing a few songs. As soon as the audience grew restless, I was supposed to stop. Only, Aldo and I had been performing Puccini, Mozart, and Romberg for a half hour and so far no one looked ready to bail. Flattering as that was, the whole point of this concert was to raise money. The necessary schmoozing couldn't happen while I commanded the floor. As much fun as I was having, it was time to bring this show to a close.

The final notes to "Quando m'en vo" rang out in the hall, and the audience applauded. When they grew quiet again, I announced, "Thank you so much for being such a wonderful audience. While this is our last song of the night, your generous donations will ensure that music and the arts continue long into the future."

I nodded to Aldo, and he began playing "Con te partiro"—"Time to Say Good-bye." Appropriate, beautiful, and one that always gets the crowd teary-eyed. In this case, I was hoping it would also get them to open their wallets.

The applause was loud and long. Both were a balm to my ego, which had suffered at my recent dry spell of performing gigs. Finding someone murdered and getting shot at had made my lack of casting seem trivial, but my confidence still appreciated the boost.

I signaled for Aldo to stand and take a bow, which he did with a flourish. The two of us then bowed together and declined when people asked us to do another tune. Millie came bursting out of the crowd, beaming. She wrapped her arms around me and whispered. "You were perfect. Gloria can't stop smiling, and Marge is ready to claw my eyes out from jealousy."

"Why would Marge claw your eyes out?"

"She thinks I helped usurp her son's glory."

"He was sick." That was the official story, and I was sticking to it.

"Marge insinuated you might have poisoned him in order to have the stage to yourself. She also thought the police might want to look more closely at the dead body you found, just in case you did the same thing to him."

I sputtered.

Millie laughed. "Don't worry about Marge. No one else around here does."

"Ladies, we should celebrate with a drink. No?" Aldo came up behind Millie and put his arm around her waist. Millie blushed. I put in my order for a glass of white wine and watched Aldo steer my aunt toward the bar. The gleam in his eye told me not to hold my breath for that wine. So I decided to go in search of my own. Too bad it wasn't that easy.

Every couple of feet I was stopped by someone who wanted to talk about my performance. The compliments were effusive and kind. Most performers would have been delighted with the attention. I was looking for a spoon so I could tunnel my way out of here.

Not that I wasn't grateful that my performance was well received. I was, but I felt awkward when people wanted to have a conversation about me with, well—me. Staged shows were easier. You got a wig and a costume, and the audience couldn't tell one performer from the other after the show was over.

After a dozen uncomfortable conversations, I grabbed my purse and ducked out the back door and into the warm night air. A few die-hard smokers were milling around the flagstone patio. Otherwise the backyard was empty, most likely due to the intense humidity. I walked to the end of the patio, trying to avoid both the smoke and conversation.

"You have a lovely voice."

So much for my avoidance technique.

Forcing my lips upward, I turned toward my new fan and blinked. "Didn't we meet the other day?" I asked, knowing full well that we had. Standing in the shadows of a large oak tree, wearing a bright yellow cocktail dress, was Coach Bennett's wife.

"I never introduced myself. My name is Carrie Bennett." She stepped into the light, and I sucked in a gulp of air. Either Carrie had had a disagreement with her makeup or she hadn't slept in days. My guess was the latter.

Shaking Carrie's hand, I glanced around the backyard for her scary other half. "I'm sorry I upset your husband. I didn't mean to."

"You don't have to worry. He's not here. Curtis doesn't like these kinds of parties."

"But he doesn't mind that you come?"

Her hand fluttered to her chest. "He doesn't know I'm

here, exactly. My friend Marge's son was supposed to play with you tonight, and I promised I'd be here to watch. Curtis wouldn't approve."

"Of supporting a friend?"

"No, of Jonathan playing piano." She took a small step backward. "My husband has firm opinions on members of his team getting involved with music and theater. I think he expressed some of them the other night."

"Jonathan's on the football team?" I found it hard to believe. The kid looked like a strong wind would blow him over.

"He has the highest field goal conversion rate in the district."

"Impressive." But something didn't make sense. "Why would your husband be upset to see Jonathan play piano?" Aside from the obvious lack of skill.

"Well, after Drew Roane quit for the choir, my husband is worried about losing other players, especially Jonathan. He tells me the two of them are best friends."

"Your husband seemed pretty angry that Drew quit."

She flinched. "I'm sorry about his behavior, but you have to understand. There's been a lot of pressure from the football boosters to have a winning season. A couple of them have even said they think Curtis might not have what it takes to coach anymore."

"Which is why he doesn't want to lose Drew." When she nodded, I added, "I thought I heard him say Drew was coming back to the team. What happened?"

Carrie clasped and unclasped her hands. "I don't know. Drew was supposed to come back to practice. When he didn't, I heard Curtis on the phone talking to someone about some plan they had. He was sure that the plan would work now that . . . things have changed."

"You mean now that Greg Lucas is dead."

Carrie straightened her shoulders. "My husband had nothing to do with that. Yes, he was angry with Greg Lucas, but he's not capable of murder. He just isn't."

I wasn't sure whether she was trying to convince me or herself. Either way, she failed. Curtis Bennett was looking guiltier by the minute.

Chapter 23

My conversation with Carrie, disturbing as it was, gave me an idea. Dodging partygoers carrying flutes of champagne, I spotted our hostess, Gloria Ockinicky, in the back corner of the living room and headed over.

"Paige, I wondered where you went." Gloria gave me an air hug—one of those lean-into-the-person-without-touching-in-case-they-have-cooties gestures. "You were fabulous tonight. Everyone is talking about it, and more important, they are writing checks."

"I just wish my Jonathan could have been here." This from a woman with football-helmet-shaped dark hair and a bright red dress. "The piano player was quite good, but you should hear my son."

"It's too bad Jonathan got so sick. The poor kid was heartbroken." Yeah, I lied. But it was for a good cause. "Actually, I thought I might leave the party early and stop by to see Jonathan. It might give him a lift to know the gig went well. He's probably feeling like he let everyone down."

Marge beamed. "That would be lovely. I've been worried about him being home alone while he's sick. Here's my card. My home address and cell are listed. The next time you need a piano player call me, and I'll make sure Jonathan is free. The two of you would be dynamic together."

Right.

I thanked Gloria for inviting me and looked around for my aunt. She was at the bar doing amaretto shots with Aldo, who was paying her extravagant compliments in between calls for more booze. Given the number of glasses stacked in front of them, I was amazed either was still talking, let alone standing. After three more shots, I convinced Millie it was time to go home. Aldo insisted on going with us—it turned out he took a cab to the gig. So I chauffeured the two of them back to Millie's and watched them stagger into the house singing "O sole mio." Then I zipped off to my next destination.

Jonathan's house.

Millie's car cornered like a beached whale, and the brakes required brute force to get them to—you know—stop. It explained a lot about my aunt's driving style.

The windows of the massive chrome-and-glass house were ablaze with light when I jammed the brakes to the floor. I rang the bell, and a few minutes later, a disheveled Jonathan came to the door. His shirt was unbuttoned, his hair was mussed, and his cheeks had a rosy flush. My sleuthing skills told me he might be entertaining a special guest. He took one look at me and frowned. "Um. Hi. Did I forget something at the party?"

"Not exactly. I was hoping you could answer a couple questions about your football team for me."

"Football?" He looked back inside the house and shifted

his weight from one foot to the other. "Well, yeah. But can we do it another time? I'm kind of busy."

"It'll just take a minute. Otherwise, I might have to go back to the party and have a chat with your mom."

"Fine." Jonathan sighed. "What do you want to know?"

"Do you know why Drew Roane quit the team?"

"Because he wanted to sing and dance?"

The way he said it made me arch an eyebrow. "Really?"

Jonathan laughed. "Coach Bennett was riding Drew at the end of last year about not being in the weight room enough. Drew got pissed. He works twice as hard as any other player, but Coach is always ragging on something. So Drew decided to get even."

"By joining the show choir."

Jonathan cracked a wide grin. "Drew always planned on coming back to the team. He was just saying he was going to join the choir to yank Coach's chain. But Mr. Lucas told Drew he knew people at Northwestern and the U of I. He promised Drew would get accepted at one of those schools. Drew's a good player, but the top scouts haven't been calling and his grades aren't exactly college material, if you know what I mean."

Which would have made Greg Lucas's offer irresistible.

A female voice called out from inside the house, and Jonathan yelled that he'd be just a minute.

"So now what?"

Jonathan jammed his hands into his pockets and shrugged. For the first time he looked genuinely confused. "I don't know. The day before Mr. Lucas was killed, Drew said someone had given him another option for college—one that didn't involve competing in that stupid choir."

"Did he say who made him the offer?"

"Nah." He shrugged. "I figured it was Coach, but Drew said it wasn't any of the teachers at our school. It sounds like his girlfriend knows the guy and introduced them. Anyway, Drew said he's waiting for proof the offer is real before coming back to practice. My boy isn't the smartest guy around, but he isn't stupid."

Guess not. Of course, if he was making deals with a murderer, then all bets were off.

I asked Jonathan to let me know if Drew ever mentioned the name of his mysterious benefactor and climbed back into Aunt Millie's Caddy. Fighting the brakes, I steered home while adding up the pieces I'd just been given. Unless I was mistaken, Devlyn was Drew's mysterious benefactor. And if Jonathan was right, Devlyn approached Drew with his offer before Greg's death. If Drew had said no, Devlyn would have had reason to kill Greg to escape Coach Bennett's blackmail threat. With a potential yes forthcoming, Devlyn's motive for murder had just been blown to bits. The more I learned, the more confused I became.

Steering down Millie's block, I slowed the car and peered into darkened driveways, trying to spot would-be shooters. Careful not to hit my car, I pulled Millie's Caddy into the garage and closed the door. Ha! Let the gunman try and get me now.

I climbed out of the car as the doorbell rang inside. My stomach tilted. Someone rang again and started knocking. I swallowed hard, walked through the laundry room into the kitchen, and peered around the corner into the living room. Everything was quiet inside, and no one was in the driveway when I arrived home. So who was at the front door? Maybe Aldo locked himself out?

The knocking started again, and I reached into my purse. My fingers closed around Millie's pink Beretta, and I slowly walked to the door. I wasn't sure if I could actually pull the trigger, but just holding it made me feel better. Taking a deep breath, I peered through the peephole. My fear transformed to frustration. Peering back at me was Detective Mike.

I opened the door. "What do you want?"

Mike laughed. "Is that how you treat all your aunt's guests?"

"I'm sure you've heard worse, and you're not a guest." Was I gracious or what?

"Your aunt called and asked me to come over." Mike pushed the door open and breezed past me. Then he noticed what was in my hand. "What the hell is that?"

"Aunt Millie's gun. She left it out in case of emergency."

"This isn't an emergency."

Fair point. I put the gun on the hallway table. "Better?"

Mike frowned. "You held it wrong."

"Huh?"

"You were holding the gun wrong. If you're going to pick one up, you need to learn how to hold it with both hands. That's the only way you're going to hit anything. If your aunt doesn't want to teach you, let me know. I'll book some time at the firing range for us."

Firing guns wasn't my idea of a romantic date. Besides, I didn't think I could fire a gun at anyone no matter what my grip on it was. To my way of thinking, the gun would either scare someone or act as a blunt object to hit them.

Still, I agreed to get lessons before picking the gun up again, and Mike seemed to breathe easier when he asked, "Where is your aunt?"

"My aunt's asleep."

"She called about an hour ago and said I needed to see you tonight." His eyes traveled up and down my silk-clad body, and his mouth curved into an appreciative smile. "She wasn't wrong about that. You look incredible with or without the gun."

My irritation receded, replaced by a warm surge of pleasure. What could I say? I was a sucker for a compliment.

Trying to avoid the pull of the heat in his eyes, I said, "Aunt Millie was a little tipsy tonight. She probably didn't mean to make that call."

"Are you sure?"

"Yes," I fibbed. I was almost positive Aunt Millie was in complete control of her matchmaking faculties when she made that call. "Sorry she wasted your time."

"I wouldn't call it a waste." Mike's eyes locked onto mine and held them. My heart flipped in my chest, and I cursed the man for being attractive. He was a menace. Mike took a step closer and added, "Besides, I was already in the neighborhood. Things were interesting around here tonight."

I blinked and took a step back. "Interesting?" I used the word "interesting" all the time, and it never meant anything good.

His eyes narrowed and lost their I-want-sex look as he folded his arms. "The doctor next door dropped by tonight. I'm guessing he was checking in on his canine patient. I watched you drop off your aunt and her friend around nine thirty. The two of them shouldn't sing in public." He smiled. "You nicked your neighbor's mailbox across the street when you were backing out. Don't worry. There wasn't any damage so I won't ticket you for that."

"Thanks." My cheeks went hot. "Anything else happen while I was gone?" So far the only interesting thing had been my lack of driving skills.

"Your friend Mr. O'Shea dropped by."

My heart jumped. "Devlyn was here? Why?"

"I don't read minds so I can't help you there. He knocked

on the door, dialed someone on his cell—which I'm assuming was you—and got back in his car."

Huh. Maybe he left a message. I unzipped my purse and went diving for my cell phone. Sure enough. Devlyn wanted to know if I was okay and told me to call him tomorrow. I was touched. Yes, the guy had a secret, but my gut told me it wasn't murder.

"Devlyn was checking up on me. He's a nice guy."

"I'm sure he is."

My stomach clenched at Mike's tone. "But?"

"But what? If you like him, that's your business. It only becomes my business if he kills someone."

"But he didn't kill anyone. Right?"

Mike took one look at my face and sighed. "What do you think you know that I should know? Something happened at the memorial service today, right?"

I considered my options. Ratting Devlyn out to Mike wasn't high on my "like" list. But if Devlyn was a killer, not ratting him out could land me six feet under. Since I wasn't interested in eternal rest, I said, "Devlyn ducked out in the middle of the service. I thought he was looking for me so I followed him." Mike's expression didn't budge as I told him about Coach Bennett's desire to have Drew Roane back on the team and his threat to reveal Devlyn's deep, dark secret.

When I was done, Mike smiled and said, "Well, if Devlyn didn't have an airtight alibi that would have put him on the top of my list. Too bad."

An airtight alibi was good. So, "Why is it too bad?"

Mike gave me a grim smile. "Because I don't like the guy."

"Why?"

"It's a guy thing." He closed the gap between us so I could feel the heat radiating off his body.

"What kind of guy thing?"

"This kind."

The last time I was surprised into immobility. This time I saw it coming. I should have ducked, run, or pointed the pink pistol at him. Instead, I let him kiss me. Worse yet, I enjoyed it. His lips were warm, and his arms felt safe as he pulled me against him. Safe was something I hadn't had a lot of in recent days, and the feeling had an aphrodisiac effect. I threw myself into the kiss with an abandon I wasn't aware I possessed.

My hands wove into Mike's curly hair and pulled him closer. Mike made a groaning sound deep in his throat that made me feel more daring. I pulled my mouth away from his and nipped at his neck. He smelled like woodsy pine-scented soap. I wasn't an outdoor person, but in this case I was ready to make an exception.

Mike's warm hands slid up and down my bare back, sending sparks of excitement shivering through me. My body wanted even more while my brain warned this was a bad idea. His fingers dipped toward the fabric covering my behind, and my brain shut down. Then Mike's mouth disappeared, and he took three steps back.

Not again. I shivered as my body yearned for the warmth of his. "What's wrong?" As if I didn't know.

"We agreed this was a bad idea." Mike sounded like he'd run a marathon. Well, I hoped he was in shape, because he was really going to start running now.

"I never agreed to anything."

"This morning we said—"

"This morning you said kissing me was a mistake. Silly me for thinking that when you kissed me tonight it meant you'd changed your mind."

"Cops can't get involved with witnesses." Yeah, I'd heard that line before. "I'd like nothing better than to hop into bed with you, but—"

"You think I was going to sleep with you?" Blood rushed to my head, and my fingers curled into fists. Mike took a step back and had the nerve to look confused. Cop school must have taught him not to engage a pissed-off woman, because he didn't say anything. Which was good, because I had plenty to say. "Look. Just because I was blowing off a little sexual steam after being shot at and scared to death doesn't mean I was going to hop into bed with you. I don't sleep around."

Mike took a step back. "I didn't say you did."

"Really? Because that isn't what I heard." My voice rang in the foyer. Yeah, I could be loud when I wanted to be, and I really wanted Mike to pay attention. And if Aunt Millie woke up, so much the better. She'd taken another swing at matchmaking and had struck out so hard she'd landed her butt in the mud. "The next time your hand touches my ass I'm ordering Killer to chew it off. Got it?"

Mike didn't get it. He gave me a condescending smile and said, "I apologize for getting carried away. Seeing you in this getup distracted me. Friends?"

Not on your life.

I marched over to the door and flung it open, careful to stay out of the doorway. If the shooter was out there, I wanted him to have a clear shot—at Mike.

Mike looked at me for a moment, then sighed and sauntered toward the door. "You know, this case won't last forever. Once it's over, you might change your mind about the friends thing. Who knows where it might lead."

He smiled at me from the stoop. I smiled back and

slammed the door. The sound of click, click, click echoed through the foyer as Killer walked in. "You're late," I snapped as I stalked upstairs and peeled off my evening attire. As far as I was concerned, this evening was over and good riddance.

Once again, Killer took up residence in my bed, but this time it wasn't his cover hogging that kept me awake. Devlyn had an alibi for Greg's murder. That put him in the clear, which was good. It also meant I was back to square one.

I tried closing my eyes and counting sheep, but instead found myself going over the suspect list. Coach Bennett enlisted Devlyn to help get his star player back. Patience didn't strike me as one of Coach's virtues, so he might have opted to take out his competition instead of waiting for Devlyn to succeed where he had failed.

Still, my gut said that for all his blustering, Coach Bennett's bark was worse than his bite. That might not be good enough for the cops, but I was operating on a different proof threshold. Besides, after tonight both the coach and his wife were never going to talk with me. Unless I found a new source for information, I was at a dead end with them. Time to move on.

Only, where to? Larry had great motive and opportunity, only the guy was gone, leaving a trail of blood and a trashed house in his wake. My stomach rolled. Larry wasn't my best friend, but the thought of him injured or worse was freaking me out. He might be guilty, but my gut believed someone wanted Larry out of the way. Why? Was it because Larry knew who the killer was? Devlyn seemed to think he did. Wait. Maybe Larry provided the killer with her alibi on the night her ex-husband was killed?

The more I thought about it, the more likely that seemed. Too bad Detective Mike already ruled out Dana as a suspect because of her alibi. That meant if I wanted to turn over that particular rock, I'd have to do it myself.

———

What the hell was that? Oof. I bolted awake as Killer scrambled over me, onto the carpet, and out the door, barking all the way. I heard Millie scream, and my feet hit the floor. Hurtling down the stairs, I raced for the kitchen, then changed directions as Millie screamed again. The front door was open. Millie was outside.

Blood pounding in my ears, I grabbed the pink gun off the hall table, ran through the front door, and felt my heart stop. Sitting in the middle of the driveway was a flaming car.

My car. And Aunt Millie was climbing into it.

Chapter 24

"Aunt Millie, stop!"

Millie didn't look up. Black smoke rose from the hood of my Cobalt as my bare feet flew down the stoop and across the driveway. I grabbed Millie as she was ready to dive into the car and pulled her back. Now that I could see into the car, I understood why Millie was acting crazy. Aldo was slumped over the steering wheel—out cold or dead. I had no idea which.

"Call the fire department and stay back," I yelled as I approached the car. The flames seemed contained to the engine—for now. I had no idea how long it would take before they spread. The car radiated with heat as I grabbed Aldo's arm and pulled.

Shit. He was belted in.

Carefully, I positioned Aldo's shiny head back against the seat and leaned over to deal with the seat belt. Damn it. Drops of sweat stung my eyes as I tried to find the release button. It had to be here. I took a deep breath and started to choke. The smoke was getting thick. Aldo's head slumped into my chest as my fingers found the seat belt release and set him free.

I shifted Also so his back was facing me. Then I wrapped my arms around his torso and pulled him free. Ugh. The little guy was heavier than he looked.

"Is he okay?" Millie appeared behind me. "Aldo?"

I didn't answer. Between the smoke inhalation and my uncertainty about Aldo's condition, I figured it was best not to try. Instead, I focused on dragging him to the relative safety of the grass. Kneeling down next to him, I took his hand and felt for a pulse. Relief washed through me. "He's alive." It was then that I noticed his state of dress. Or undress. Aldo was wearing a white tank, black boxer shorts, white tube socks, and black dress shoes.

Somewhere in the distance, I could hear sirens. A pink-robed Aunt Millie knelt next to Aldo and held his hand while telling him everything was going to be okay. I hoped she was right as I stood up and took a couple of steps closer to what used to be my car.

My legs started to shake and my throat burned as I watched the smoke billow out from the hood. This couldn't have been an accident. I walked around so I could see inside the car. Keys were dangling from the ignition. I had no idea why Aldo had decided to take my car for a joyride, but doing so had almost cost him his life.

I couldn't breathe. Tears leaked from the corners of my eyes. I was scared. Someone wanted me dead and didn't care who they took out in the process.

Sirens screamed, and doors slammed behind me. Heavy footsteps charged up the driveway. The cavalry had arrived.

"He's over here." Aunt Millie's voice traveled over the noise. She was waving her arms so hard she tilted backward onto Aldo, who had been sitting upright. The momentum sent Millie and Aldo sprawling onto the grass.

The paramedics charged up the driveway with a stretcher and looked from Millie to Aldo, trying to decide who was the one most in need of attention. A firefighter directed me to move to the grass. I did as the firefighters turned on the hose and doused the remaining flames. The fire was out within seconds. The fear remained.

Mike's Mustang parked at the edge of the driveway. Cop lights blinked from his back window. He climbed out and made a beeline for me.

"We have to stop meeting like this." Detective Mike's eyes belied his light tone. They were glittering with frustration, anger, and worry.

"Someone blew up my car." I was a master of the obvious.

"They did a bad job. The car is still in one piece."

"You say that as though it's a bad thing."

His smile was grim. "The person behind this isn't a pro. That's good. He'll make a mistake."

"He already made a mistake. Aunt Millie's friend Aldo was in the car. Not me." My heart squeezed as I watched the paramedics load Aldo into the ambulance waiting on the street. Millie waved at me, tightened the belt on her robe, and climbed in after him. Seconds later, the ambulance backed up and drove off.

"The fuse must have been connected to the ignition. Does anyone else typically drive your car?"

"No." My throat clenched.

A firefighter walked over to Mike and whispered in his ear. Mike whispered back then turned to me. "I'm going to take a look at the car. Then I might have some more questions for you and your aunt. In the meantime, you should go inside and put some clothes on."

Yikes. I was wearing an oversized Northwestern University T-shirt that reached just below my ass and nothing else. Feeling Mike's eyes on my bare skin, I raced inside the house and locked the door behind me. My legs shook as I walked up the stairs. I reached my room, sat on the edge of the bed, and hugged a pillow to my chest as tears began to fall. My shoulder and neck muscles ached. My stomach clenched. It hurt to breathe.

Something warm and fuzzy rubbed against my bare legs. Killer jumped up on the bed and whined as he curled up next to me. I must be in bad shape if the dog that wanted me to starve was being nice.

Wiping away the tears, I scratched Killer behind the ears and got up. Sitting here crying wasn't going to make things any better. I pulled on my favorite dark-wash jeans and a stretchy black T-shirt and went to find my toothbrush. It was hard to feel brave with morning breath.

Armed with sexy clothes and a minty-fresh mouth, I marched down the stairs. I pushed the fear to the side and focused on the white-hot anger building inside me. Anger made me feel powerful and kept the tears at bay. Both were good.

The fire truck was pulling away as I walked back into the sunshine. A bunch of neighbors had come out and were milling in the street. Mike was down at the bottom of the driveway talking to a uniformed officer. He spotted me, nodded at the officer, and trotted up the drive.

"The department will send over a tow truck so our techs can take a better look at the car. We think the bomb was made with gas cylinders that were wired into the ignition." He tucked his hands in his back pocket. "It probably produced an impressive burst of fire to start, but didn't do the kind of damage other devices might have."

I looked at my singed Cobalt and tears threatened to reemerge. "Is that supposed to make me feel better?"

He shrugged. "Make sure you and your aunt keep your cars parked in the garage overnight from now on. And you'll want to contact your insurance carrier. Give them my name and number if they have any questions."

I hadn't even thought about contacting my insurance agent. Yippee. More fun.

"Do you have any idea who did this?" I asked.

Mike straightened his shoulders and tried to look confident as he said, "Not yet, but it's only a matter of time."

I just hoped when that time came, I was still alive to enjoy it.

Mike went through the "stay inside and out of trouble" routine and promised to let me know if there were any developments. He turned to leave, and I remembered a question I'd forgotten to ask last night.

"Did you ever find Larry?"

I could see the answer reflected in Mike's eyes. Larry was still missing, and no one had a clue where to look for him.

No one except me.

It was well after noon before the last of the police officers pulled away and the neighbors went indoors. Millie had called to let me know Aldo was fine. The doctors said his blood pressure shot up and caused him to black out. They would be monitoring him for a few more hours before sending him home. Millie planned on keeping Aldo company, which meant I was free to borrow her car. Since the car had been parked in the garage all night, I was relatively certain it wouldn't explode the minute I cranked the gas. Still, I held my breath and prayed to the patron saint of fire retardancy that I wouldn't get blown to bits.

The pink Caddy roared to life and no flames burst forth. My day was improving. I pulled the car out of the driveway and went in search of Dana Lucas, careful not to take out any lawn ornaments along the way.

Dana's red Jeep was in her driveway. I parked Millie's car at the curb, grabbed my purse, and stalked up to the door. My nerves were taut as I rang the bell and unzipped my purse halfway. Coming here was a risk. If Dana was the one who lit my car on fire, she'd have no qualms about killing me in broad daylight. Still, I was banking on her son's presence being a deterrent. And if not . . . I reached into my purse and closed my fingers around cool steel.

The door swung open, and a red-eyed Dana stood in the doorway. The woman was just as intimidating up close as I remembered, although she looked far more upset today than she had at her ex-husband's memorial service.

Her eyebrows knit together as she stared at me. "Yes? Can I help you?"

Clearly, my attendance at her yoga class made zero impression on her. I relaxed my grip on the gun. If Dana was the one taking shots at me, she'd know what I looked like.

"We met at your yoga class the other day. My name is Paige Marshall."

She forced a smile. "Right. You were the one who found my ex-husband dead. Sorry I didn't recognize you. You look different today."

Probably because I wasn't red-faced and covered in sweat. Talking a deep breath, I said, "I was hoping you could help me find my boss, Larry DeWeese. He's been missing since yesterday morning."

Dana froze. Slowly she said, "Why are you asking me?"

"Because you and Larry were seen together outside the country club on Wednesday night."

"Who said we were together?"

"Larry did."

Dana's eyes went wide. "Larry wasn't sure who we could trust. So he said we shouldn't tell anyone."

"He knew I was looking into Greg's murder. I guess he figured I could be trusted." Dana's bottom lip trembled. She wanted to share her secrets with someone. Now I just needed to convince her that someone was me. "I know about Larry's financial problems and about *the song*."

That did it.

Dana stepped back and waved me into the house. Running a hand through her spiky hair, she led me down the hall to a country-style kitchen and poured herself a large glass of red wine. She drained the glass and nodded for me to take a seat at the kitchen table. "Do you want some?"

I watched her pour another helping. After the morning I'd had, I could use a drink. Too bad I needed a clear head. I declined and asked, "Have you heard from Larry recently?"

"Not a word." She took a seat at a table topped with white tile, and I pulled out the chair opposite her. "He was supposed to call me yesterday before Greg's memorial service, but I never heard from him. I just know something terrible has happened."

Tears crept down Dana's cheeks, and her shoulders began to shake. I grabbed a tissue out of my purse and passed it over. "Because Larry thought he knew who murdered Greg?"

Dana cried harder. "I think so, yes. But he never told me who it was. He wanted to keep me safe. Not like Greg. He never cared about anyone but himself."

"What did you and Larry do on Wednesday night after you left the club?" Maybe they crossed paths with the murderer without Dana realizing it.

"My son, Jacob, was at a sleepover. I told Larry we were coming here to have a quiet dinner, but my lawyer was waiting to talk to him. Greg's entire career was based on the song he stole from Larry. I was trying to help Larry get what was rightfully his."

"That was generous since you must have gotten part of that money in your divorce settlement."

"I didn't see a dime." Dana's eyes glittered with anger and tears. "Greg and his lawyers convinced the judge that he'd written the song long before I was married to him. That I didn't deserve to reap the rewards of any premarital success."

Ouch.

"The lawyer thought Larry had a good case. Then Greg was murdered and Larry decided to call off the lawsuit."

"Why?"

She sniffled. "Larry thought my son would be named as Greg's sole beneficiary, and he didn't want to take away the money or my son's good memories of his father."

Dana dissolved into tears again.

"Is that what you argued about outside Greg's house the other day?"

Dana stiffened. "How do you know we argued?"

The truth wasn't going to help me, and I couldn't come up with a plausible lie. So I did the next best thing—I stayed quiet and hoped for the best. My heart thudded in my chest as the seconds ticked by.

Finally, Dana's shoulders slumped, and she nodded. "We were there to look for Greg's will. Larry found a copy of it in Greg's files along with the original handwritten version of the song that Greg stole. The song was in Larry's handwriting. A judge would have to rule in his favor, but Larry didn't want to pursue it anymore. He insisted he'd find another way to pay off his bills."

Huh. Dana looked like she was seriously in love with Larry. Which only added to my confusion. "Why haven't you told any of this to the police? This information might help them find him."

"I promised Larry I wouldn't."

Damn. I was hoping she wouldn't say that. Larry's unwillingness to reclaim his stolen music or the profits made from it seemed to strip away his motive for murder—unless he wanted it to look that way. I couldn't help but remember the e-mail quoting a large amount of money for services to be rendered by the mysterious Kris. Larry might have set up his own disappearance and dropped hints about knowing who the killer was just to throw the cops off the scent.

Of course, one thing about Dana was still bothering me. "When I was at class the other night, the other two students acted like they were scared of you."

Dana knocked back the rest of her wine and smiled. "I'm a tough teacher."

"Yes, I know." I rested my arms on the table and leaned forward. "But that isn't what they were referring to. They said you told them something, and whatever it was made them very nervous."

Her lips pursed, and her eyebrows knit together. Dana was in deep thought. Suddenly, she threw back her head and barked out a laugh. "Holy crap. They think I killed Greg."

"Why would they think that? I mean, most divorced couples don't go around killing each other." Although, I, for one, believed if any divorcée would take a whack at her former spouse, it was Dana.

She smiled. "A couple weeks ago, Greg blew off a weekend trip he'd planned with our son. He followed that act by sending me a child-support check written on a closed account. I found out about both right before class, and I might have said a few things I shouldn't have."

I raised an eyebrow.

Dana laughed again. "Okay, I think I said something like if Greg was smart, he'd go into hiding; otherwise, I'd tie him up with my yoga straps and beat him to death with the heel of my shoe. Yoga equipment is mostly made of cloth or foam, otherwise I would have chosen something more appropriate. Greg thought my yoga teaching was a joke." She gave me a sadistic smile. "Turns out I got the last laugh."

Chapter 25

Climbing back into the Caddy, I was more confused than when I'd arrived. Dana was in the clear. That was good, but I still had no idea where Larry was. That was bad, especially since I was now seriously considering him as a suspect in Greg's murder.

Not sure what else to do, I cruised over to Larry's house. Maybe he'd turned up since last I checked.

Nope.

The place was empty and locked up tight. If any clues inside led to his whereabouts, the cops would have to find them. I wasn't about to break and enter with the neighborhood watch on duty. She was camped out on her front porch with her binoculars at the ready. The good news was, if Larry came back, she'd send up smoke signals to the cops.

The only other place that might hold answers about Larry was the school, and I still didn't have a key. Tomorrow was the first day of classes, albeit a shortened one. The decision to start the school week on a Tuesday seemed odd to me.

Wasn't the school week supposed to start on a Monday? To top it off, tomorrow's school day was less than three hours long—just enough time for kids to visit every class, figure out where the classrooms were located, and meet the teachers.

Larry had asked me to sing for all his classes in the hopes of interesting some of the kids in voice lessons. I'd agreed. Without Larry there, I wasn't sure if the sub would want me to perform, but I figured I'd show up just in case. Besides, I had to attend a show choir meeting immediately after school. I hoped Larry would turn up before then. If not, I was in charge.

Suddenly, it struck me. Starting tomorrow, I was a teacher.

Yikes.

This revelation shouldn't have been a surprise, but it was. Teenagers would be looking to me to help them achieve their goals. They may not like it, but they needed me—especially now that Larry was missing in action. This might not be the career I wanted, but for now it was the one I had, and I didn't want to let the kids down.

I pulled into Millie's garage, went inside the house, and dialed Devlyn. If I was going to give this teaching thing my all, I needed to be prepared.

Devlyn answered on the first ring. "Are you okay? You didn't call me back last night."

Oops. Between Mike's late-night visit and the car explosion, I'd totally forgotten. "Sorry. Things have been a little crazy."

I explained about last night's gig and this morning's car excitement. The latter had Devlyn freaking. "Oh my God. Is your aunt's friend okay? Are you okay? Do the police have any leads?"

Yes. Yes and no. "The police are working on it."

"I don't like the idea of you being alone."

Neither did I. A quick lap of the house told me Millie wasn't around, and Killer didn't count as company. In a crisis I wasn't sure who he'd attack—me or an intruder.

"Millie should be home soon." I hoped.

"We still have some work to do on our choreography. Do you want me to come over?"

Yes. No. Crap. I wanted to practice for tomorrow, but while Mike said Devlyn was in the clear, he also didn't trust Devlyn. What if Mike was right? I didn't feel comfortable being alone with him.

"Are you still there?"

Oops. "Yes. I'm trying to remember when Detective Kaiser said he was going to drop by." A murderer wouldn't want to stop by if the cops were coming for a chat. Right?

"If he's coming over, I should definitely be there. He might try to intimidate you or something."

After last night's kiss, I would agree with the "or something." Huh. Devlyn had passed that test, but I wasn't feeling any better about being alone with him. "Do you think Felicia would want to come over?" I asked.

Devlyn paused before answering. "I can ask. We can give her a demonstration of our dancing prowess and see if she thinks it'll work with the costumes."

Sounded good to me. Felicia might not be big, but she looked scrappy. If Devlyn turned out to be a bad guy, I'd have an ally ready to do damage with acrylic nails.

Devlyn promised to check with Felicia before swinging over. If she couldn't make it, I'd call the whole thing off. Impressing the kids tomorrow wasn't worth dying over.

I headed for the stairs to grab my dance bag and froze

as I heard the front door handle rattle. Someone was trying to get in. The front door swung open, and Aunt Millie strolled in followed by a very happy-looking Aldo. Someone at the hospital had taken pity on the world and given Aldo a pair of green scrubs to wear. Millie was also wearing scrubs on the bottom, but was sporting a GOT DRUGS? T-shirt on top. She spotted me and smiled. "Look who got a clean bill of health from the doctors."

"I'm glad you're okay, Aldo." The tightness in my chest eased as the little Italian man gave me a toothy grin.

"Oh, Aldo's just fine." Aunt Millie steered the man in question toward the kitchen. "His heart just got a little excited when he saw flames shooting from the engine. The doctors said his blood pressure shot up and he passed out. But just to be certain, they asked that someone keep an eye on Aldo for a couple days."

"That makes sense to me."

Aldo took a seat at the table, and Aunt Millie beamed. "See, Aldo. I told you Paige wouldn't mind."

"Mind what?"

My aunt grabbed the coffeepot and filled it with water. "Well, Aldo lives alone in a retirement community condo. They have strict rules about overnight guests."

"The ladies on the condo board donna like the idea of anyone not married having the sex," Aldo quipped as he smoothed the white tufts of hair behind his ears. "I thinka they haven't gotten any in a vera long time. They do not-a remember how nice it is. At our age, you forgeta things when you haven't-a done them for a while." He waggled his bushy eyebrows at my aunt.

She giggled and blushed. "Anyway, I insisted Aldo stay here for the next couple of days." Aunt Millie hit start on the coffeepot and wiped her hands on a towel as Killer trotted into the room. He spotted Aldo, parked his rump on the floor, and began to growl.

"Oh, stop that, Killer." Millie gave Aldo an apologetic smile. "Between the break-in, the shooting, and the car explosion, Killer is feeling a little protective. Aren't you, sweetheart?"

When put that way, I had no idea why Aldo would want to stay here. The fainting spell must have affected his brain. Although, by the way Aldo's eyes were following Millie's backside, I had no doubt his brain wasn't the one doing the thinking. For some reason his blatant interest in my aunt made me happy.

Killer bared his teeth again.

Millie sighed and pulled a rawhide out of the cupboard. "You'll just have to find a way to get along with our guest." Killer snagged the rawhide between his teeth and settled onto the rug next to the back door. His eyes never left Aldo as he gnawed. Creepy.

"Devlyn and I were planning on rehearsing in the living room," I mentioned. "But I can call and cancel." If Aldo needed peace and quiet, I was going to do my part. He'd already had one medical scare because of me. I wasn't about to add another.

"You need a piano player?" Aldo cracked his knuckles.

"Aunt Millie doesn't own a piano."

Aldo wagged a wrinkled finger at Millie. He began listing reasons why a piano was a necessary investment as the doorbell rang. Devlyn had arrived. The minute I opened the door, he grabbed me and squeezed. Then a voice behind Devlyn said, "It's hot out here. Are we going in or am I going home?"

Devlyn let go. Oxygen and blood began to flow, and Felicia strolled in the door in skin-tight black jeans, a low-cut red tank top, and four-inch heels. An enormous silver bag was slung over her shoulder. "Devlyn said you needed an audience for your rehearsal. I hope you don't mind, but I have to cut out early. I have a date."

Not a surprise.

"Well, then," I said. "I guess we should get to work."

I retrieved my dance bag and a CD player from upstairs. When I came back down, Millie, Aldo, and Felicia were seated against the back living room wall. Devlyn was in the middle of the carpeted floor stretching. Something I probably should have done. Oh well. A pulled muscle was the least of my worries.

Devlyn helped me set up the machine, then hit play. It was showtime. The intro started, and Devlyn and I strutted our stuff. The double turns and spins were harder to do on carpet, but I was grateful for the soft landing material in case I took a dive.

Nope. Devlyn lifted me up onto his shoulder. I hit the final pose, and he even got me back down to the floor without either of us getting bruised. Things were looking up.

Aunt Millie and Aldo applauded. Felicia cocked her head to one side and asked us to do it again with a couple modifications. Her ideas were good, so we worked them into the dance. It took four more tries, a lot of sweat, and one face-plant into the carpet (by me) before Felicia declared it fabulous. "Not even Chessie Bock can find fault with that routine."

"I think Chessie could find fault with just about anything." Devlyn wiped his face with a towel.

I tended to agree. "Especially anything that has to do with me."

"That girl doesn't realize how lucky she is to have you teaching her." My aunt climbed to her feet with a frown.

"At this point, I'd settle for a cease-fire." Sad, but true.

Devlyn shrugged. "Chessie will come around. I've directed her in a lot of shows and had her in class. Trust me. She's ambitious. Once she realizes someone can help her reach her goals, she becomes their biggest fan."

Fan? Something told me that was never going to happen.

"Well, I should get dinner started." Aunt Millie hoisted herself up off her chair. "Devlyn, would like to join us? I'm making spaghetti and meatballs."

I psychically sent Devlyn a message: Run. Save yourself.

"That sounds great. Thank you."

Either my psychic powers sucked or Devlyn was a glutton for punishment.

Beaming, Aunt Millie bounded off to the kitchen with Aldo trailing behind her. Felicia glanced at her watch and said, "I have forty-five minutes before my date. What other numbers do you have to show me?"

Ugh.

We went through two other songs we'd started working on. Thank God one was a slow number. Felicia gave us a couple ideas to work with, then got up to leave. "Devlyn, would you mind if I have a private moment with Paige? Just some girl stuff we need to discuss."

Devlyn gave Felicia a wounded look and walked over to the other side of the room with his water bottle. Felicia lowered her voice and said, "I think you should keep an eye on Devlyn. Just in case . . . you know . . ."

I couldn't imagine how Felicia could know about Devlyn's interaction with the North Shore High School football coach. That meant I had no idea what she was talking about. "In case of what?"

"As the theater teacher, Devlyn spends a lot of time with his students."

"And?"

Felicia rolled her eyes. "If he wanted them to be nice to you, they would. They might also follow his instructions if he wanted someone scared off or maybe killed?"

I blinked. "You think Devlyn ordered his students to kill Greg Lucas?"

"I don't know what to think." Felicia twisted her hands together as her eyes bore into mine. "But I do know that I don't want anything to happen to you." She reached out and touched my hand. "I heard about the note you found in your bag. That sounds like something a teenager would do to piss you off, don't you think? Devlyn could have set that in motion. He told me last week that he'd seen you in a lot of shows. He could have known about that review."

My stomach clenched at the idea of Felicia reading that review. Was that vain? Yes. At this moment, did I care? No.

I turned and watched as Devlyn practiced tangoing across the carpet. Detective Mike said Devlyn had an airtight alibi, but what if Felicia was onto something? Maybe Coach Bennett knew Devlyn had instructed a student to kill Greg and was blackmailing him with that information. It seemed far-fetched, but anything was possible.

Killer trotted in from the kitchen, walked over to Devlyn, and bumped his head against Devlyn's hand. Devlyn gave him a couple of pats and then continued dancing. Seeing Killer be nice to Devlyn made me even more nervous. The dog was a menace. Perhaps it recognized one of its own.

"Just think about what I said." Felicia reached down to pick up her bag. "Devlyn was right when he said Chessie was ambitious. She'd sell her soul to get ahead. If Devlyn promised her a leg up . . . well, I just think you should be careful." With a jaunty wave at Devlyn, Felicia sashayed into the foyer and out the front door.

"So, what terrible thing did she have to say about me?"

I jumped as Devlyn appeared at my side along with his new best friend, Killer. I hadn't heard him move. His stealth was unnerving.

"What makes you think she had something bad to say about you?"

Devlyn laughed. "Felicia loves gossip. The only reason she'd remove a member of her audience is if she's gossiping about them. So what wonderfully awful thing am I guilty of?"

I could tell the truth or lie. What the hell . . .

"She thinks you convinced Chessie and her friends to murder Greg Lucas and terrorize me."

Devlyn's mouth spread into a goofy smile as he started to laugh. "Felicia's outdone herself. Normally, she just busies herself with gossip about affairs and cross-dressing. I'm glad she saved something so sinister for me. I think I make a great puppet master, don't you?" He pretended to pull strings on a marionette.

"She also thinks Chessie was behind the threat in my bag."

Devlyn stopped laughing and pursed his lips together. "Now that you mention it, that sounds like something Chessie would do. But I didn't put her up to it. And I certainly would never ask a student to kill someone for me. You know that."

Maybe. "I saw you and Coach Bennett talking in the hallway yesterday."

Devlyn froze. His eyes met mine, and his voice was dangerously quiet as he cocked an eyebrow. "And what do you think you heard?"

"Coach Bennett is blackmailing you into helping him get his star player back on the team."

"Blackmail is a strong word."

"He's threatening to reveal whatever secret you're hiding unless you help him. What would you call it?"

"I concede the point." He crossed his arms and cocked his head to one side. "And now you're wondering what that secret is."

"Do you blame me?" I asked.

"No, but I do expect you to trust me."

"I barely know you."

Devlyn ran a hand through his dark hair and blew out a loud burst of air. "Okay. Yes, I have a secret. Yes, Curtis Bennett knows what it is. He let me know what he discovered and asked me to do a favor for him. End of story."

Funny, but it sounded like the story ended just as it was getting to the good part. The two of us stared at each other for what seemed like forever. My heart pounded in my throat. I swallowed hard as Devlyn's eyes pleaded with me to believe him. I wanted to. I really did. But I needed to be sure. Not making sure might raise the body count. "Are you going to tell me what Coach Bennett has on you?"

His shoulders stiffened. "Are you asking me if I killed Greg Lucas?"

Yes. "I don't know. Am I?"

Devlyn shook his head, turned on his heel, and stalked over to his gym bag. With Killer at his heels, he shoved his towel into the bag and zipped it shut.

"I thought you were different. Guess I was wrong." Turning to me, he said, "Tell your aunt I'm sorry I had to leave. I just lost my appetite." Without another word, he marched to the front door and slammed it shut behind him.

Killer looked up at me and rumbled a low, menacing growl followed by several loud barks. Translation: What the hell were you thinking? Answer: I wasn't. No, I didn't think

Devlyn ordered his students to kill Greg Lucas. But after everything that had happened, I couldn't shake the twinge of doubt that I might be wrong. And now I'd upset the only person interested in helping me make a success of my job. After that performance, I doubted Devlyn would show up at tomorrow's rehearsal. I was officially on my own.

My head began to throb as Aunt Millie popped out of the kitchen. "Dinner is served."

Oh goody. Well, maybe Millie's terrible cooking would finally come in handy. If I was lucky, I'd contract food poisoning.

Chapter 26

No such luck. For the first time ever, the food from Aunt Millie's kitchen was not only edible, it was tasty. Too bad I had no interest in eating it. My stomach was still churning from my confrontation with Devlyn. I was thankful neither Millie nor Aldo noticed my lack of appetite or Devlyn's disappearance. They only had eyes for each other.

After thirty minutes of languorous looks and compliments on each other's lack of aging (which was sweet, considering Aldo's bald head had more wrinkles than a best-in-show mastiff), I excused myself and headed upstairs. Maybe preparing for tomorrow's half day of school would take my mind off Devlyn's hurt and angry expression.

With Larry missing in action, I had no idea whether I'd still be singing for each class. Figuring it was best to be prepared, I sorted through my music and picked pieces I hoped would impress the students. I threw some dance clothes into my bag and a can of Mace. Then I vowed to check the bag before I left in the morning just in case Millie decided to add her own pink accessory. There was no way I was taking a gun into a school no matter how scared I was.

That settled, I pawed through my wardrobe looking for something suitably hip but professional. I decided on a black-and-white diagonally striped dress, a thick red belt, and killer red heels. If nothing else, the boys might decide to give me the benefit of the doubt based on the heels alone.

Aunt Millie and Aldo asked me to join them for a rollicking game of Yahtzee. The rattling dice jangled my already taut nerves, but I had nothing better to do with my evening. Besides, seeing Aunt Millie look so happy was good for the soul.

After losing for the tenth time, I asked Millie if she could give me a lift to school tomorrow morning and then called it a night. I was whupped.

Too bad I couldn't sleep. Visions of Aldo's inert body, Devlyn's angry face, and Felicia's dire warnings played in my head. It was no use. After an hour and a half of pretending sleep was moments away, I turned on the light and grabbed a notepad and pen from the desk. Propping myself up on the pillows, I started listing my suspects: Larry, Dana, Coach Bennett, Devlyn, and Eric. Eric wasn't really a suspect, but the cops had questioned him so I included him.

I then listed everything else I'd learned since. Which, surprisingly, was a lot. I chewed on the cap of the pen as I studied the list. It was all interesting, but I had no idea which information was important.

On a whim, I crossed out everything that specifically had to do with Devlyn, Coach Bennett, Dana, and Greg's theft of Larry's music. What was left?

Someone had tried to run Greg off the road earlier this year. Someone also let the air out of his tires. Both happened long before Drew Roane quit the football team or Greg hit on Chessie. Someone was pissed at Greg back in May and early June—right before school let out for the summer. Then nothing terrible happened to Greg until school was ready to start again. Was that a coincidence? I didn't think so.

The murderer had to be someone who was out of town for the summer. When the murderer came back, Greg did something to push that person over the edge and he died.

It made sense. Or maybe I was just hoping it made sense. Still, asking around couldn't hurt. What was more natural at the beginning of the school year than asking what people did for their summer vacation?

———

Millie dropped me off at Prospect Glen High School. Since she'd canceled everything on her agenda yesterday, she was in a hurry to catch up and zipped off the minute I closed the car door. I went down to the choir room. No Larry. Not a surprise.

I checked in with the front office. Larry hadn't called in sick, which meant the secretaries were unaware of his absence. Not sure what else to do, I gave the staff Detective Mike's phone number and informed them that Larry had disappeared over the weekend. While the office staff digested that information and scrambled to find a qualified sub (while I had a master's degree in music, I wasn't certified), I went back to Larry's office to search for any clues I might have missed.

The office's organization hadn't improved since my last snooping expedition. If anything, there was more clutter. Stacks of class syllabi were perched precariously on top of the office calendar and other assorted notes and office supplies. Knowing the syllabi were going to be needed today,

I moved them to the top of the choir room piano and went back into Larry's office.

The desk calendar caught my eye. I'd looked at it before, but this time I was looking for something specific. The months of July and August showed lots of notations—several meetings with the Choir Boosters board members, a music educators' seminar at Northwestern University, and even a meeting with Devlyn to discuss options for the school musical.

Larry was in the area for most if not all of the summer. If my current theory was correct, that geographical proximity put him out of the running as Greg's murderer. It also took Devlyn out of the picture. Detective Mike would probably find a hundred flaws with my reasoning, but I didn't care. My gut told me I was right. At this point, my gut was all I had to go on.

I dug through the rest of Larry's desk drawers. A large envelope held a stack of photographs from competitions. I quickly flipped through them. Larry, Felicia, and the show choir kids were all prominently featured. Judging by the different costumes and hairstyles, the photos had been taken at a number of different competitions spanning the past two or three years. In the background of a few photographs, I could see Greg Lucas leering at Felicia's backside. I flipped to the last photo. There was Larry wearing a goofy grin. My heart ached. I hoped he'd have a chance to smile at the camera like that again.

I grabbed the printed class rosters from the corner of the desk and headed into the choir room. I could hear the chatter of teens and the slamming of lockers in the hallway. Classes began in fifteen minutes. I had no idea what would happen when they started, but I'd do my best.

Two girls opened the door, took one look at me sitting

behind the piano, and giggled. Three boys in droopy denim and T-shirts came in behind.

"Where's Mr. DeWeese?" asked a girl in a short purple skirt and way too much eye makeup.

Good question. I wished I knew.

Trying not to sound concerned, I said, "Mr. DeWeese had an emergency. He won't be here today, but he left his class syllabus so we can get started."

"Are we still having the show choir meeting after school?"

My stomach clenched. "Of course we are." I gave the girl a perky smile. "Mr. DeWeese wouldn't have it any other way."

Kids scrambled to take their seats as the bell rang. No Larry. No certified teacher to save the day. It was all me. Yikes.

I checked Larry's schedule. First period—Freshman Choir. Yippee. After taking attendance, I handed out the syllabus, then gave the entire class the "Mr. DeWeese had an emergency" song and dance.

Now what?

Since the kids had never seen me before, I introduced myself and my position at the school. I also mentioned I'd be teaching a select number of voice students during the school day. The kids hung on my every word. Weird.

We went over the calendar of events for the semester, which included the fall and winter concerts—both were mandatory. The students asked a few questions, and I answered them as best as I could. After twenty minutes, the bell rang. Yay! One class done. Only eight more to go.

As the kids grabbed their stuff and filed out, a large woman with even larger glasses ran through the door and almost took out two whispering girls. The woman spotted me and lumbered over.

Breathing hard, she sputtered, "I'm sorry I'm late. In all my years I've never gotten a call to substitute teach on the first day of class. Then I couldn't find my keys and there was a train . . ." Her voice trailed off, and she shrugged.

I let out a sigh of relief. This woman was a teacher, and that meant she was in charge. Since Larry wasn't present and the substitute teacher didn't play the piano, I opted out of singing for the students. Instead, I just introduced myself to the classes and left it at that. That worked great until the last period of the day—Chorale—the top choir and home to my show choir students, including Chessie Bock.

When Chessie strutted into the classroom holding hands with Eric, she took one look at me and rolled her eyes. In a way it was comforting to know some things never change. Eric waited for Chessie to turn her back before waving. If nothing else, my foray into detecting had gotten him on my side. That was something, right?

The minutes passed uncomfortably fast. Chessie glared at me through most of the period. Or maybe it wasn't a glare. Out of the corner of my eye, I watched as she shot me nervous glances. Chessie was worried about something, which made me wonder if Felicia was right.

Once the bell rang, the substitute teacher headed for the door and all eyes looked to me. "The show choir meeting won't start for another ten minutes," I said with more confidence than I felt. "Once all the other team members arrive, we'll talk about plans for this year's season." My eyes locked with Chessie's, and I smiled. "Ms. Bock, I would like to see you in Mr. DeWeese's office for a moment."

Without waiting for Chessie's reaction, I turned on my heel and headed for the door. Kids behind me snickered and did the "oooo" sounds adolescents reserve for times when someone is called out.

"Yeah?" Chessie hovered in the doorway. Her attitude was belligerent, but her eyes looked scared. It was the scared I was interested in.

"Come on in and shut the door."

Chessie looked like she wanted to protest, but she followed my instructions and took a seat on the piano bench.

Smiling, I said, "I just thought you should know threatening notes aren't going to make me up and quit."

Her eyes went wide. Direct hit. "What notes?" Her voice was devoid of its usual swagger.

"I think we both know what I'm talking about." Our eyes met for several seconds. I felt a small burst of satisfaction when Chessie looked away first. "Having those kinds of threats on your record wouldn't look so great to college admissions boards."

Chessie gasped. Clearly, she hadn't thought about her antics interfering with her college applications.

I sat down on Larry's chair and leaned forwarded. "Here's what I'm thinking. If you admit to me you wrote the notes and apologize, I'll pretend the whole thing didn't happen." Chessie looked like I'd hit her over the head with a wet fish. Through the office window, I could see the rest of the show choir kids stroll through the choir room door. "Why don't you take some time to think about it? You can give me your answer after the meeting. Okay?"

Without giving her a chance to agree, I stood, turned the doorknob, and walked out of the office. Grabbing my dance bag, I headed for the bathroom to change—just in case Devlyn put in an appearance.

Once I had put on my tights, T-shirt, and black dance skirt, I walked back into the choir room. A stone-faced Chessie refused to look at me as I did a quick head count. Forty students. We were four short. Two stragglers came through the door and found seats in the back. I waited another couple minutes, hoping Devlyn would decide to show. The final students poked their heads into the room, and the back of my neck started to sweat.

"Hi. As you all know, my name is Paige Marshall. I'll be working with Music in Motion this year. I might also be running the first couple rehearsals for Singsations if Mr. DeWeese's emergency lasts longer than expected." I wasn't sure if this last part was true, but it was the best I could come up with. Larry had conveniently left rehearsal, performance, and competition schedules so I handed them out and let the kids look over them. Then I went over the rules.

"All Music in Motion team members are allowed two unexcused absences. If you have more than two, you will be removed from the team and a member of Singsations will be tapped to join the squad." When I was a teen, we would have rebelled at the idea of being kicked out of a program for having only two absences. Not these kids. My team nodded while the other squad leaned forward with hope blazing in their eyes.

Huh. Maybe I was wrong about the willingness of kids to bump someone off for their teacher. These kids looked like they'd happily shove someone off a cliff in order to climb the ranks. Scary.

I answered a few questions about the rehearsal schedule and glanced at the door. Devlyn wasn't coming. Not that I blamed him, but still . . .

Taking a deep breath, I said, "Today, I'm going to announce the song selection for Music in Motion. We'll be working on—"

The choir room door swung open, and Devlyn strolled in wearing lime green sweats and a gray Prospect Glen T-shirt. "Sorry, I'm late. I was busy fielding questions about auditions for the fall play. Are we ready to show them the number that's going to help them compete for first place this year?"

My heart gave a happy flutter as the kids leaned forward in anticipation. Mouthing "thank you" to Devlyn, I put our accompaniment disk into the CD player and cranked the volume. Devlyn and I took our places, and music filled the room. It was showtime.

Perhaps it was my delight over Devlyn's appearance and implied forgiveness that made me forget my nervousness. Instead, I just had fun. I sang the soprano part. Devlyn added his own baritone harmony to the mix, and we turned, twirled, and hand slapped through the song. I struck a pose. Devlyn strutted around me. I held out my hand, and he twirled me against his chest and down I dipped. We danced and sang our hearts out then he grabbed my hips, I jumped, and up I went onto his shoulder. Ta-da!

The kids went wild, and I heard a number of gratifying "holy crap" exclamations as Devlyn smoothly set me down onto the floor. I hit off on the CD player as the kids started chattering.

"Is all the choreography like that?"

"I thought Chessie said she didn't know how to sing show tunes."

"What are the costumes going to look like?"

"Is the Singsations stuff going to be this hard?"

"I don't think I can do the lift."

"That's going to take forever to learn."

Devlyn put his hands up, and the room got quiet. "I think you'll all admit Paige is ready to take Music in Motion to the next level. If you aren't up to it, make sure you tell her now so someone else who is ready can take your spot."

Silence.

Devlyn glanced toward me and winked. I winked back. It felt good to be on the same side again.

A couple of choir members asked to see the routine again. I looked at Devlyn. He nodded, and away we went. I could see the girls watching me closely. The boys all studied Devlyn. By the time we were done, the only ones applauding were the Singsations kids. My students were already discussing getting together for additional practices outside of rehearsals to brush up on their dance.

"Mr. DeWeese, Mr. O'Shea, and I are excited about working with all of you this year. The sheet music Mr. DeWeese ordered should be in by the end of the week. Our first music rehearsal will be next Monday. We'll start learning some of the basic steps next rehearsal. Got it?"

They nodded.

"Good. I'll see you all tomorrow."

The excited group gathered up their stuff and headed for the exit. In the middle of the kids was Chessie trying to make a break for it.

"Miss Bock," I said, projecting my voice over the exuberant chitchat. "I believe you had something to tell me."

Chessie stopped walking. Eric tugged on her hand. For a moment I wondered if she'd decide to walk out the door with him. Finally, she said something to Eric, turned around, and walked back into the room. Eric shrugged and trudged out the door with the rest of the crowd.

Devlyn leaned over and whispered, "Are you sure confronting Chessie now is a good idea?"

"Trust me."

Chessie stood next to the piano. She had developed an intense interest in her purple flip-flops as the rest of the students left.

"So what did you think of the routine?" I asked.

"It was pretty good."

High praise.

"I'm hoping the judges think it's better than pretty good," Devlyn joked. "That routine needs to bring down the house." He waited for Chessie and me to agree with him, but neither of us spoke. We just looked at each other.

The silence stretched on for several long seconds. We were playing a game of chicken. The first one to speak lost. It wasn't going to be me.

"Okay. Fine. I wrote those notes. Only it wasn't all my idea. Someone told me to do it."

Chapter 27

"Someone told you to write Ms. Marshall threatening notes?"

I was glad Devlyn spoke because I was too stunned.

"Well, sort of." Chessie bit her lip. "Once Mr. DeWeese told us you were going to be in charge of the team I knew we had to make you quit. Otherwise we'd be throwing away everything we'd worked for. So I did some research online and found that review."

If ever I ran into that reviewer, I was going to deck him in the mouth. "And?"

"Your bag was out in the open, so I put the printout in. I figured things were so busy no one would see me doing it." Her chin rose. "You didn't."

"But somebody did."

Slowly she nodded.

"Who?"

"I don't know," Chessie said. Devlyn shot her a look of disbelief, and her defiant attitude crumbled. "I really don't know. Honest. I got an e-mail around seven o'clock on Friday night saying what a great idea the note was and that another note left in your mailbox on Saturday morning would really put the pressure on. It worried me that someone saw me, because I was so careful, but I liked that someone else agreed with me. Eric was against me doing anything to get rid of you."

Sighing, I asked, "Was the e-mail signed?" Another head shake. "Did you recognize the e-mail address?"

"No," she admitted. "But lots of my friends have created new e-mail addresses recently so I assumed it was just one of them. I mean, who else could it have been?"

I lifted an eyebrow in doubt. An epidemic of e-mail address changes seemed far-fetched to me. Devlyn didn't agree. "We see this every year with seniors applying to colleges. I've had to update my files a dozen times already to keep track of kids who have changed their addresses to something more professional."

Damn. That made sense. "Did the person say why they thought Saturday morning was a good time to drop off another note?"

Chessie chewed on the end of a lock of hair. "The e-mail mentioned something else would happen around lunchtime. We'd have a one-two punch. Or one-two-three if you count my first note."

The pride in her voice pissed me off. "Do you know what the e-mailer's punch was?" Before she could say anything, I answered the question. "Gunshots. While I was standing at the bottom of my aunt's driveway reading your note, someone tried to kill me. Someone you helped."

The girl's face drained of color, and her eyes flew to Devlyn's face for confirmation. The minute he nodded, her lip trembled and she started to cry.

My gut instinct is normally to sooth away tears. I can't help it. In this case, I was happy to let Chessie cry. Scaring the crap out of me and aiding and abetting a murderer were pretty good mistakes to cry over.

After a few minutes, the flow of tears ebbed, and Chessie started snuffling. Devlyn handed her a tissue, and she wiped her face. Taking a shaky breath, she asked, "Will I go to jail?"

"No." Although it wasn't the worst idea I'd heard. Chessie heaved a sigh of relief, but I wasn't done yet. "However, I want that e-mail address."

"I'll have to look for it when I get home. My parents won't pay for me to have a phone with Internet access."

Devlyn pointed at the door. "You'll go to the library computer and get it now." His tone meant business. Chessie must have thought so, too, because she grabbed her bag and scurried toward the door, promising to return shortly. When she was gone, Devlyn ran a hand through his hair and sat hard on the piano bench. "Well, that was unexpected."

"Not entirely," I said. The slight tremor in my voice ruined the Zen sound I was going for. "Felicia and you both agreed on one thing last night—the notes sounded like something Chessie would do."

"Felicia was also right about someone putting Chessie up to writing one of the notes, which means the rest of her theory might be dead on. Frankly, I'm surprised you're still in the same room with me." His tone was bitter, his eyes angry. He was waiting for me to run.

My feet stayed firmly in place. "I'm sorry I didn't trust you. I do now."

Devlyn stood up. "You shouldn't trust me."

Uh-oh. My feet twitched. "You didn't kill Greg Lucas." I was sure the person who did was out of town all summer. Wasn't I?

"I haven't been honest with you. We both know that."

"Everyone has secrets."

"But not everyone gets blackmailed over them. Thank God that's finished."

I blinked. "Drew Roane rejoined the team?"

Devlyn smiled. "I got the call this morning. Coach Bennett's happy."

"'All's well that ends well,' right?" I thought my Shakespeare quote would make the drama teacher in him smile.

Nope. He frowned. "Remember when we talked about teenage girls and the trouble they can cause for teachers? I saw it for the first time when I was student teaching. A senior girl thought I was cute. She was always trying to schedule private acting lessons with me. Anyway—"

The door burst open, and Chessie stomped in waving a piece of paper. "I got it." She handed the page to me, and her eyes glistened with tears. "While I was in the library, I made a decision. If you need me to talk to the police about the notes and the e-mail, I will. I don't care if it shows up on my school records. I was stupid and mean, and I deserve whatever happens because of it."

I was floored. She wasn't just saying this in hopes of getting herself off the hook. She meant it. This Chessie wasn't the same self-absorbed, egotistical girl I'd come to know and resent. For the first time, I could see the budding adult under the teenage angst, and I was impressed.

"I'll talk to Detective Kaiser. There might be a way for him to take your statement without notifying the school administration about your actions."

"Really?" Her eyes filled with hope, then suspicion. "Why are you being so nice?"

I laughed. It felt good to laugh. "Maybe because I remember what it's like to be a teenager who screwed up. Besides, I need you to help win competitions this year. I think we have a chance. Don't you?"

Chessie smiled. The first real smile I'd seen from her since I'd taken the job. "Are the rest of the dance numbers as good as the one you showed us today?"

"They will be," I promised.

"Then, yeah," she said. "I think we have a really good chance. See you tomorrow?"

When I nodded, she gave a wave and walked out the door.

"Damn it," Devlyn said, looking at his watch. "I'm supposed to be helping a couple seniors pick out their college audition monologues. They're waiting for me in the theater. It won't take long. Can you wait?"

I didn't have a car. Unless I called Aunt Millie, I had no choice. "Can you give me a lift home?"

"Absolutely." He grinned as he sprinted toward the door. "Meet you back here in fifteen or twenty minutes."

The minute he was gone, I looked down at the paper in my hands: showchoirfan42@gmail.com. Huh. No wonder Chessie thought the e-mail was from one of her friends. It certainly sounded that way to me.

I packed up my stuff, put the CD player away, and got the room ready for tomorrow. While lining up the chairs, I realized Chessie had given me an additional piece of the puzzle. The murderer had to have been in the field house the last day of camp. Considering at least two hundred parents, kids, and teachers had been present, this didn't completely narrow the list down. But it was a start.

I grabbed my purse and found a pen. Then, using the piano as a desk, I started jotting down notes. Thanks to Mike, I knew Devlyn had an airtight alibi and was in the clear. So were Dana and Coach Bennett. If either of them were in that field house, the kids and staff would have been talking about it. The only two left from my original suspect list were Larry and Eric. Eric didn't have an alibi, but his parents had him on lockdown after coming home. I didn't see him picking up a gun or rigging my car with explosives. Which left Larry.

My gut said no. Which meant the killer was someone I'd never considered.

"Oh, thank God you're still here." Felicia poked her head into the room. Her eyes looked freaked, and she teetered slightly on her heels. "I don't know who else to tell. I mean, I could call the police, but I'm not sure that's the right thing to do."

"What's going on?" I shoved the paper back in my purse and zipped it partially shut. "Did someone else get hurt?" The fact that we were just down the hall from the first murder scene made my heart jump.

Felicia clasped her hands in front of her and shook her head. She was wearing a large pink sewing smock over her clothes. It engulfed her petite frame, making her look small and vulnerable. "I checked my e-mail while I was working in the costume shop. Most of the messages were just beginning-of-school stuff. A few students asked for letters of recommendations. I wasn't even paying attention to the sender when I opened one and . . ." Her eyes went wide. "I think the murderer e-mailed me."

She grabbed my hand and tugged. I could feel her fingers trembling as she hurried me down the hallway toward the dressing rooms at the back of the theater. Her voice was high and breathy as she continued to chatter. "E-mails can be faked, but this looks real to me. I just can't believe it. He isn't a killer. At least, I would never have believed it, but he confessed."

Somewhere to my left, I could hear Devlyn's voice. He must be finishing up with his students. I thought about asking him to come with us, but Felicia was on a mission. She pulled me through a back hallway and into the scene shop at the very rear of the building. I sneezed as the smell of sawdust hit me.

"The costume shop is back here. My e-mail is open on the laptop. Please read it. If you think it's real, we'll call the police."

Felicia let me enter the fluorescent-lit room first. Three mannequins greeted me near the door. A closed closet door and shelves filled with bolts of fabric took up the back wall. Two long tables sat in the center of the room. A tiny desk sat in the left rear corner, a darkened laptop open on it.

I took a seat at the desk and clicked the mouse, and a password protected text box appeared. Felicia leaned over from behind me to type. Her breath was shallow and fast as her fingers pressed the keys. She hit enter, and the open e-mail flashed on the screen.

The message wasn't long. I started reading and went cold.

Felicia,

I am sending this to you because you might understand what I have done. Last Wednesday, I decided Greg Lucas was finished pushing me around and arranged to meet him at the theater that night. I told him that I was going public. That I would tell everyone I'd written his famous song unless he paid me the money that was rightfully mine. Greg laughed in my face, and something inside me snapped. I grabbed the microphone off the stand, and I killed him. I never meant to do it or to let a student take the blame for it. You have to believe me.

Larry

The e-mail address of the sender read showchoirfan42@ gmail.com. The same address Chessie gave me. I swallowed hard as blood pounded in my head.

"What do you think?" Felicia whispered behind me.

My legs barely held me upright as I stood and turned around. "We need to call the police."

"Oh my God! You think this is real? Larry killed Greg."

"Yes." No. I had never been so certain or so scared. Blood pounded in my temples, and the back of my neck began to sweat. Larry hadn't written this e-mail. Felicia had.

Chapter 28

An icy streak of fear swirled through me as I smiled at Felicia. "Everything's going to be okay. Let me call Detective Kaiser. He'll know how to handle this."

Felicia took a deep breath, gave me a shaky smile, and nodded. Thank God. I turned to grab my purse off the desk and felt the prick of something cold and sharp against the back of my neck.

"Give me the phone." Felicia's voice was no longer weak or whispery.

Oh shit! The metal jabbed deeper into my neck, and pain shot through my spine. Fear gripped my heart and squeezed hard.

"What are you doing, Felicia?" I asked trying to sound confused, though I wasn't. All the pieces had been there waiting for me to put them together. And I had—too late.

Felicia laughed, deep and throaty. The room spun for a moment as I felt drops of blood ooze from where Felicia's weapon bit into my neck. The sharp pain vanished, replaced by the minor sting of the wound. I slowly turned. Felicia met my eyes, and she smiled as she stepped back. Scissors glinted in Felicia's right hand.

I breathed a momentary sigh of relief, thinking I could outrun her and the scissors given half a chance. Then she reached into her sewing-smock pocket and pulled out a small silver gun. "You know what I'm doing, Paige. Give me your cell phone, please."

I dragged my eyes away from the gun so I could look squarely at Felicia. "What do you mean?"

She pouted behind the raised weapon. "I was hoping when I brought you down here that you would believe the e-mail. But you didn't." She nodded toward my hand. "Your phone. I can't have you calling anyone right now. You've caused enough trouble."

My hand shook as I passed over my only lifeline to help. She took it and placed it on the table behind her with a satisfied nod.

Trying hard not to hyperventilate, I asked, "Why don't you think I believe Larry killed Greg?" I couldn't help asking. The professional performer in me was curious even as the rest of me shrank back in fear.

She shrugged. "Your left eyebrow twitched. You do that when you lie. I saw it the other day when I asked if you knew who the detective's other suspects were."

Detective Mike was right, and I was screwed. "So what now?"

"I have to kill you." The regret in Felicia's voice gave me a tinge of hope.

"Like you killed Greg?" I asked trying to quell the fear long enough to come up with a way out of this room alive.

"He wasn't a good man. Greg used people and threw them away when he was done."

"You had an affair with him." Devlyn said Felicia had a thing for Greg. The photos in Larry's office showed Greg leering at her. She must be the affair mentioned in Greg's divorce.

Her eyes blazed. "It wasn't just an affair. We were a team. Do you know how much I sacrificed for him? What I did to help his career? His wife never supported him. She never understood."

"And you did."

"Greg and I are both creative personalities. Dana couldn't do the things I did for him."

"What kind of things?" Felicia seemed to want to talk, and I was more than willing to let her. Hell, the longer she talked, the better chance I had of Devlyn coming to look for me. I'd left my dance bag in the choir room. He'd know I was still somewhere in the school. I hoped to God that would be enough for him to start up a search.

A small, sad smile crossed Felicia's red painted lips. "Greg knew his choir didn't have the talent to win solely on their own merit. So I helped."

"By making ugly costumes for our team?"

She laughed. The combination of her laughter and the gun made my stomach heave. "I didn't have to work hard on that one. Last year's coach was clueless. Not like you. You understand what it takes to win."

"Thanks." I think.

"Greg understood winning, too." Felicia leaned back against the table and sighed. "The judges get tired of the same team taking first year after year. They needed a reason to vote for his team. I helped him with that, too." The sultry, knowing smile she gave me made me pretty sure verbal arguments hadn't been part of her strategy.

"You must have loved Greg a lot to go to such lengths for

him." Larry's photos included shots of some of the judging panels. A couple of the men looked old enough to be Felicia's grandfather.

"I did." Her lower lip trembled. "The two of us were going to conquer the world together—him with his music, and me with my fashion designs. He said we'd go public with our relationship once the divorce was final and his money was secure."

"What happened?" As if I couldn't guess.

Her eyes narrowed. "He said we still had to be careful. He'd convinced the judge to give him control of the money he'd made with his music, but that could change if Dana appealed. We had to be patient. Greg promised when the time was right, he'd use his money to finance my first collection."

"You mean he was going to use Larry's money."

She shrugged. "Larry didn't know how to capitalize on his music. Greg saw an opportunity, and he took it."

"Which is what he did with you, right? He knew you loved him, saw an opportunity to advance his career, and took it."

"He loved me," Felicia yelled as she stood up straight. The gun in her hand trembled as her face contorted with rage. Icy terror snaked through my chest. "He loved me, and then he pushed me away. I tried to get him to see reason, but he wouldn't take my calls."

"So you let the air out of his tires."

"I knew he'd have to wait for a service truck, and I wanted to talk to him face-to-face."

"But he didn't want to talk to you?"

"He said I needed to move on. That he already had. He made a mistake," she whispered. Her eyes glinted with hurt, anger, and a love-struck gleam that scared the shit out of me. I needed to get away from Felicia—now.

I edged closer to the desk and tucked my hand behind me, hoping Felicia wouldn't notice. "You hit him with your car."

She chuckled again. "Larry's car. I told him mine was at the shop and I needed to run an errand during show choir practice. He handed over his keys without asking where I was going. Larry still trusts people even after everything."

"But Larry figured it out." Which was why he traded in his car for a new one.

"When he read the newspaper report, he came over to my place and asked if I was the driver. I told him how Greg dumped me. How I'd learned he'd been cheating on me the entire time we were together. When I saw him in the street looking so smug, I couldn't help myself." Her smile said differently. "Larry suggested I go away for the summer to get some distance. He said it would make me feel better. I thought it had." She gnawed at her lip. For the first time she looked confused. Some of the red of her lipstick had smudged onto her teeth, making her look even scarier.

My hand brushed the edge of my purse, then found the opening. Wallet. Gum. Eye shadow. Checkbook.

Eureka!

My fingers closed around the can of Mace. At least, I hoped it was the can of Mace and not a tube of lipstick.

"So what happened when you came back?" I asked, easing the Mace toward my pocket.

"Greg found me the first day of camp. He told me how much he missed me. He wanted me back. This time we'd get married. I wanted to believe him." Her eyes got a faraway look, and I slipped the Mace into my pocket while she was lost in a memory. "Wednesday, I waited for him in my car after camp ended. I figured I'd surprise him."

"You saw him hitting on Chessie." I took a step to the

right, and Felicia's eyes narrowed. Her trigger finger twitched, sending goose bumps racing up my arms.

"I decided to give him one more chance. I called and asked him to meet me at the theater. He jumped at the opportunity. He thought I was going to let him help select the costumes for the choir. That I was going to do everything I did for him before. He even wanted me to talk him up to you. Greg said he was going to finesse you into helping his team." I held my breath as Felicia glared at me. "When I told him I wouldn't, he got angry. He told me how stupid I was to believe he was ever going to spend his money on my no-talent designs. That I was only good for one thing and even that wasn't so great. And he laughed. The next thing I knew, he was bleeding as I wrapped the microphone cord tight around his neck." Her eyes met mine. "I'm not sorry I killed him, but I'll regret killing you. I tried to scare you, but you just wouldn't go."

Yikes. "People might believe that Larry killed Greg, but me? No one will believe that." Raw desperation clawed at my throat, making me sound breathy and weak.

I fingered the Mace can in my pocket. There was the nozzle. I would only get one chance at this.

"They'll believe what I want them to believe. Now, open that door, please." Felicia pointed to the door next to me.

My left hand gripped the door handle while my right tightened on the Mace. I swung the door open and saw a set of stairs leading down.

A jab in my back told me to move.

One step.

Two steps.

Three.

The stairs were steep. Felicia's heels clicked behind me

as she followed me down. Fear pressed against my chest. I was going to die.

Four.

Five.

I could see fabric at the bottom of the stairs.

Six.

It was a costume storage room. I heard a moan to my right as I stepped off the stairs.

Larry.

He was bound and gagged, but alive. Larry's eyes widened as Felicia's heels clicked against the final steps, and he let out a muffled yell. I pulled the Mace out of my pocket and said a prayer. Taking a deep breath, I turned and fired.

Felicia screamed and grabbed at her eyes. She lost her balance and fell backward. Her head hit the edge of a step, and suddenly there was a loud explosion.

Shit!

White heat seared through my left upper arm. My legs muscles trembled and threatened to collapse. My eyes blurred with tears as the world faded for a moment before coming back into full color. I had no time to think about the pain or the blood dripping onto the floor. A shrieking Felicia sat up and pulled the trigger again.

A fake fur coat to my right took a slug to the upper chest, and I sprayed my Mace again, hoping to keep Felicia shooting blind. The smell of the Mace had me gagging and backing away, trying my best not to inhale.

"You bitch!" she gasped as she struggled to her feet and fired again. A straw cowboy hat bit the dust two feet from where I was standing.

A piece of straw landed on my bleeding arm. Too close. I wasn't sure how long the Mace would impair Felicia's vision. If I wanted to live, I had to find a better weapon—fast.

I took a step to my left. Felicia swung in my direction and fired. The bullet dug into the wall just above my head. We were in the farthest, deepest part of the school. Worse yet, the entire theater wing had been soundproofed to prevent potential disturbances to other classes. To put it bluntly, I was screwed.

My heart slammed against my chest. Panic and pain swirled through me. Not sure what else to do, I reached behind me and grabbed a gaudy metal-and-rhinestone tiara off the shelf and threw it to my right.

Felicia fired at the sound. Hope slashed through the panic as I grabbed the next two things I could get my hands on— a British Bobby helmet and an ugly Pepto-Bismol pink handbag. I let the first one sail—right at Felicia. That one missed. It thudded behind her on the stairs. She turned around and fired, and I let the handbag fly.

Direct hit to the back of the head.

The gun went off again as Felicia spun wildly looking for me. I grabbed a Roman gladiator chest plate off the shelf and charged. I could see in Felicia's face the minute she heard me move. The gun aimed as I raised the metal chest plate above my head and swung with everything I had.

The gun fired. The bullet struck somewhere to my left as the metal plate smashed down on Felicia's head with a satisfying clang. "Oof." Felicia collapsed to the ground. If this was a theatrical production, the curtain would come down and the audience would go wild. Instead, I grabbed a pair of fishnet stockings, tied up Felicia, checked that Larry was breathing, and went to call for help—hyperventilating and bleeding all the way.

Whoever said art mimicked life was lying—big time.

Chapter 29

Felicia was waking up when Detective Kaiser, Devlyn, and what looked to be the entire Prospect Glen Police Department tromped down the stairs. Devlyn took one look at me and turned white. Guess I looked even worse than I felt, which was pretty bad.

Detective Mike looked around at the dazed Felicia, the disheveled Larry, and bloody me, and yelled, "What the hell is going on here?"

"Fe-fe-fe-li-ci-a ki—"

"Felicia killed Greg Lucas." I cut Larry off before he spit on himself. I'd freed him from his bindings while waiting for the cavalry to arrive. The man was happy, freaked, and angry all at the same time. The combination meant it was almost impossible for him to get a word out without stuttering a half dozen times. "She also tried to kill me and was going to frame Larry for it." I'd already told Mike this once on the phone, but it bore repeating.

Detective Mike put Felicia under arrest and told her she

had the right to remain silent. Given the way she started shrieking about Greg deserving everything he got, I doubted she was going to take advantage of that right. I was just bummed I couldn't really enjoy watching Felicia being carted away in cuffs. The searing pain in my arm combined with the blood loss had made me nauseous and shivery.

Thank God the paramedics showed up, took one look at the gunshot wound, and gave me a shot of something that took the edge off everything.

They also decided I needed a trip to the hospital. As far as they could tell, the bullet had passed clean through the fatty part of my upper arm. Most likely there was no permanent damage done except to my pride. Hello? *Fatty part?*

Mike had questions he needed answered, but he decided my need for medical attention was more pressing. He promised to drop by Millie's place later to do the cop thing. Then he turned his attention to Larry. As the paramedics helped me up the stairs, Detective Mike fired off questions. Hearing Mike try to keep his cool while Larry tripped over his answers was kind of amusing. Or maybe that was just the drugs talking. Hard to tell.

The doctors at the hospital confirmed my fatty arm problem. I also got stitches, pain meds, and an antibiotic. Yippee. Aunt Millie arrived just as I was begging to go home. Her face was white. Her eyes were wide and filled with fear. The minute she spotted me sitting in my emergency room cubical, her whole body trembled.

Then the moment was gone. She straightened her shoulders and marched over to give me a hug. "Thank God you're okay. Your parents would never have let me hear the end of it if anything happened to you while living under my roof."

Tearing up, I hugged her back and asked, "Can we get

out of here? I'm starving." Who knows—maybe if I played the victim card just right, she'd drive through McDonald's.

Sadly, there was no French fry therapy for me. Instead, Millie had dinner waiting at home. My intestines clenched in anticipation. There was no way my aunt could make edible meals two days in a row.

Turns out I was right and wrong. A quick taste told me the pork roast was not only edible, it was delicious. So were the apple and onion stuffing, mashed potatoes, and green beans almondine. And they were all made by Aldo. Maybe I could convince him to marry Aunt Millie and cook for me all the time. His taste in clothing was a touch eccentric—today he was sporting a lime green smoking jacket and purple velvet pants—but I could learn to love his style. Especially since it came with a homemade apple tart for dessert.

The doorbell rang halfway through dinner. Detective Mike had arrived to take my statement. Aldo put another place setting at the table and insisted Mike join us. Being reminded that I had almost died killed my appetite. Oh well—not eating was a good way to work on my fatty arm problem.

Once Mike had shoveled down half his dinner, he got out his cop book and asked me for a rundown of today's events. I gave him the highlights. When I was done, he gave me a funny look and asked, "How did you know the e-mail wasn't from Larry? I looked up the account. It was registered under his name."

I wasn't surprised. Felicia had covered herself pretty well. Thank goodness she'd missed a few details. "Dana and Larry were meeting with an attorney on Wednesday night. The attorney thought Larry had a good case, which meant Larry didn't have a reason to blackmail Greg later that night. Not when he could humiliate him in court."

"Dana told me she was with two of her yoga students on Wednesday night."

I smiled. "Dana probably got the dates wrong." AKA—she lied. Dana must have thought her relationship with Larry would look like an additional motive for murder. Mike's expression told me he and Dana were going to have a heart-to-heart. "Is Larry okay? How did he end up in the costume shop?" I asked.

Mike nodded while sucking down more pot roast. When he swallowed, he said, "Felicia showed up in the middle of the night on Saturday and begged Larry to go with her to the police station. When he went to get dressed, she hit him over the head and knocked him out. He was still pretty hung over, so it wasn't hard to do. She stashed him at her place for the day and moved him to the school late Saturday night using one of the dollies from the scene shop. Then she ransacked the place looking for Greg's pitch pipe. You were right about that."

Score one for me.

Mike added, "Felicia said she never really wanted to kill you, but after Larry sobered up and started to talk, she realized she didn't have much of a choice. She planned on putting your dead body on the stage to mimic Greg's along with a note from Larry confessing to the crimes."

"So Felicia officially confessed?"

"Her lawyer isn't too happy, but her confession was totally by the book. She even confessed to planting Eric Metz's phone on Wednesday morning, the shooting on Saturday, and rigging your car to explode. Turns out, she'd bought that device off the Internet back in the spring and planned on using it on Greg Lucas's car. But she changed her mind. She thought it would scare you off." He laughed. "Guess she doesn't know you all that well."

Neither did Mike. Otherwise he wouldn't have kissed and ditched me twice. The way he was looking at me now made me almost think about forgiving him.

We were clearing away dishes and setting out dessert when the doorbell rang again. Killer barked himself silly as Millie hustled to the front door. I knew who it was the minute Killer gave a happy yip. Devlyn had arrived with Larry in tow.

Devlyn and Larry followed Millie and Killer into the kitchen. The minute Devlyn saw me, he pulled me into his arms and planted a kiss on top of my head. "Don't ever disappear like that again. I came back to the choir room, and your stuff was still there, but you were gone. After ten minutes I knew something was wrong, but Captain America over here wouldn't do anything about it. He said you probably went out to lunch and forgot your dance bag."

Mike glared at Devlyn and puffed out his chest. "Some of us operate in the real world, where facts matter."

"The fact is you should be thanking Paige. She solved Greg's murder for you."

That went over well. "Thanking her? She's lucky I didn't arrest her for the stunts she pulled."

I really didn't want to be in a cell next to Felicia. One sleepover with a deranged killer was enough.

Thank goodness Devlyn realized he'd pushed too far and apologized. Mike asked if I could come down to the station tomorrow for a formal statement. No cell-block bunking for me. Hurray!

After we set a time for my police-department visit, Mike headed out, and the rest of us settled down to enjoy dessert. We all looked at one another. Now that Mike was gone we could talk freely, but no one seemed to know where to begin. The silence was making me jumpy so I turned to Larry and said, "I thought you would have been with Dana tonight. She was really worried about you."

Larry blushed. "I was with D-d-dana earlier, but we both thought she should talk to her son tonight. Now that Fe-fe-licia is behind bars and talking to the police, everyone is going to know about the song Greg stole from me. We don't want Jacob to learn about his dad's past from the newspapers or the kids at school. Jacob has had it hard enough."

"He's lucky to have you and Dana on his side," I said. "And it's nice to hear you'll get the acknowledgment for your music that you deserve."

Millie and Aldo were confused so Devlyn and Larry filled them in on the college music theft. While they talked, a large knot of guilt settled into my stomach. The kitchen lights were bright, allowing me to see every bump and bruise Larry had suffered at Felicia's hands. He was a nice guy, and I'd suspected him of murder. I was a schmuck.

When Millie and Aldo were up to speed, I said, "I'm sorry I thought you might have killed Greg Lucas."

Larry waved off my apology with his fork-holding hand, sending a piece of cinnamon apple flying. His ears turned pink as Killer raced across the floor and gobbled it up. "No, I'm the one who should be sorry. I was so worried about the police suspecting Dana that I let them think you could be a suspect. I should have realized it was Felicia right away. You're not to blame for anything."

"That's not exactly true." My conscious begged I come clean about everything even though it would most likely get me fired. Or maybe it was my burning curiosity over Larry's payment to a hit man that had me admitting, "I figured out the password to your e-mail. One of the messages made me think you hired someone to kill Greg Lucas."

Larry looked confused, which was way better than angry. "What e-mail made you think that?"

"A guy named Kris said he would kill for fifteen hundred dollars."

Larry blinked. Then he started to laugh. "Kris is a professional Broadway choreographer. I really wanted to take Greg down this year, and my choreography sucked. Only, I didn't have the cash to pay her." His face colored at the admission of his monetary problems, and I held my breath, waiting for Larry to sack me.

Devlyn smiled. "Well, you're lucky you don't need her. Wait until you see what Paige and I have come up with. The kids were blown away."

"Even Chessie Bock?" Larry said, sounding surprised.

"Especially Chessie Bock."

Larry grinned. "I can't wait to see it. Although I don't think Paige should dance until her shoulder is feeling better."

I was stunned. "You mean you're not going to fire me for breaking into your e-mail?" Or his car—although he didn't technically know about that one.

"You have to work with Chessie." Larry laughed. "Trust me—that is more than punishment enough."

———

Devlyn drove Larry home, and Millie and Aldo headed upstairs to watch television before going to bed. My arm was throbbing, so I popped another pain pill and took a shower. I then camped out on the living room floor with the pugs and a book while waiting for the pill to kick in.

The pain in my arm was starting to ebb as the doorbell rang again. I opened the door and was surprise to see Devlyn standing on the stoop.

"Did you forget something?" I asked as he stepped inside.

He looked different. No smile. No twinkle in his eyes. His expression was unreadable. "You've heard everyone else's secrets today, but I never got a chance to tell you mine."

"You don't have to," I insisted.

"But—"

"You're my friend, but that doesn't give me the right to know everything about your life. You don't owe me any explanations, but I owe you an apology. I shouldn't have—"

One minute I was apologizing, the next I was being kissed senseless. Devlyn's arm snaked around my waist and drew me close as his mouth insisted I respond. As much as I wanted to, I couldn't. I was confused. Again.

Taking several steps back, I blinked up at him. "What do you think you're doing? You're gay."

"Not exactly."

"What does that mean?"

He sighed. "I wasn't kidding when I said teenage girls pursue teachers. My first two years of teaching, I had more than one student make passes at me. Some wanted roles in the shows or passing grades. A few liked the danger of pursuing a teacher. The choir teacher walked in on one girl taking off her top as a demonstration of how far she'd go to get the lead in the musical."

"Holy crap!"

Devlyn laughed. "My thoughts exactly. Thank goodness the student had a reputation for pursuing teachers. The teacher didn't report the incident, but encouraged me to find a different job. The following year, I started teaching at Prospect Glen. I also incorporated a lot more pastels into my wardrobe, started the rumor about myself, and had my friend Phillip come to a couple of events with me."

"You're not gay."

He shook his head.

In my drug-addled mind, something clicked. "Detective Mike knows."

"I had a date Wednesday night. Detective Kaiser had to talk to her in order to verify my alibi."

Great. This was the second guy this week who was involved with another woman while kissing me. My man karma sucked.

Devlyn took a step closer. My heart skipped several beats as he gave me a sexy smile. "In case you were wondering, I told the girl I was interested in someone else."

My mouth went dry as he leaned in again. His lips touched mine, and this time I knew what to do. Only, his mouth was gone before I had a chance to do anything.

I was about to protest when Devlyn brushed a finger along my cheek and said, "You've had a long day, and I'm not going to take advantage of that. I want you to trust me, which means we have to get to know each other for real." He walked to the front door, opened it, and turned back. "But consider this fair warning. I think the two of us make a great team, and I plan to prove it to you. Starting tomorrow."

Tomorrow.

My show choir had its second rehearsal tomorrow. For the first time since I took the job, I realized I wasn't dreading it.

In fact, as I smiled at Devlyn's handsome face disappearing behind the door, I thought teaching show choir might turn out to be fun.

At least, until a real job came along.